STORY **EVAN STANLEY**

ART **ADAM BRYCE THOMAS** (#37 & 40)
EVAN STANLEY (#38-40)
BRACARDI CURRY (#38-39)

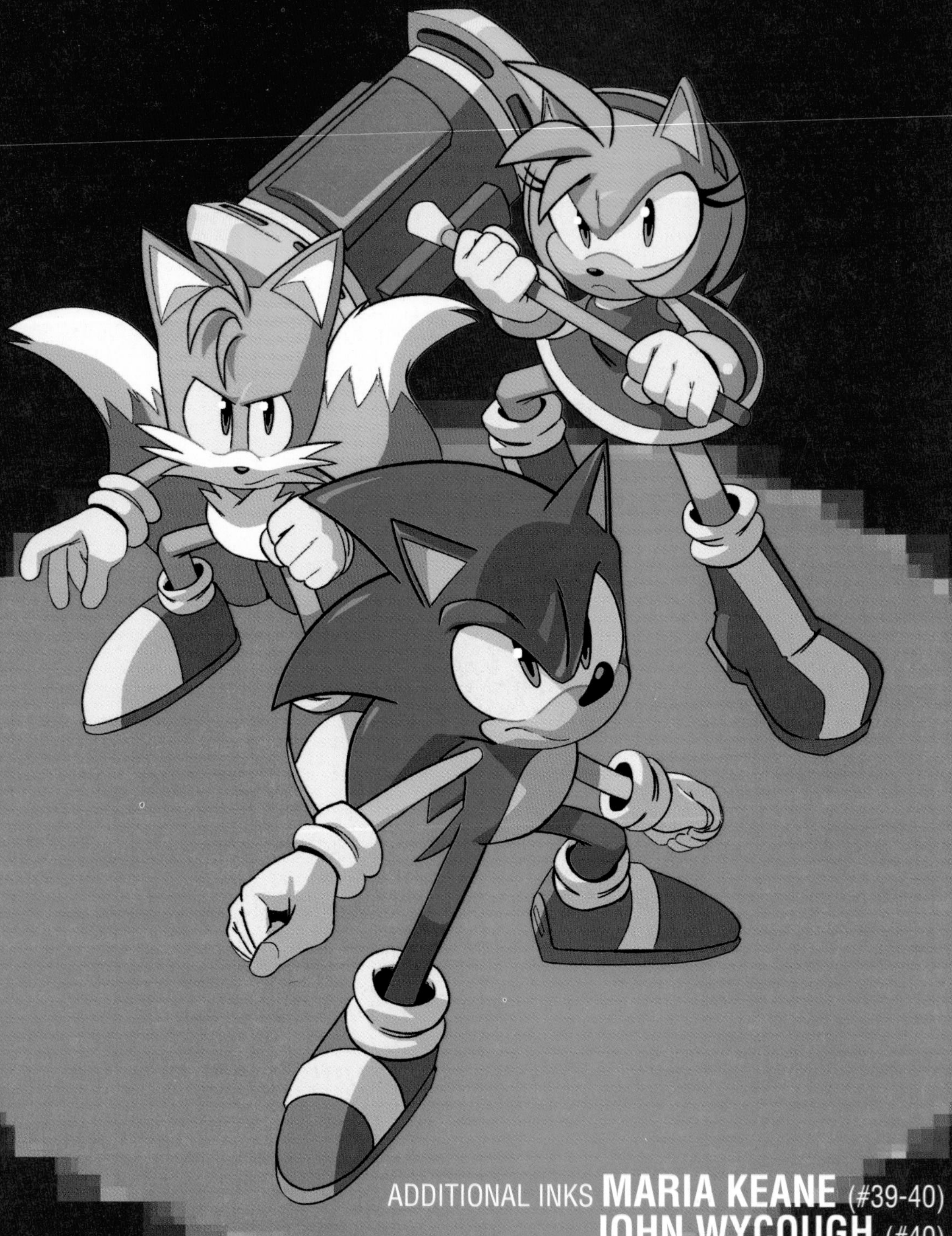

ADDITIONAL INKS **MARIA KEANE** (#39-40)
JOHN WYCOUGH (#40)

COLORS **REGGIE GRAHAM** (#37)
MATT HERMS (#38-39)
HEATHER BRECKEL (#40)
LEONARDO ITO (#40)

LETTERS **SHAWN LEE**

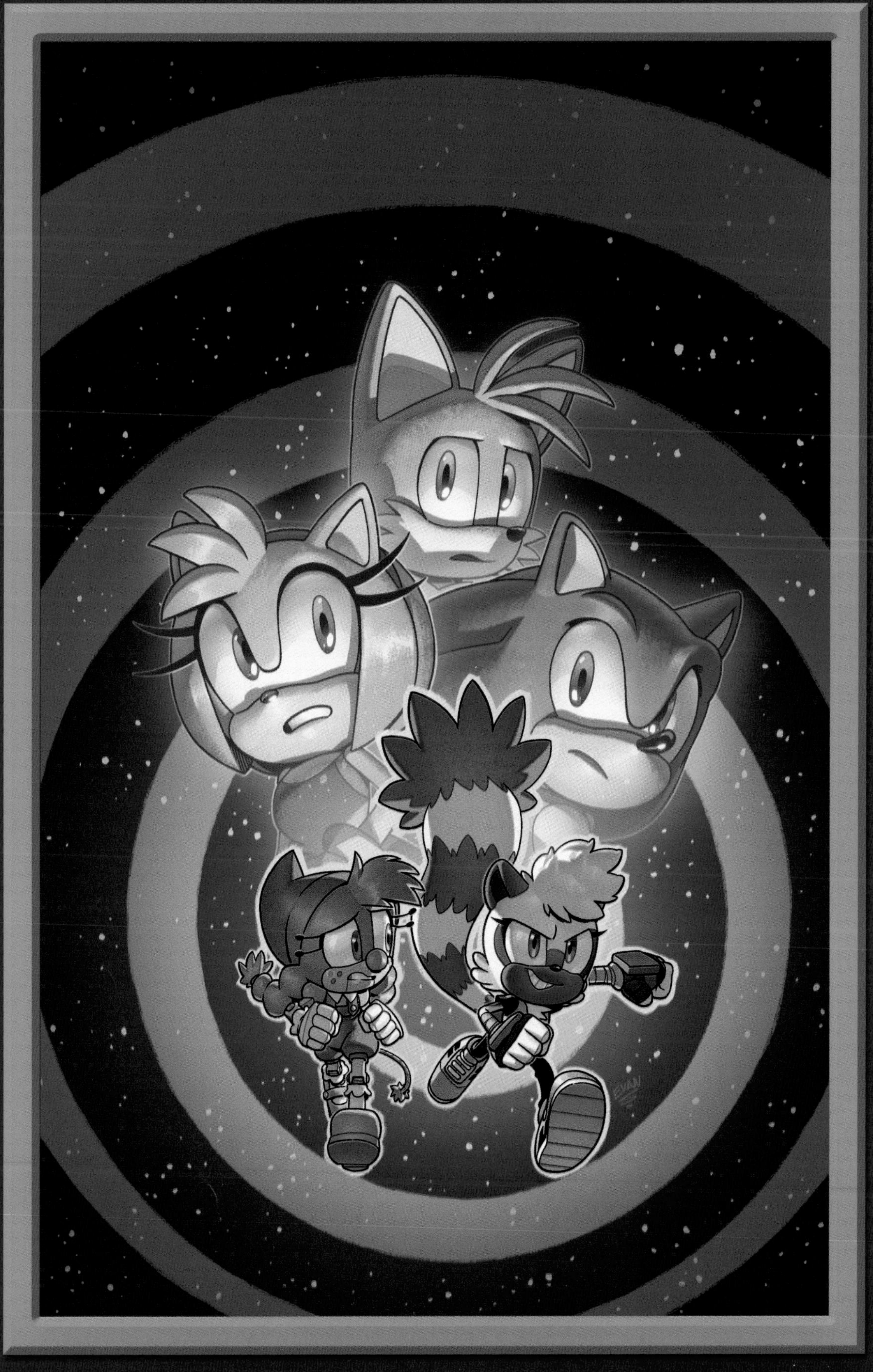

ART BY **EVAN STANLEY**

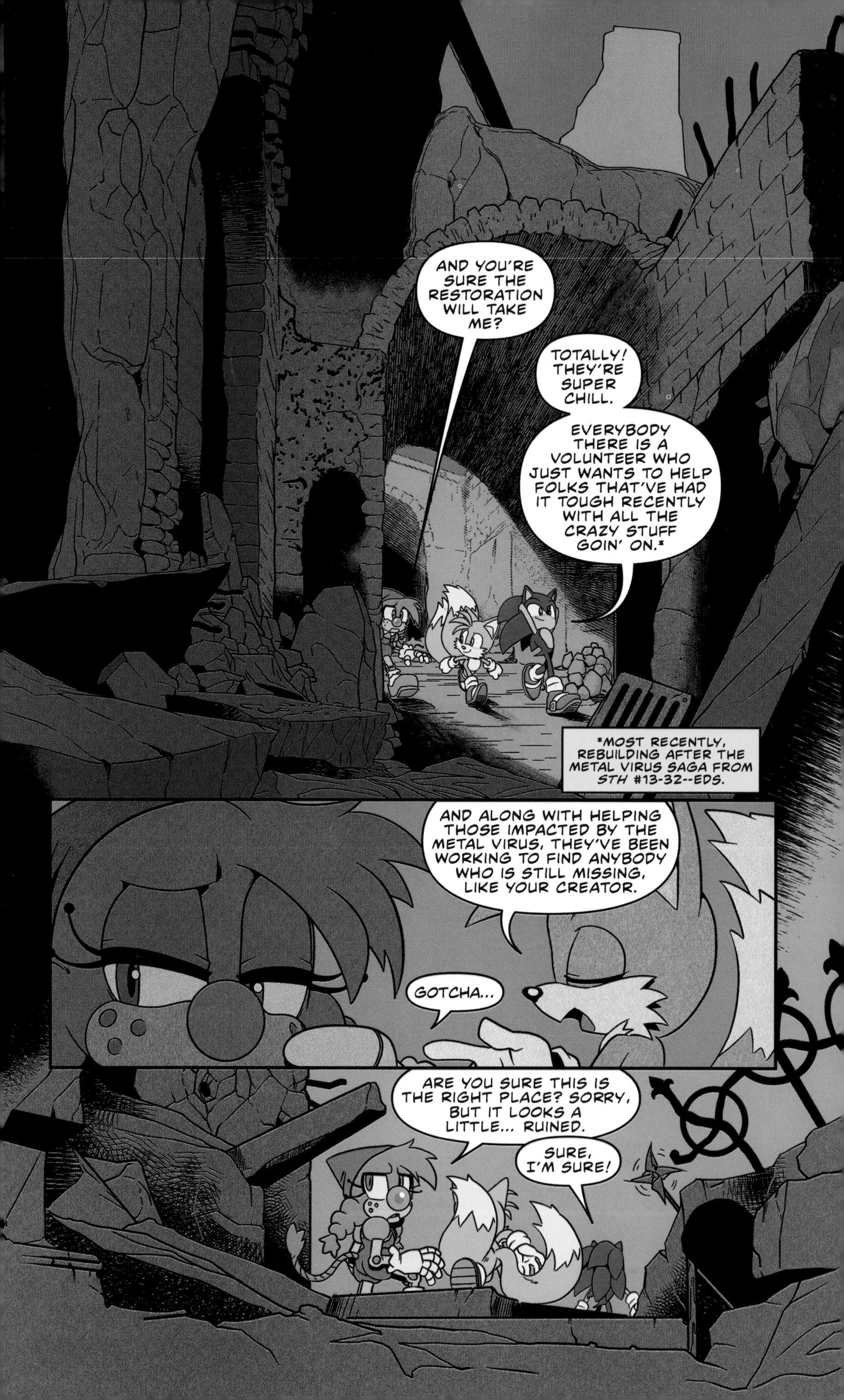
AND YOU'RE SURE THE RESTORATION WILL TAKE ME?
TOTALLY! THEY'RE SUPER CHILL.
EVERYBODY THERE IS A VOLUNTEER WHO JUST WANTS TO HELP FOLKS THAT'VE HAD IT TOUGH RECENTLY WITH ALL THE CRAZY STUFF GOIN' ON.*
*MOST RECENTLY, REBUILDING AFTER THE METAL VIRUS SAGA FROM STH #13-32--EDS.
AND ALONG WITH HELPING THOSE IMPACTED BY THE METAL VIRUS, THEY'VE BEEN WORKING TO FIND ANYBODY WHO IS STILL MISSING, LIKE YOUR CREATOR.
GOTCHA...
ARE YOU SURE THIS IS THE RIGHT PLACE? SORRY, BUT IT LOOKS A LITTLE... RUINED.
SURE, I'M SURE!

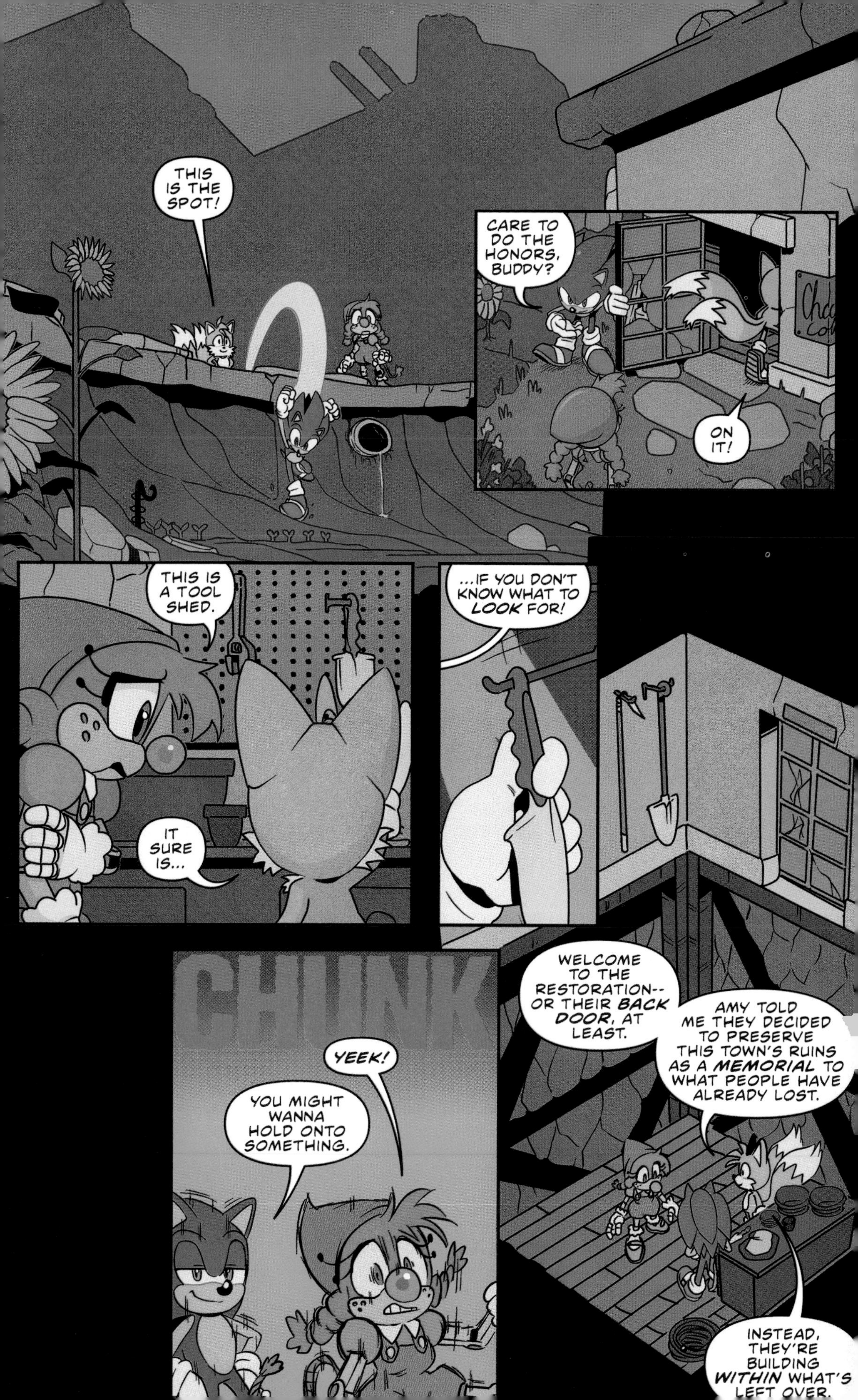
THIS IS THE SPOT!
CARE TO DO THE HONORS, BUDDY?
ON IT!
THIS IS A TOOL SHED.
IT SURE IS...
...IF YOU DON'T KNOW WHAT TO LOOK FOR!
CHUNK
YEEK!
YOU MIGHT WANNA HOLD ONTO SOMETHING.
WELCOME TO THE RESTORATION-- OR THEIR BACK DOOR, AT LEAST.
AMY TOLD ME THEY DECIDED TO PRESERVE THIS TOWN'S RUINS AS A MEMORIAL TO WHAT PEOPLE HAVE ALREADY LOST.
INSTEAD, THEY'RE BUILDING WITHIN WHAT'S LEFT OVER.

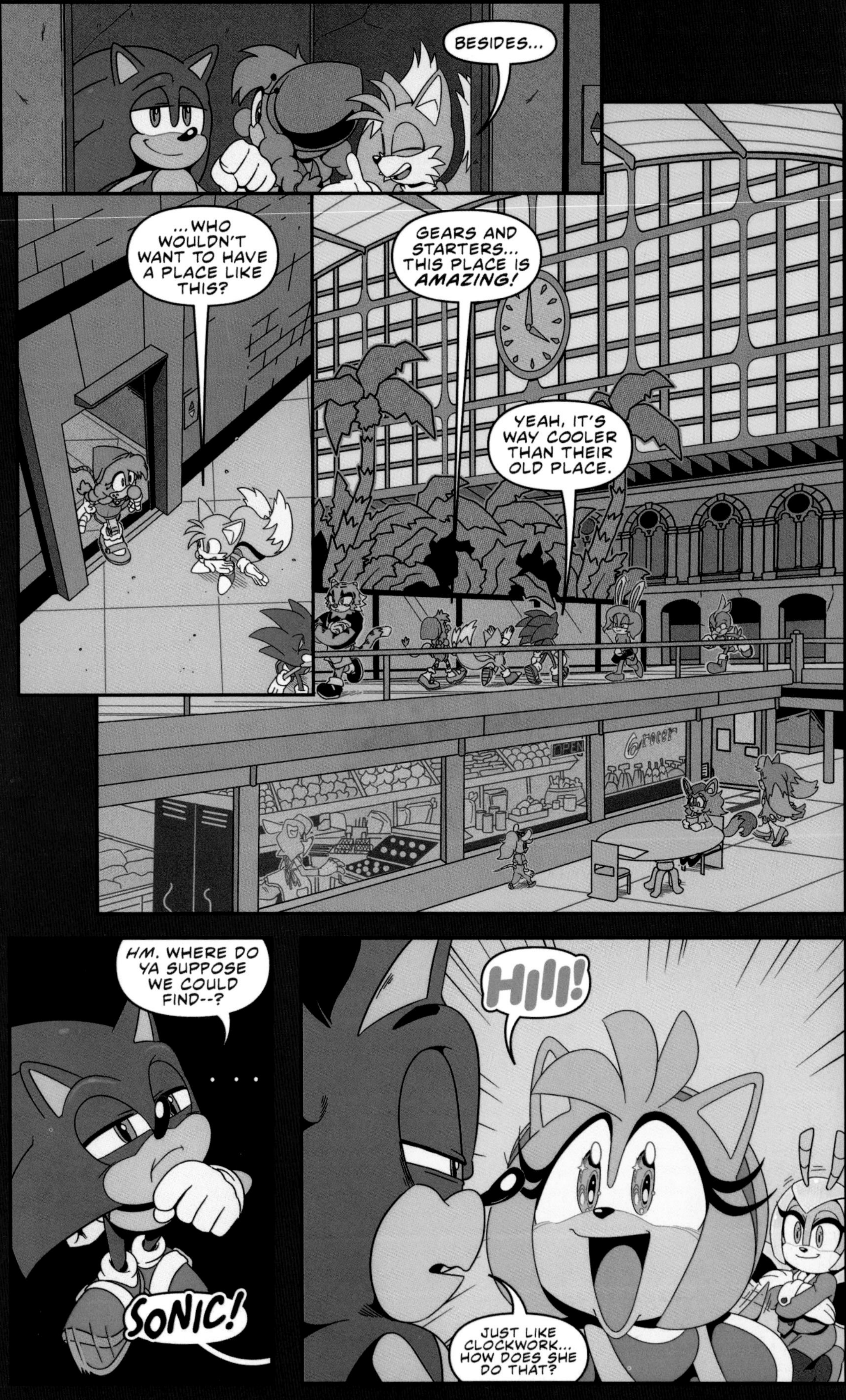
BESIDES...
...WHO WOULDN'T WANT TO HAVE A PLACE LIKE THIS?
GEARS AND STARTERS... THIS PLACE IS *AMAZING!*
YEAH, IT'S WAY COOLER THAN THEIR OLD PLACE.
OPEN
Grocer
HM. WHERE DO YA SUPPOSE WE COULD FIND--?
...
SONIC!
HIII!
JUST LIKE CLOCKWORK... HOW DOES SHE DO THAT?

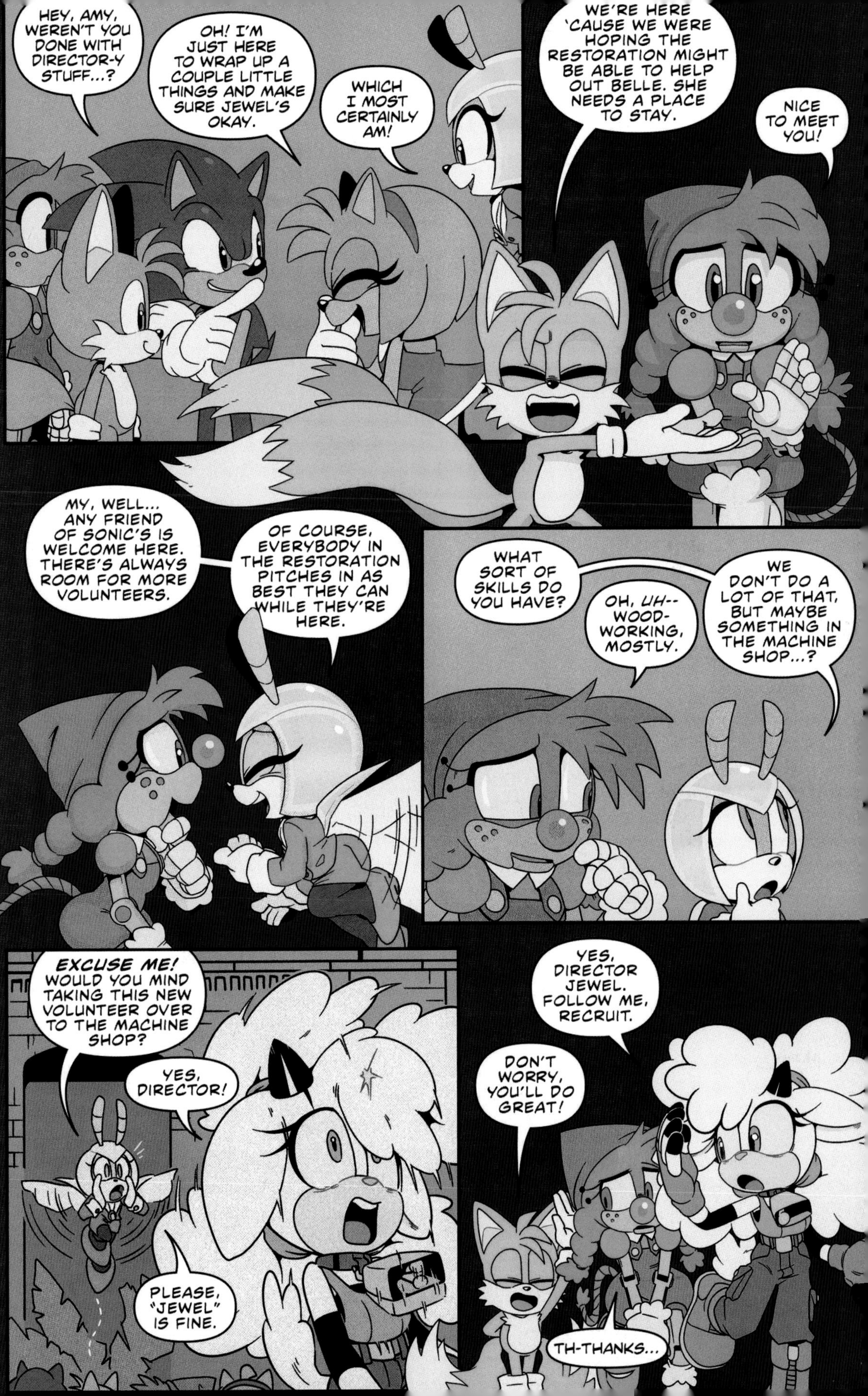
HEY, AMY, WEREN'T YOU DONE WITH DIRECTOR-Y STUFF...?
OH! I'M JUST HERE TO WRAP UP A COUPLE LITTLE THINGS AND MAKE SURE JEWEL'S OKAY.
WHICH I MOST CERTAINLY AM!
WE'RE HERE 'CAUSE WE WERE HOPING THE RESTORATION MIGHT BE ABLE TO HELP OUT BELLE. SHE NEEDS A PLACE TO STAY.
NICE TO MEET YOU!
MY, WELL... ANY FRIEND OF SONIC'S IS WELCOME HERE. THERE'S ALWAYS ROOM FOR MORE VOLUNTEERS.
OF COURSE, EVERYBODY IN THE RESTORATION PITCHES IN AS BEST THEY CAN WHILE THEY'RE HERE.
WHAT SORT OF SKILLS DO YOU HAVE?
OH, *UH*-- WOOD-WORKING, MOSTLY.
WE DON'T DO A LOT OF THAT, BUT MAYBE SOMETHING IN THE MACHINE SHOP...?
EXCUSE ME! WOULD YOU MIND TAKING THIS NEW VOLUNTEER OVER TO THE MACHINE SHOP?
YES, DIRECTOR!
PLEASE, "JEWEL" IS FINE.
YES, DIRECTOR JEWEL. FOLLOW ME, RECRUIT.
DON'T WORRY, YOU'LL DO GREAT!
TH-THANKS...

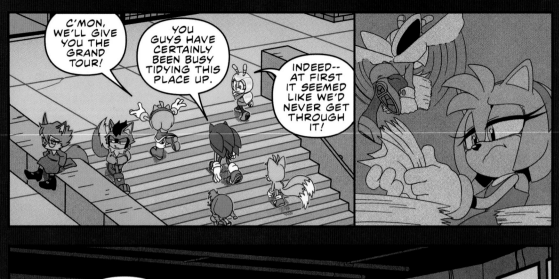

C'MON, WE'LL GIVE YOU THE GRAND TOUR!

YOU GUYS HAVE CERTAINLY BEEN BUSY TIDYING THIS PLACE UP.

INDEED-- AT FIRST IT SEEMED LIKE WE'D NEVER GET THROUGH IT!

BUT YOU CAN DO ANYTHING IF YOU TAKE IT ONE STEP AT A TIME...

HERE *YOU* ARE. IF I HAVE TO LOOK AT ANOTHER EQUIPMENT REQUISITION FORM, I'LL SCREAM.

...AND HERE WE ARE!

UHM, MS. JEWEL? SHOULD PROBABLY HAVE A LOOK AT THIS...

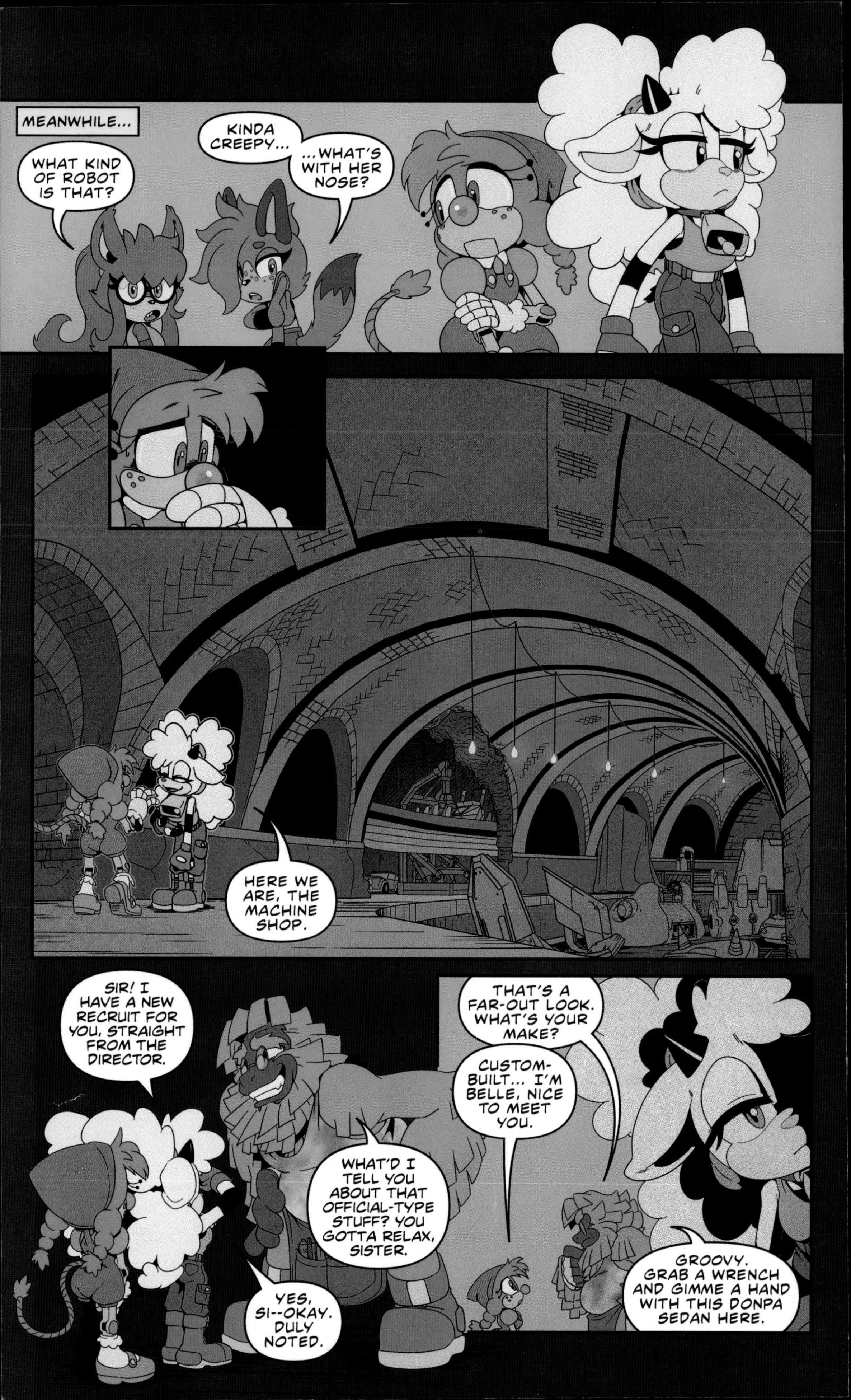
MEANWHILE...
WHAT KIND OF ROBOT IS THAT?
KINDA CREEPY...
...WHAT'S WITH HER NOSE?
HERE WE ARE, THE MACHINE SHOP.
SIR! I HAVE A NEW RECRUIT FOR YOU, STRAIGHT FROM THE DIRECTOR.
WHAT'D I TELL YOU ABOUT THAT OFFICIAL-TYPE STUFF? YOU GOTTA RELAX, SISTER.
YES, SI--OKAY. DULY NOTED.
THAT'S A FAR-OUT LOOK. WHAT'S YOUR MAKE?
CUSTOM-BUILT... I'M BELLE, NICE TO MEET YOU.
GROOVY. GRAB A WRENCH AND GIMME A HAND WITH THIS DONPA SEDAN HERE.

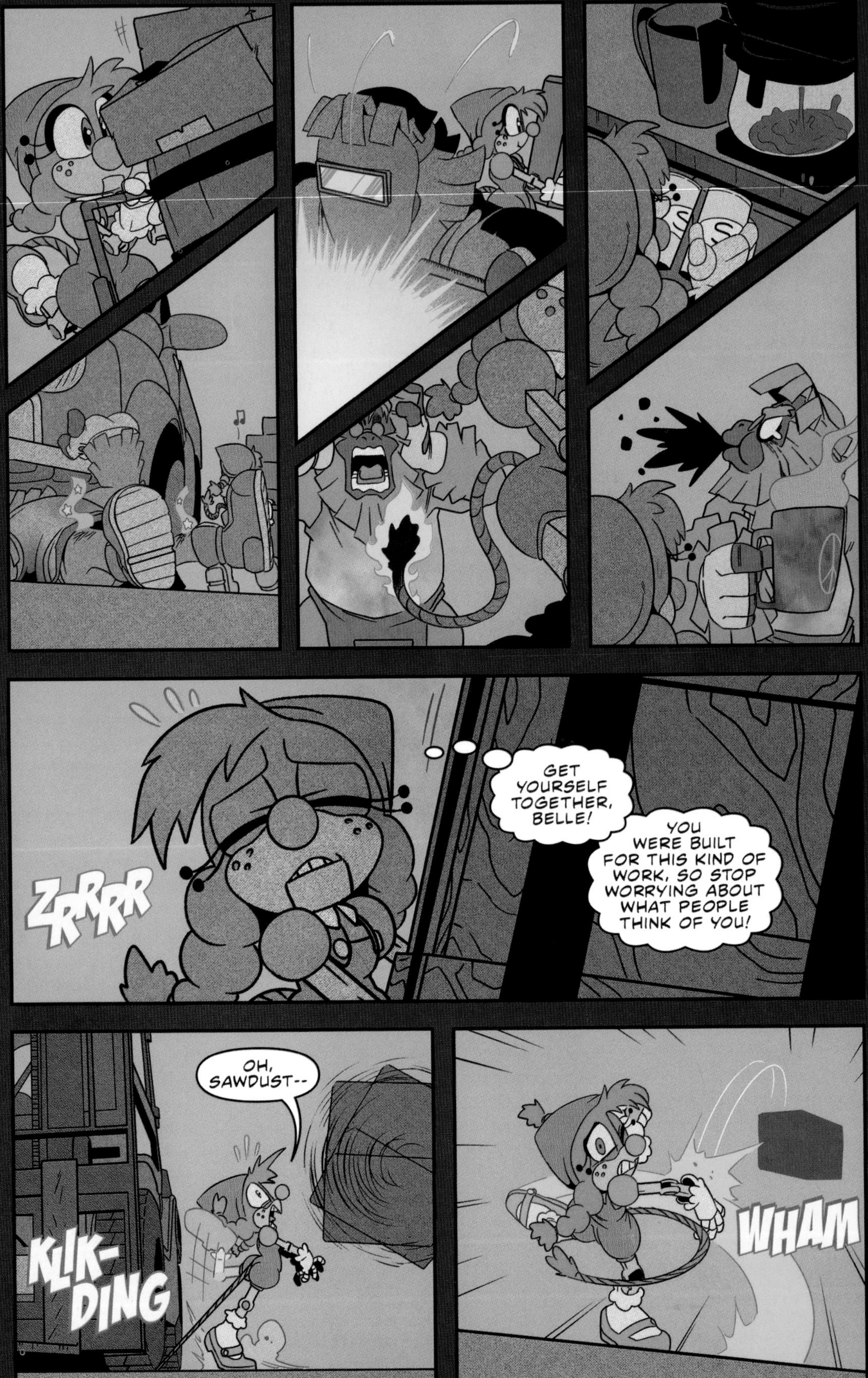
GET YOURSELF TOGETHER, BELLE!
YOU WERE BUILT FOR THIS KIND OF WORK, SO STOP WORRYING ABOUT WHAT PEOPLE THINK OF YOU!
ZRRRR
OH, SAWDUST--
KLIK-DING
WHAM

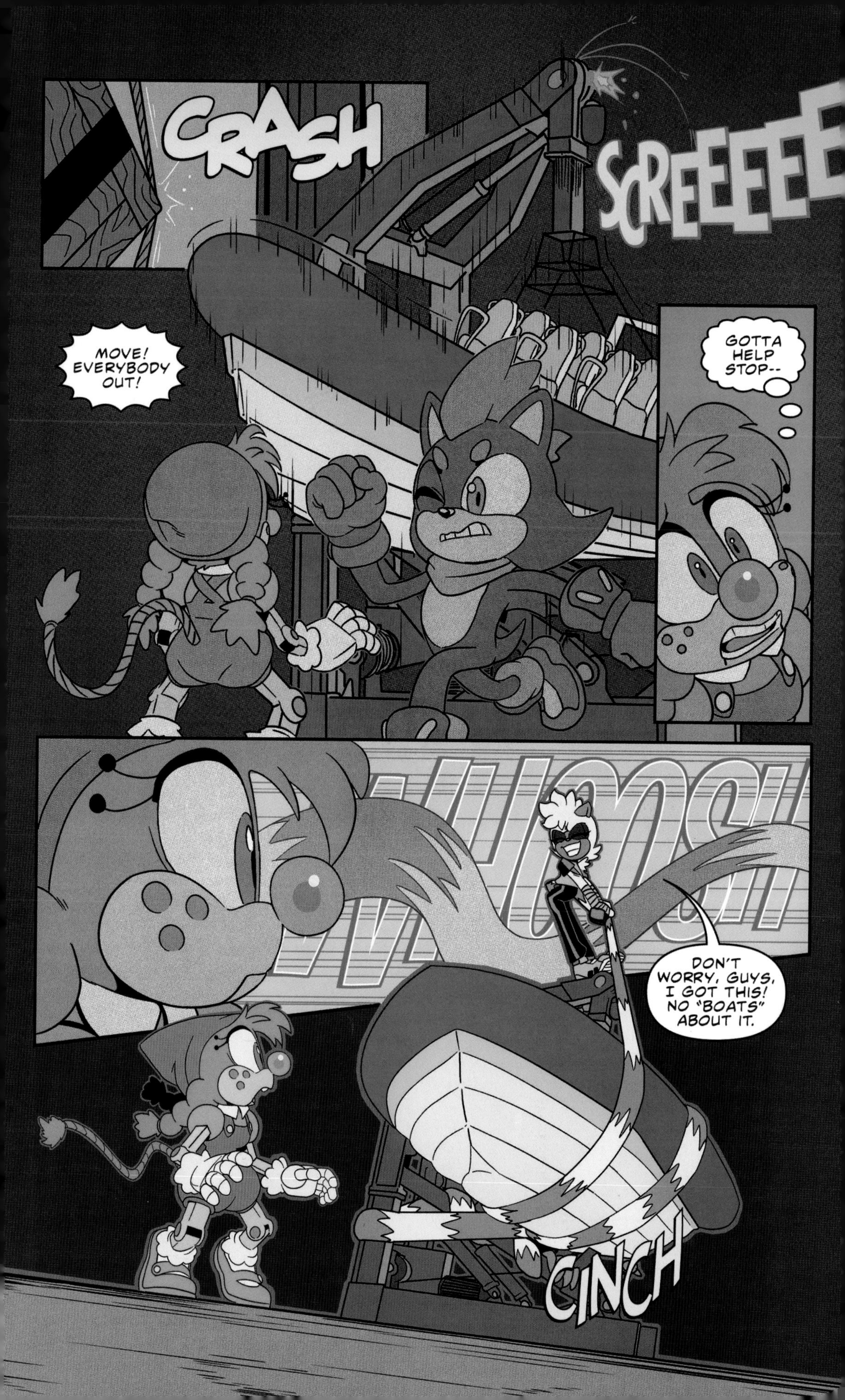
CRASH
SCREEEEE
MOVE! EVERYBODY OUT!
GOTTA HELP STOP--
WHOOSH
DON'T WORRY, GUYS, I GOT THIS! NO "BOATS" ABOUT IT.
CINCH

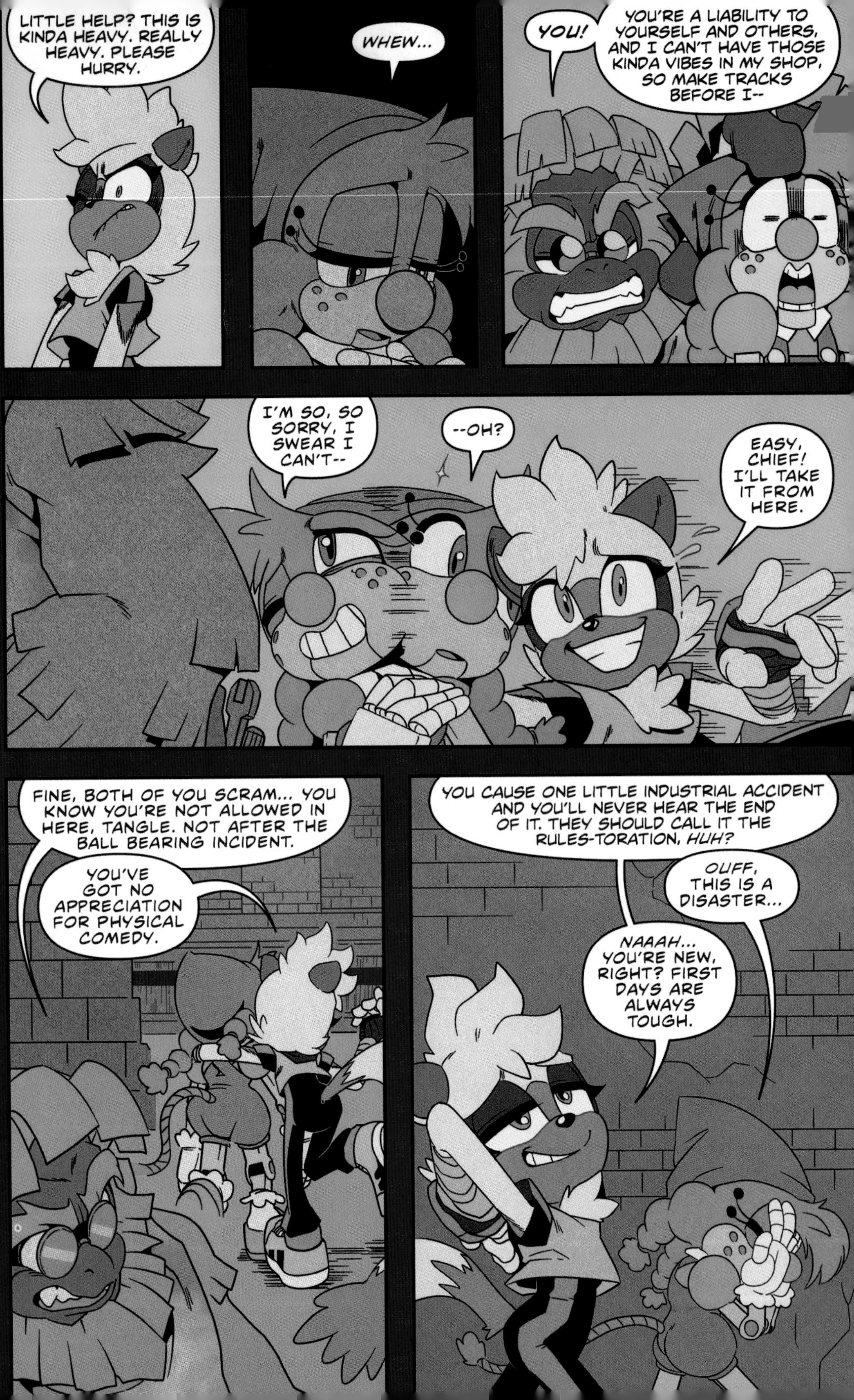
LITTLE HELP? THIS IS KINDA HEAVY. REALLY HEAVY. PLEASE HURRY.
WHEW...
YOU!
YOU'RE A LIABILITY TO YOURSELF AND OTHERS, AND I CAN'T HAVE THOSE KINDA VIBES IN MY SHOP, SO MAKE TRACKS BEFORE I--
I'M SO, SO SORRY, I SWEAR I CAN'T--
--OH?
EASY, CHIEF! I'LL TAKE IT FROM HERE.
FINE, BOTH OF YOU SCRAM... YOU KNOW YOU'RE NOT ALLOWED IN HERE, TANGLE. NOT AFTER THE BALL BEARING INCIDENT.
YOU'VE GOT NO APPRECIATION FOR PHYSICAL COMEDY.
YOU CAUSE ONE LITTLE INDUSTRIAL ACCIDENT AND YOU'LL NEVER HEAR THE END OF IT. THEY SHOULD CALL IT THE RULES-TORATION, HUH?
OUFF, THIS IS A DISASTER...
NAAAH... YOU'RE NEW, RIGHT? FIRST DAYS ARE ALWAYS TOUGH.

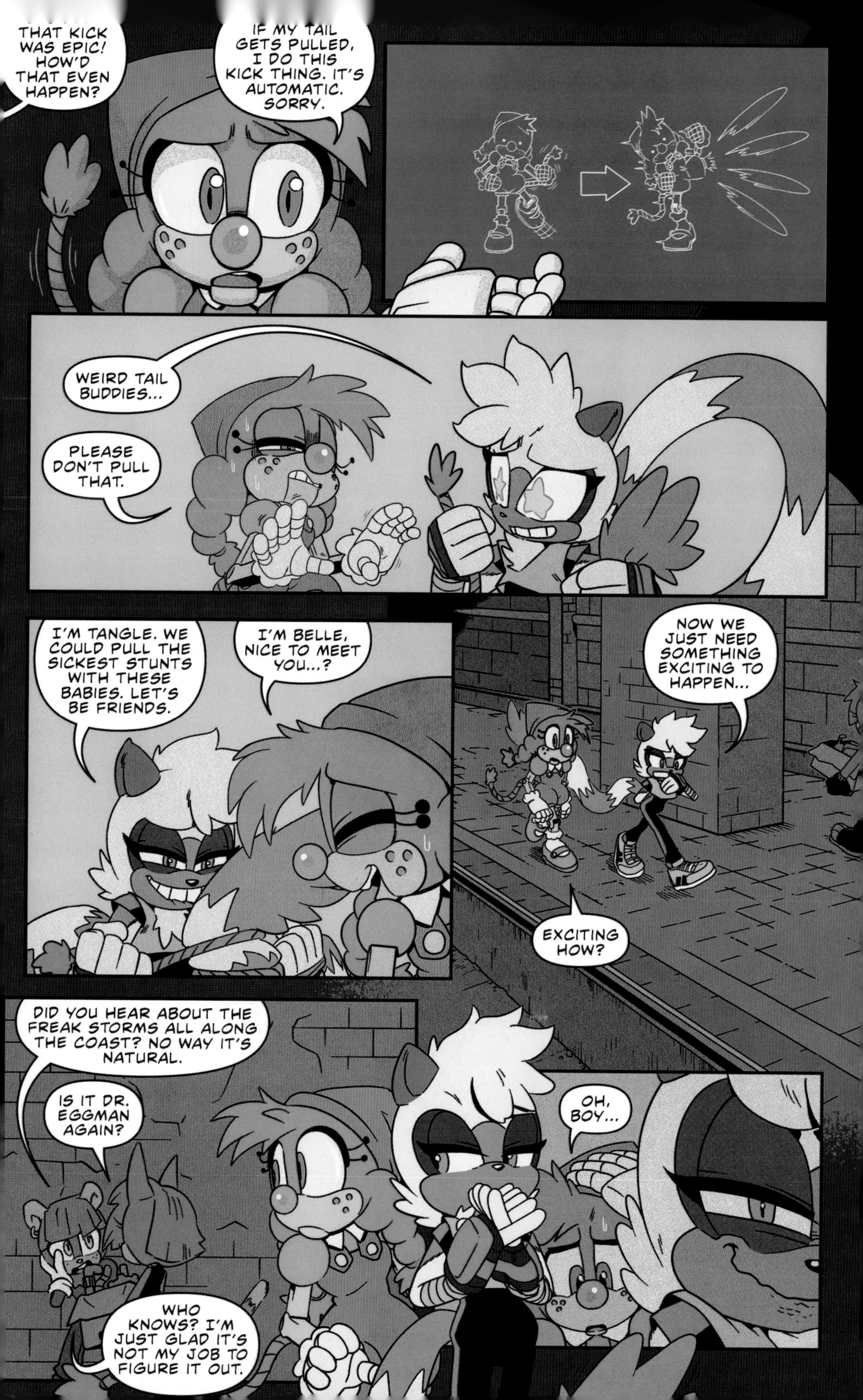
THAT KICK WAS EPIC! HOW'D THAT EVEN HAPPEN?
IF MY TAIL GETS PULLED, I DO THIS KICK THING. IT'S AUTOMATIC. SORRY.
WEIRD TAIL BUDDIES...
PLEASE DON'T PULL THAT.
I'M TANGLE. WE COULD PULL THE SICKEST STUNTS WITH THESE BABIES. LET'S BE FRIENDS.
I'M BELLE, NICE TO MEET YOU...?
NOW WE JUST NEED SOMETHING EXCITING TO HAPPEN...
EXCITING HOW?
DID YOU HEAR ABOUT THE FREAK STORMS ALL ALONG THE COAST? NO WAY IT'S NATURAL.
IS IT DR. EGGMAN AGAIN?
OH, BOY...
WHO KNOWS? I'M JUST GLAD IT'S NOT MY JOB TO FIGURE IT OUT.

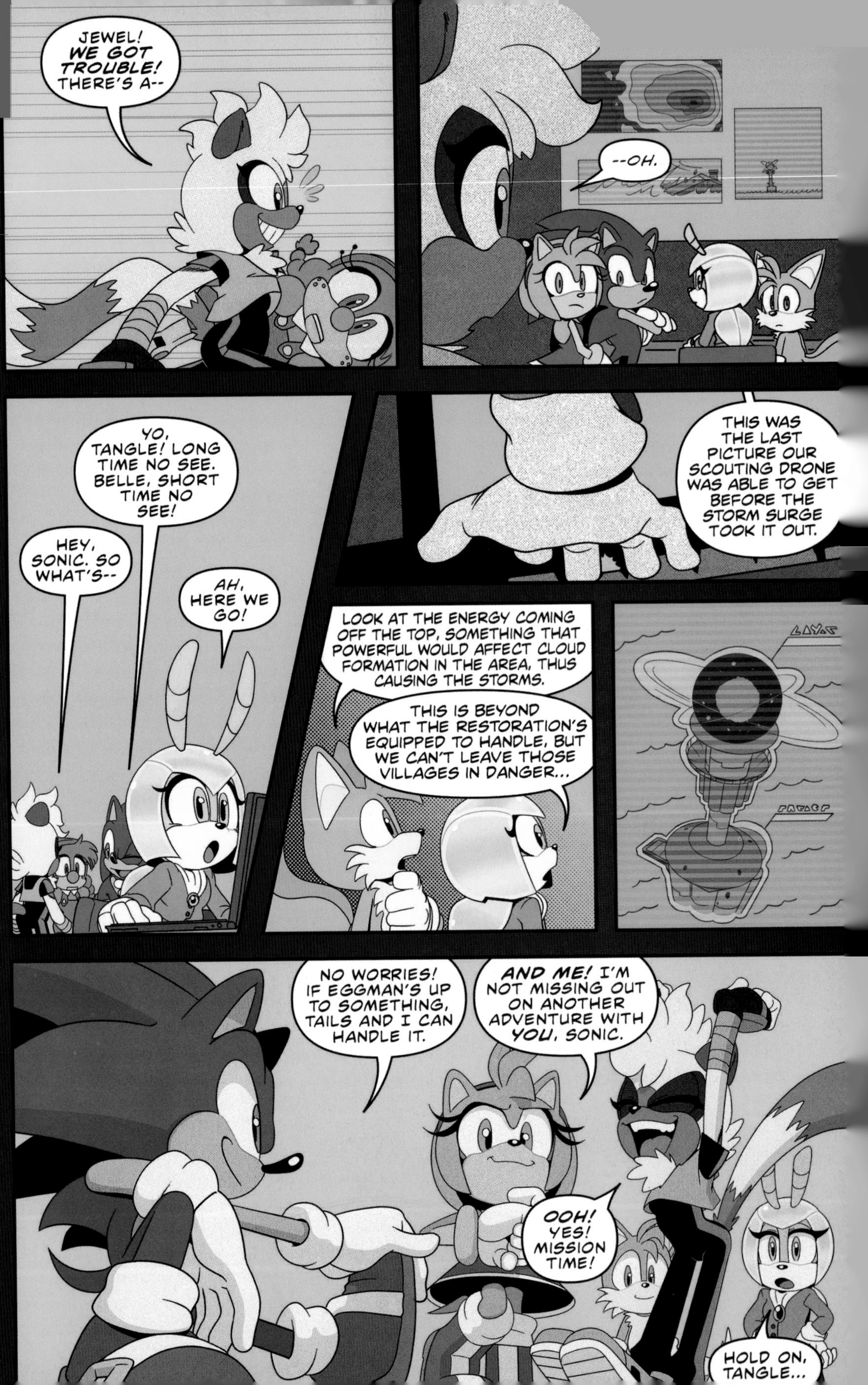
JEWEL! WE GOT TROUBLE! THERE'S A--
--OH.
YO, TANGLE! LONG TIME NO SEE. BELLE, SHORT TIME NO SEE!
HEY, SONIC. SO WHAT'S--
AH, HERE WE GO!
THIS WAS THE LAST PICTURE OUR SCOUTING DRONE WAS ABLE TO GET BEFORE THE STORM SURGE TOOK IT OUT.
LOOK AT THE ENERGY COMING OFF THE TOP, SOMETHING THAT POWERFUL WOULD AFFECT CLOUD FORMATION IN THE AREA, THUS CAUSING THE STORMS.
THIS IS BEYOND WHAT THE RESTORATION'S EQUIPPED TO HANDLE, BUT WE CAN'T LEAVE THOSE VILLAGES IN DANGER...
NO WORRIES! IF EGGMAN'S UP TO SOMETHING, TAILS AND I CAN HANDLE IT.
AND ME! I'M NOT MISSING OUT ON ANOTHER ADVENTURE WITH YOU, SONIC.
OOH! YES! MISSION TIME!
HOLD ON, TANGLE...

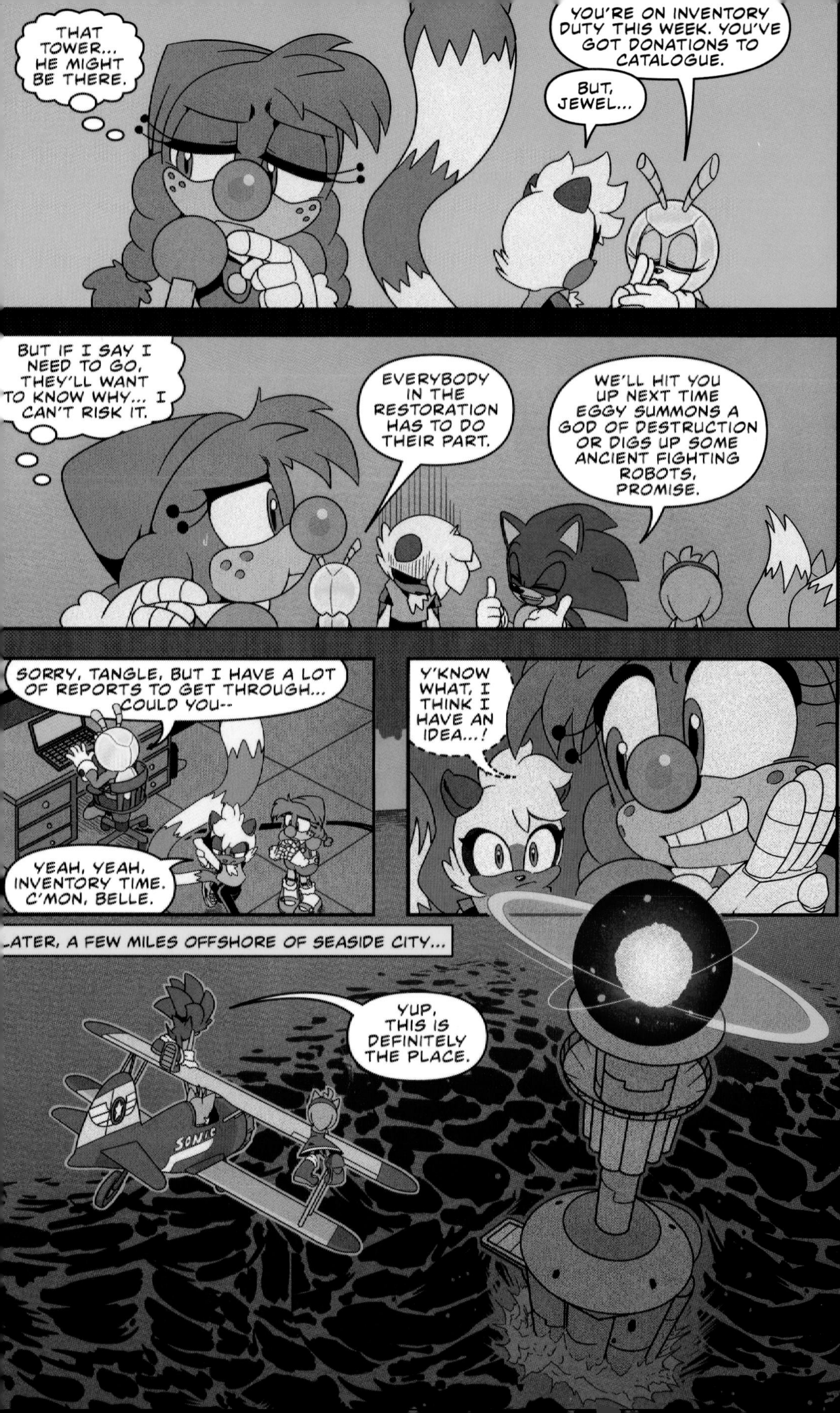
THAT TOWER... HE MIGHT BE THERE.
YOU'RE ON INVENTORY DUTY THIS WEEK. YOU'VE GOT DONATIONS TO CATALOGUE.
BUT, JEWEL...
BUT IF I SAY I NEED TO GO, THEY'LL WANT TO KNOW WHY... I CAN'T RISK IT.
EVERYBODY IN THE RESTORATION HAS TO DO THEIR PART.
WE'LL HIT YOU UP NEXT TIME EGGY SUMMONS A GOD OF DESTRUCTION OR DIGS UP SOME ANCIENT FIGHTING ROBOTS, PROMISE.
SORRY, TANGLE, BUT I HAVE A LOT OF REPORTS TO GET THROUGH... COULD YOU--
YEAH, YEAH, INVENTORY TIME. C'MON, BELLE.
Y'KNOW WHAT, I THINK I HAVE AN IDEA...!
LATER, A FEW MILES OFFSHORE OF SEASIDE CITY...
YUP, THIS IS DEFINITELY THE PLACE.
SONIC

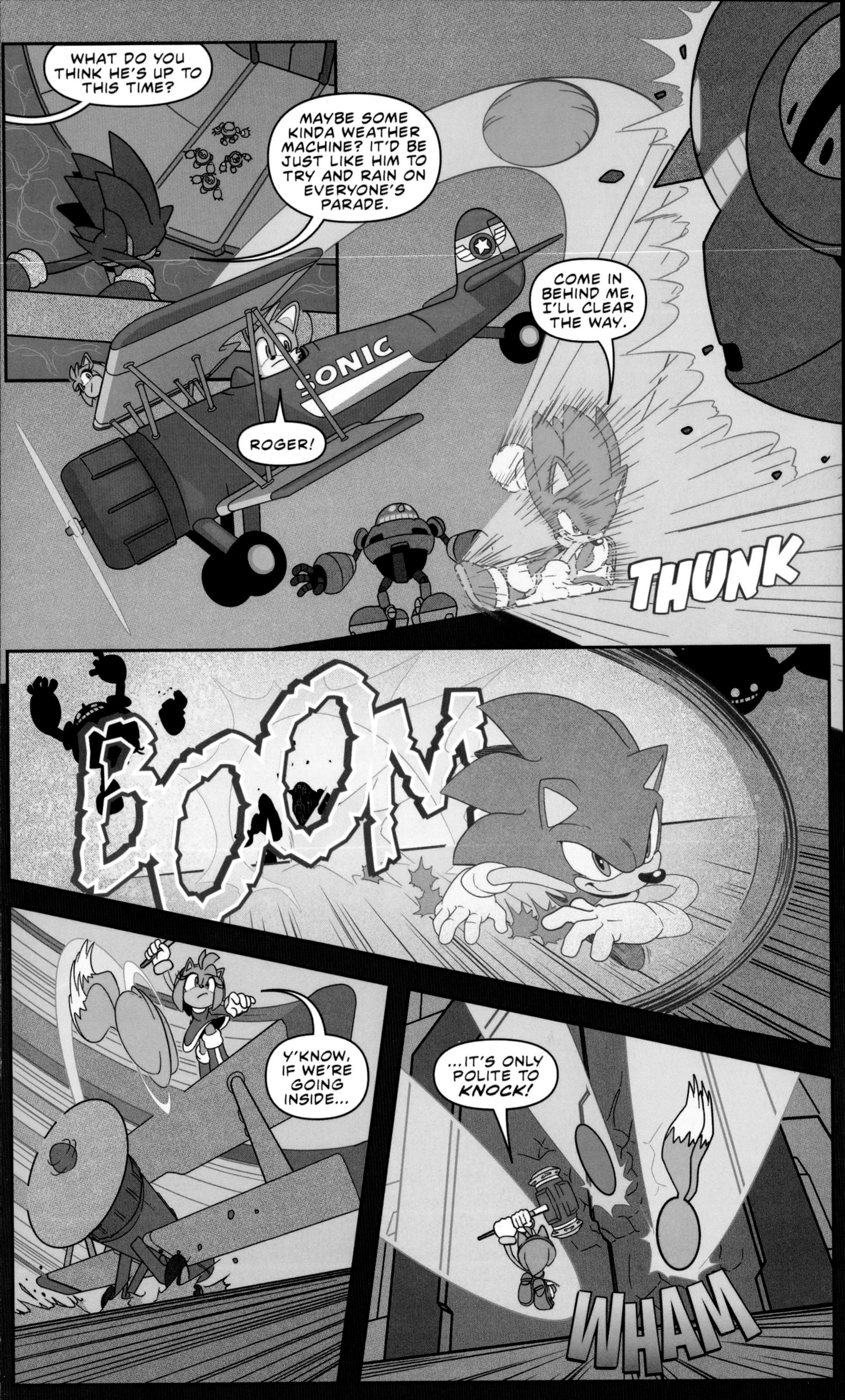
WHAT DO YOU THINK HE'S UP TO THIS TIME?
MAYBE SOME KINDA WEATHER MACHINE? IT'D BE JUST LIKE HIM TO TRY AND RAIN ON EVERYONE'S PARADE.
SONIC
COME IN BEHIND ME, I'LL CLEAR THE WAY.
ROGER!
THUNK
BOOM
Y'KNOW, IF WE'RE GOING INSIDE...
...IT'S ONLY POLITE TO KNOCK!
WHAM

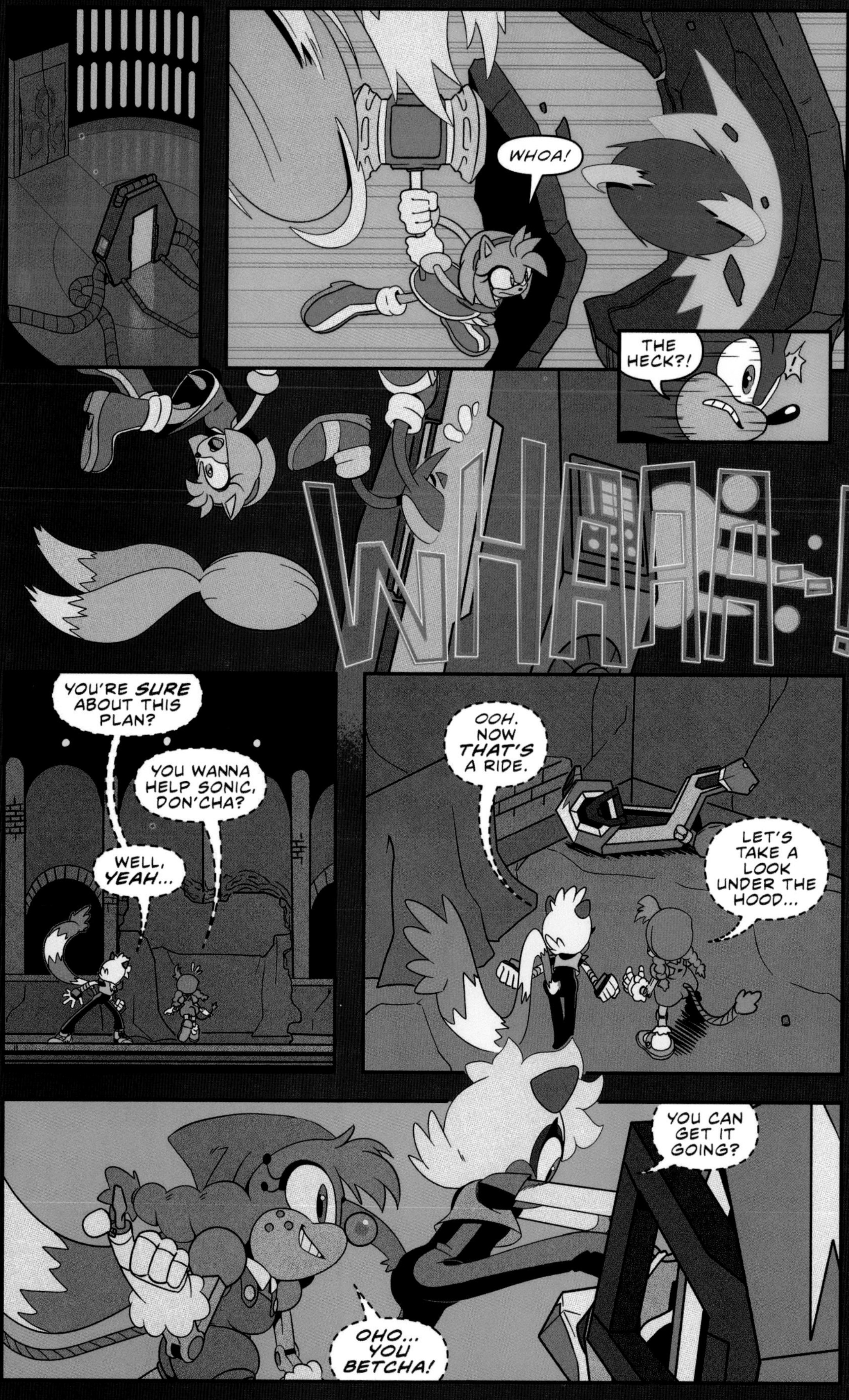
WHOA!
THE HECK?!
WHAAA--!
YOU'RE SURE ABOUT THIS PLAN?
YOU WANNA HELP SONIC, DON'CHA?
WELL, YEAH...
OOH. NOW THAT'S A RIDE.
LET'S TAKE A LOOK UNDER THE HOOD...
YOU CAN GET IT GOING?
OHO... YOU BETCHA!

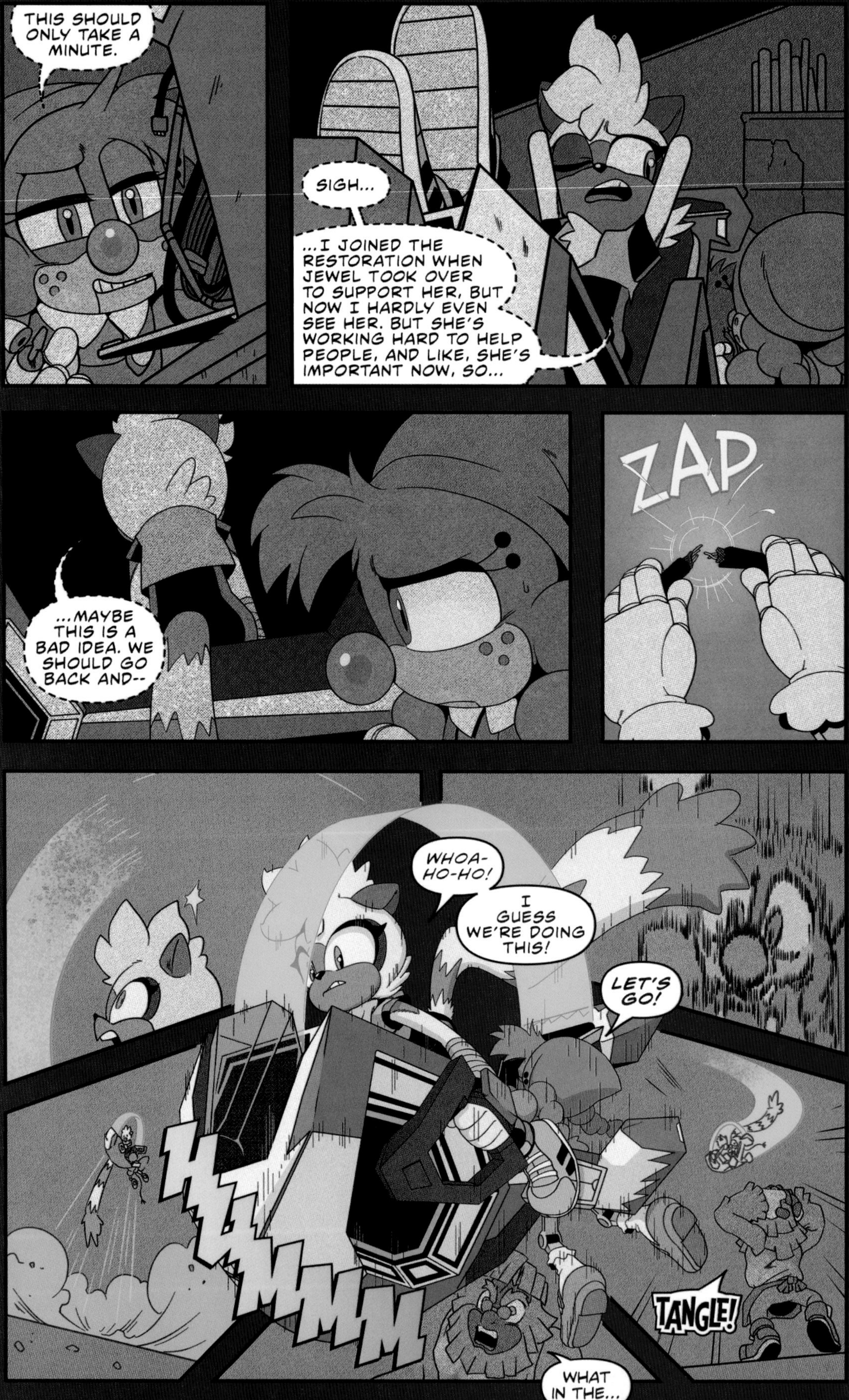
THIS SHOULD ONLY TAKE A MINUTE.
SIGH...
...I JOINED THE RESTORATION WHEN JEWEL TOOK OVER TO SUPPORT HER, BUT NOW I HARDLY EVEN SEE HER. BUT SHE'S WORKING HARD TO HELP PEOPLE, AND LIKE, SHE'S IMPORTANT NOW, SO...
...MAYBE THIS IS A BAD IDEA. WE SHOULD GO BACK AND--
ZAP
WHOA-HO-HO!
I GUESS WE'RE DOING THIS!
LET'S GO!
HMMMMM
TANGLE!
WHAT IN THE...

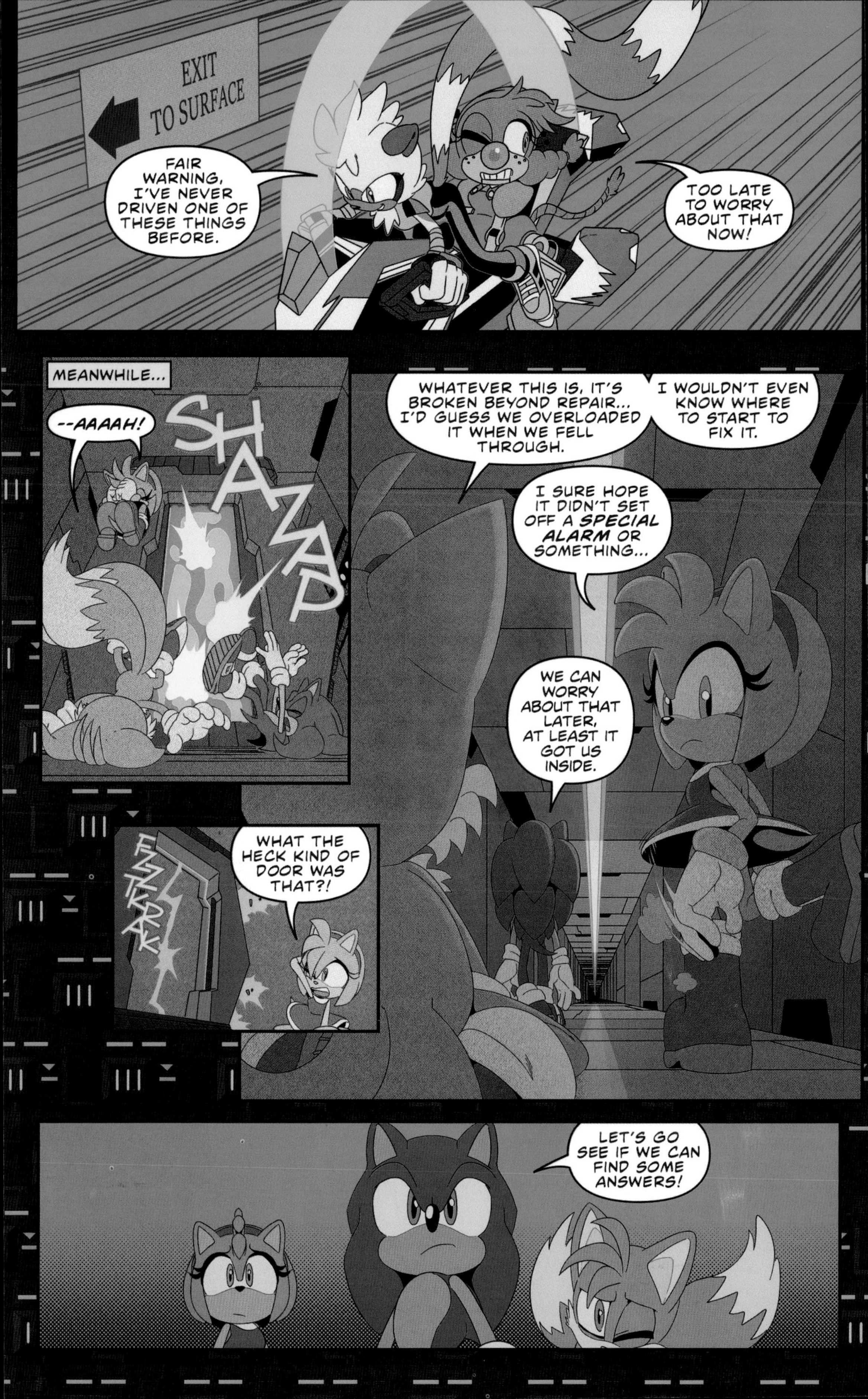

EXIT TO SURFACE
FAIR WARNING, I'VE NEVER DRIVEN ONE OF THESE THINGS BEFORE.
TOO LATE TO WORRY ABOUT THAT NOW!
MEANWHILE...
--AAAAH!
SHAZAAP
WHATEVER THIS IS, IT'S BROKEN BEYOND REPAIR... I'D GUESS WE OVERLOADED IT WHEN WE FELL THROUGH.
I WOULDN'T EVEN KNOW WHERE TO START TO FIX IT.
I SURE HOPE IT DIDN'T SET OFF A SPECIAL ALARM OR SOMETHING...
WE CAN WORRY ABOUT THAT LATER, AT LEAST IT GOT US INSIDE.
FZZKRAK
WHAT THE HECK KIND OF DOOR WAS THAT?!
LET'S GO SEE IF WE CAN FIND SOME ANSWERS!

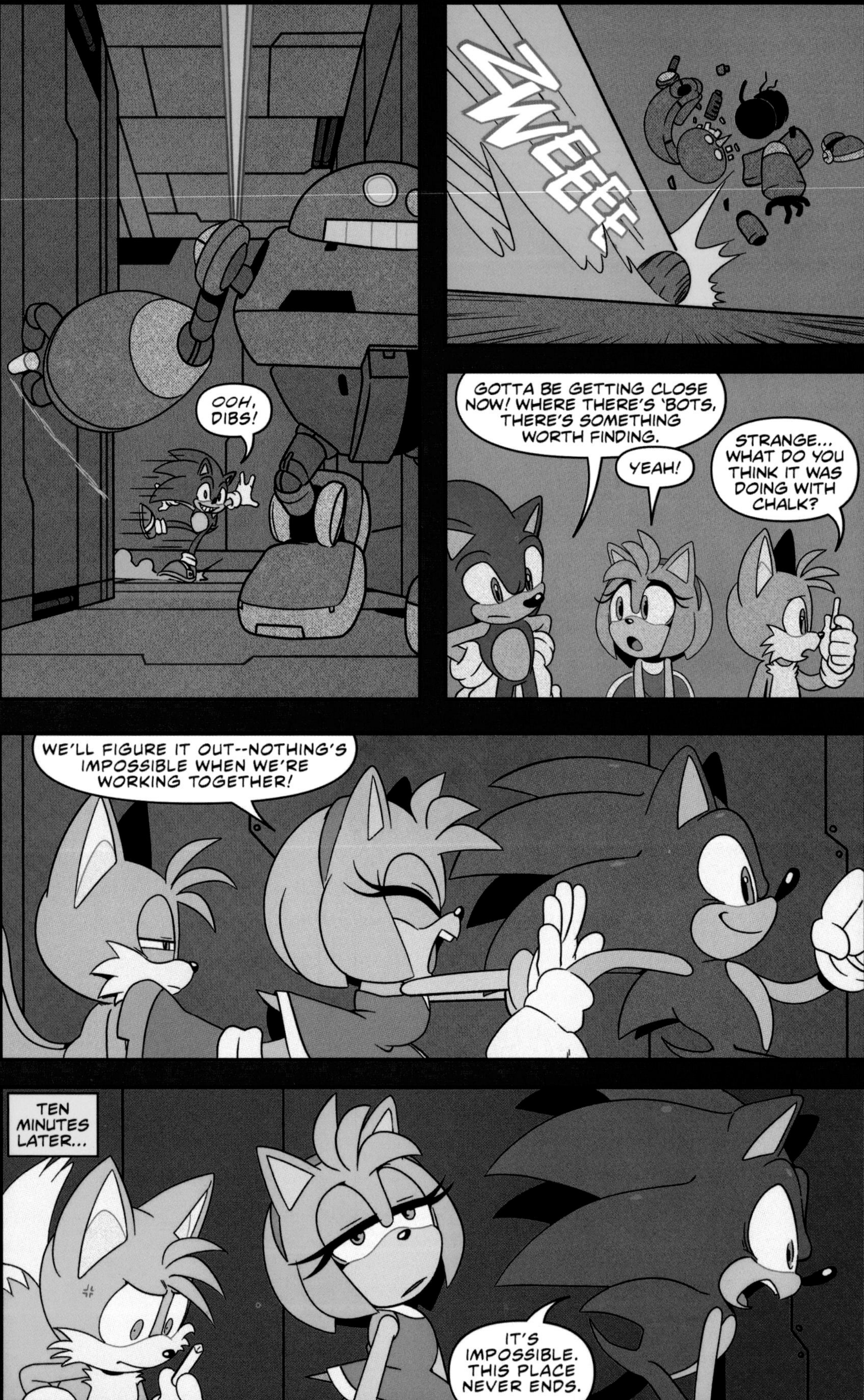
ZWEEEE
OOH, DIBS!
GOTTA BE GETTING CLOSE NOW! WHERE THERE'S 'BOTS, THERE'S SOMETHING WORTH FINDING.
YEAH!
STRANGE... WHAT DO YOU THINK IT WAS DOING WITH CHALK?
WE'LL FIGURE IT OUT--NOTHING'S IMPOSSIBLE WHEN WE'RE WORKING TOGETHER!
TEN MINUTES LATER...
IT'S IMPOSSIBLE. THIS PLACE NEVER ENDS.

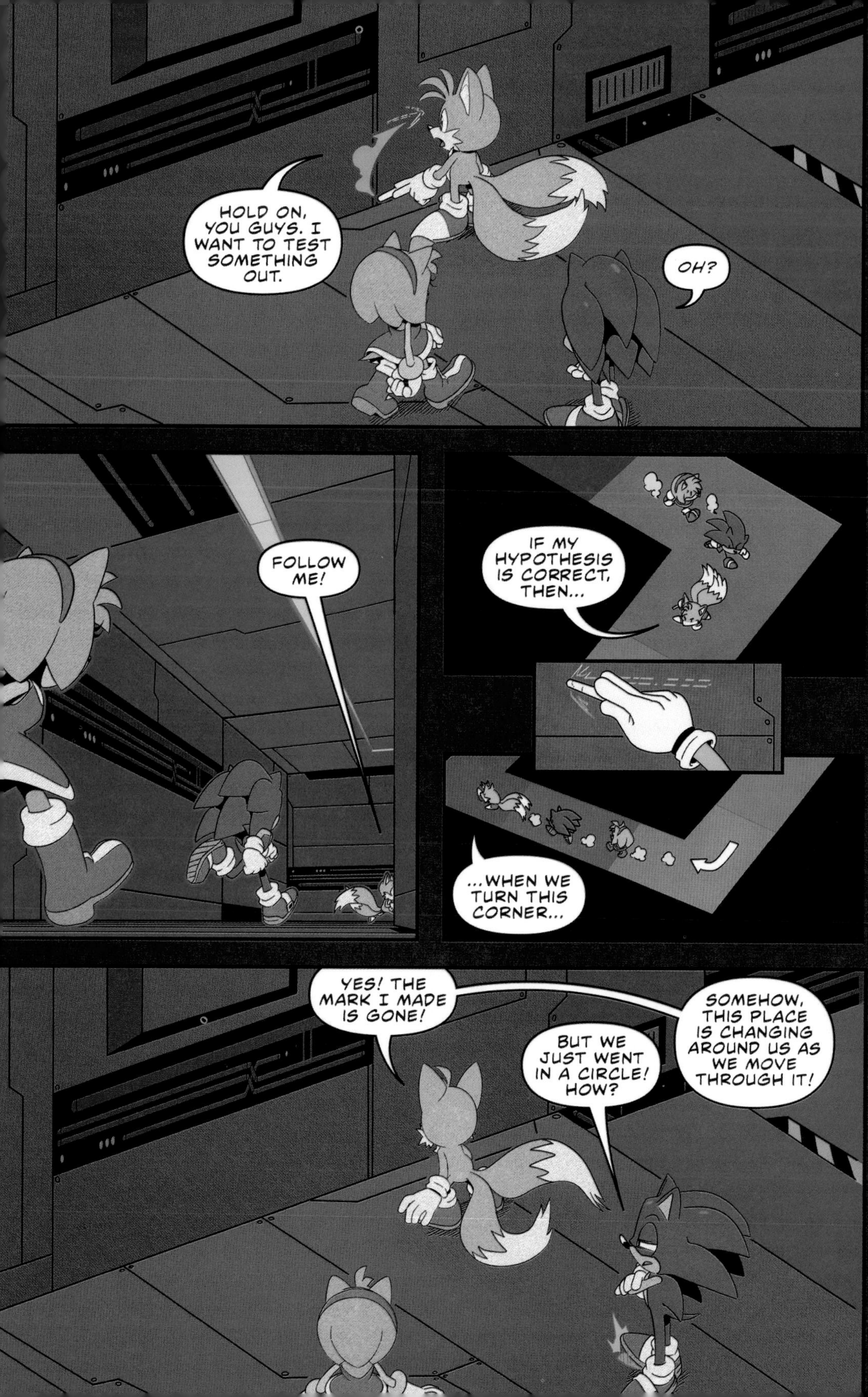
HOLD ON, YOU GUYS. I WANT TO TEST SOMETHING OUT.
OH?
FOLLOW ME!
IF MY HYPOTHESIS IS CORRECT, THEN...
...WHEN WE TURN THIS CORNER...
YES! THE MARK I MADE IS GONE!
BUT WE JUST WENT IN A CIRCLE! HOW?
SOMEHOW, THIS PLACE IS CHANGING AROUND US AS WE MOVE THROUGH IT!

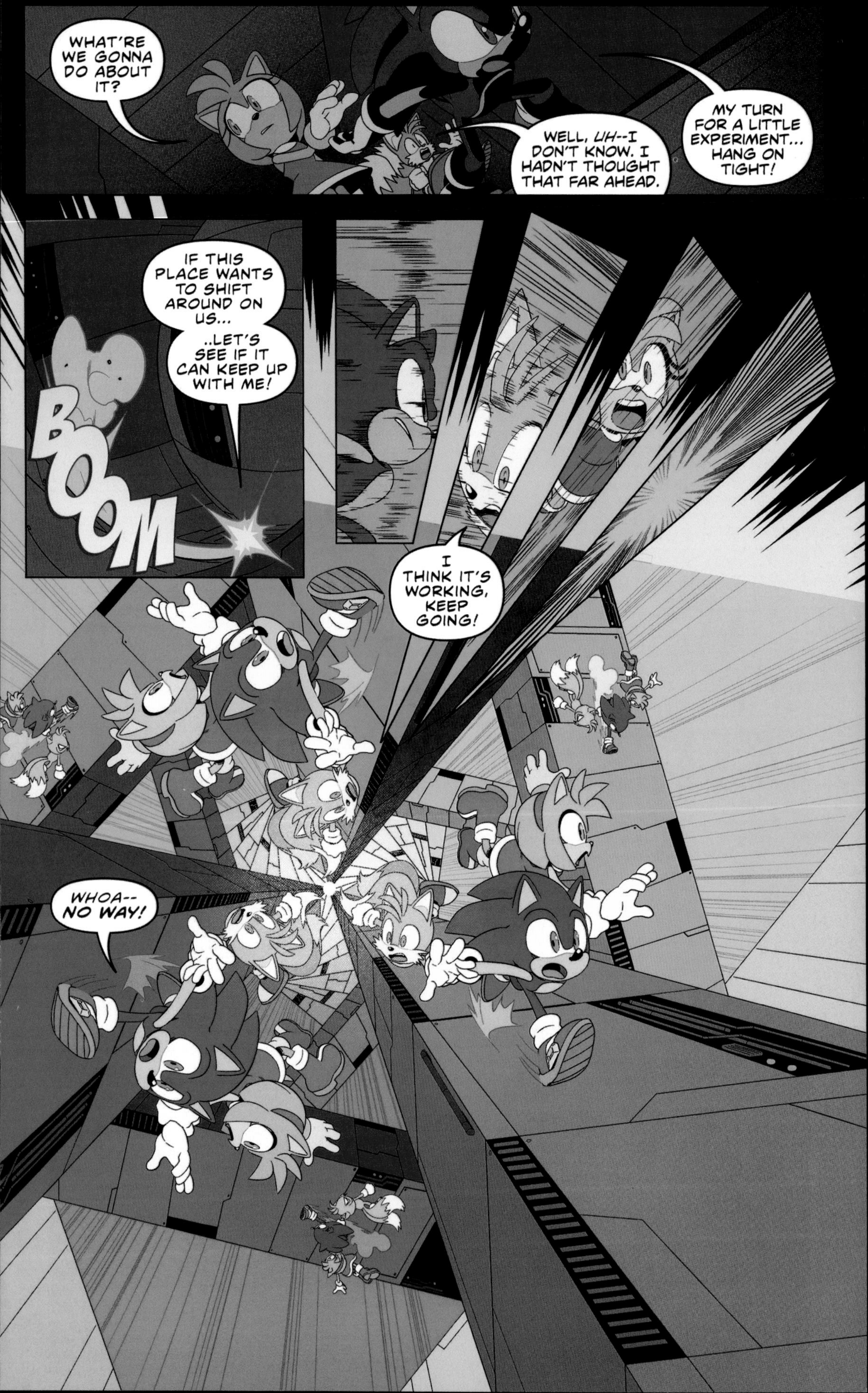
WHAT'RE WE GONNA DO ABOUT IT?
WELL, *UH*--I DON'T KNOW. I HADN'T THOUGHT THAT FAR AHEAD.
MY TURN FOR A LITTLE EXPERIMENT... HANG ON TIGHT!
IF THIS PLACE WANTS TO SHIFT AROUND ON US...
..LET'S SEE IF IT CAN KEEP UP WITH ME!
BOOM
I THINK IT'S WORKING, KEEP GOING!
WHOA-- NO WAY!

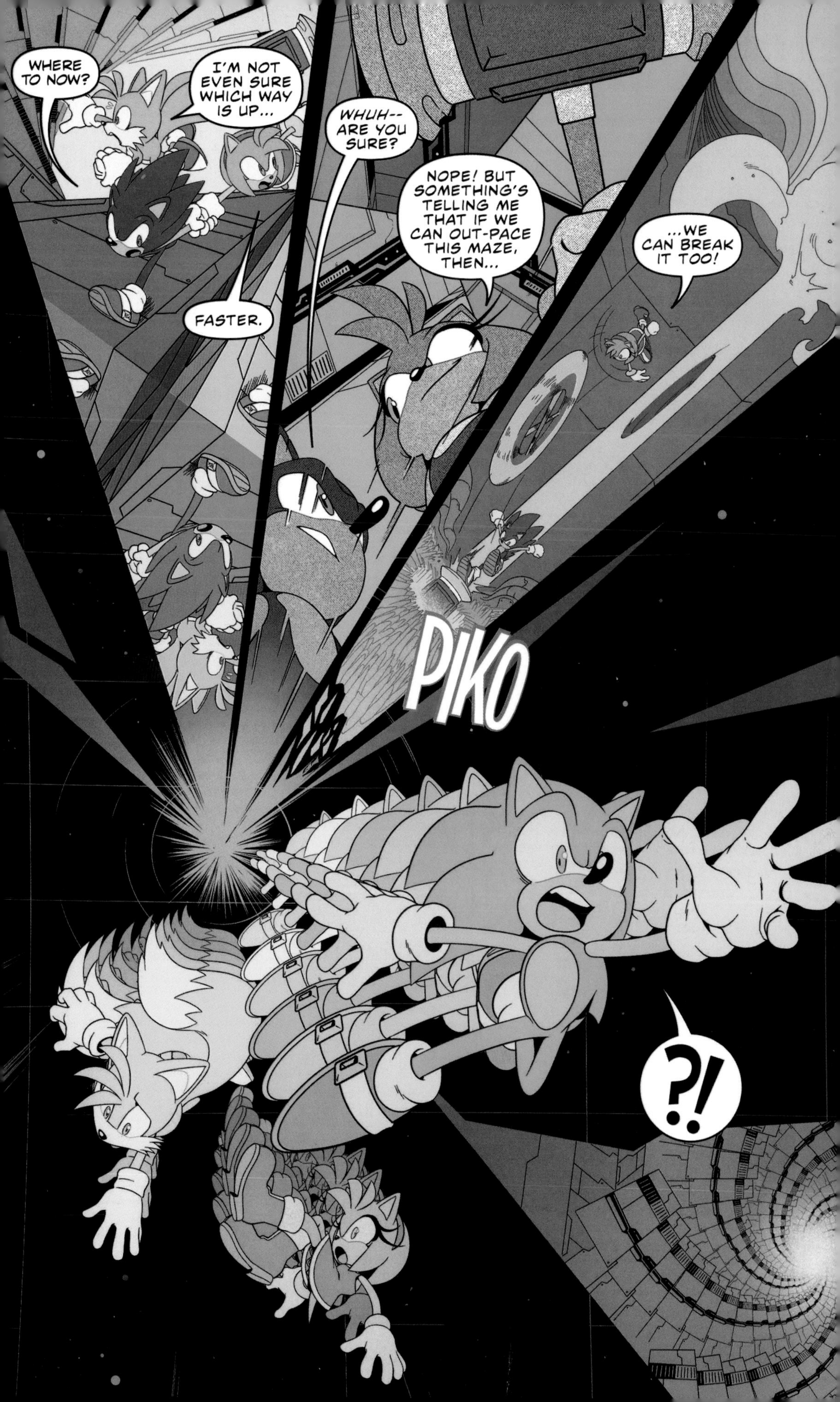
WHERE TO NOW?
I'M NOT EVEN SURE WHICH WAY IS UP...
FASTER.
WHUH-- ARE YOU SURE?
NOPE! BUT SOMETHING'S TELLING ME THAT IF WE CAN OUT-PACE THIS MAZE, THEN...
...WE CAN BREAK IT TOO!
PIKO
?!

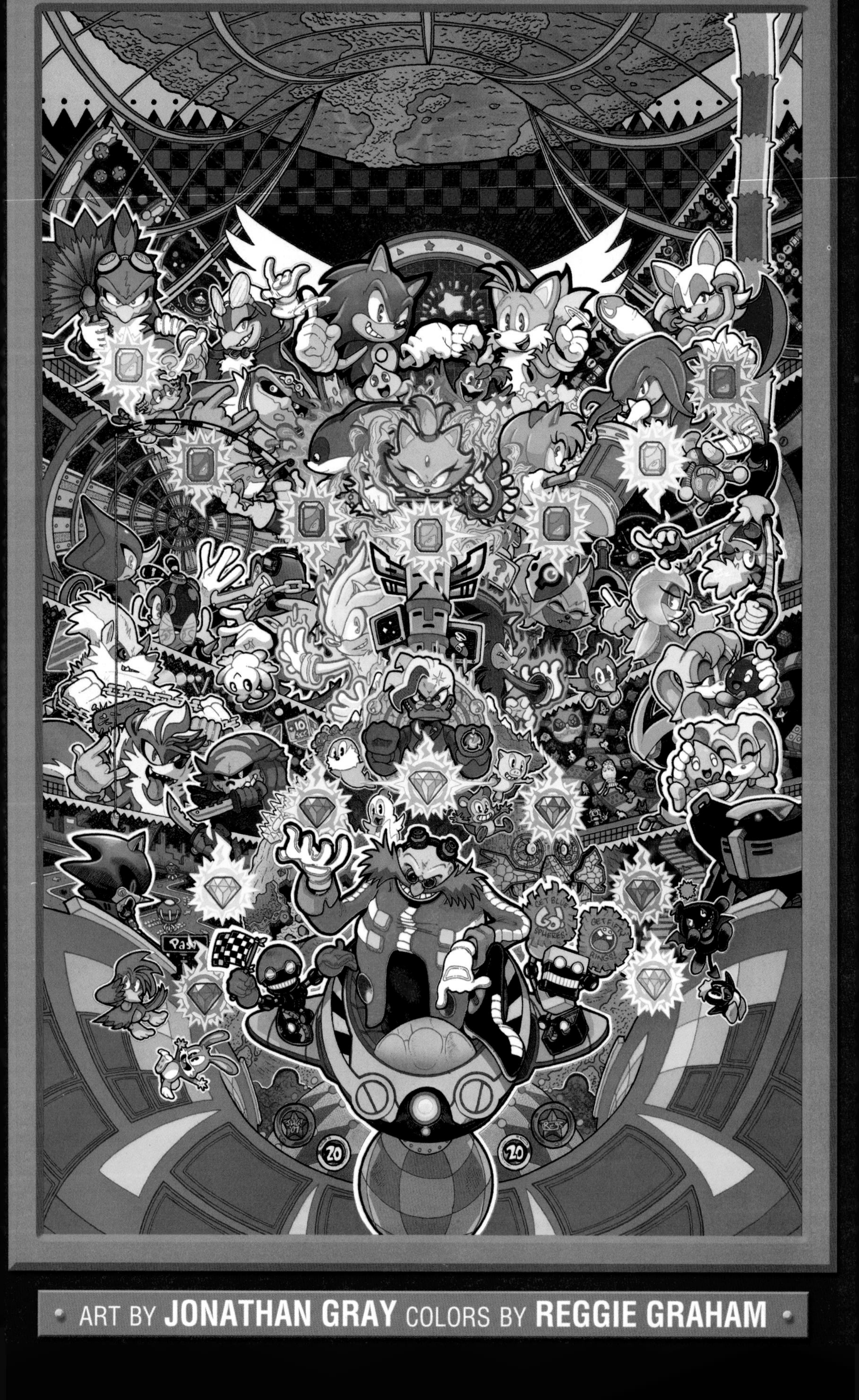
GET BLUE SPHERES!
GET FIFTY RINGS!
20
20

ART BY **JONATHAN GRAY** COLORS BY **REGGIE GRAHAM**

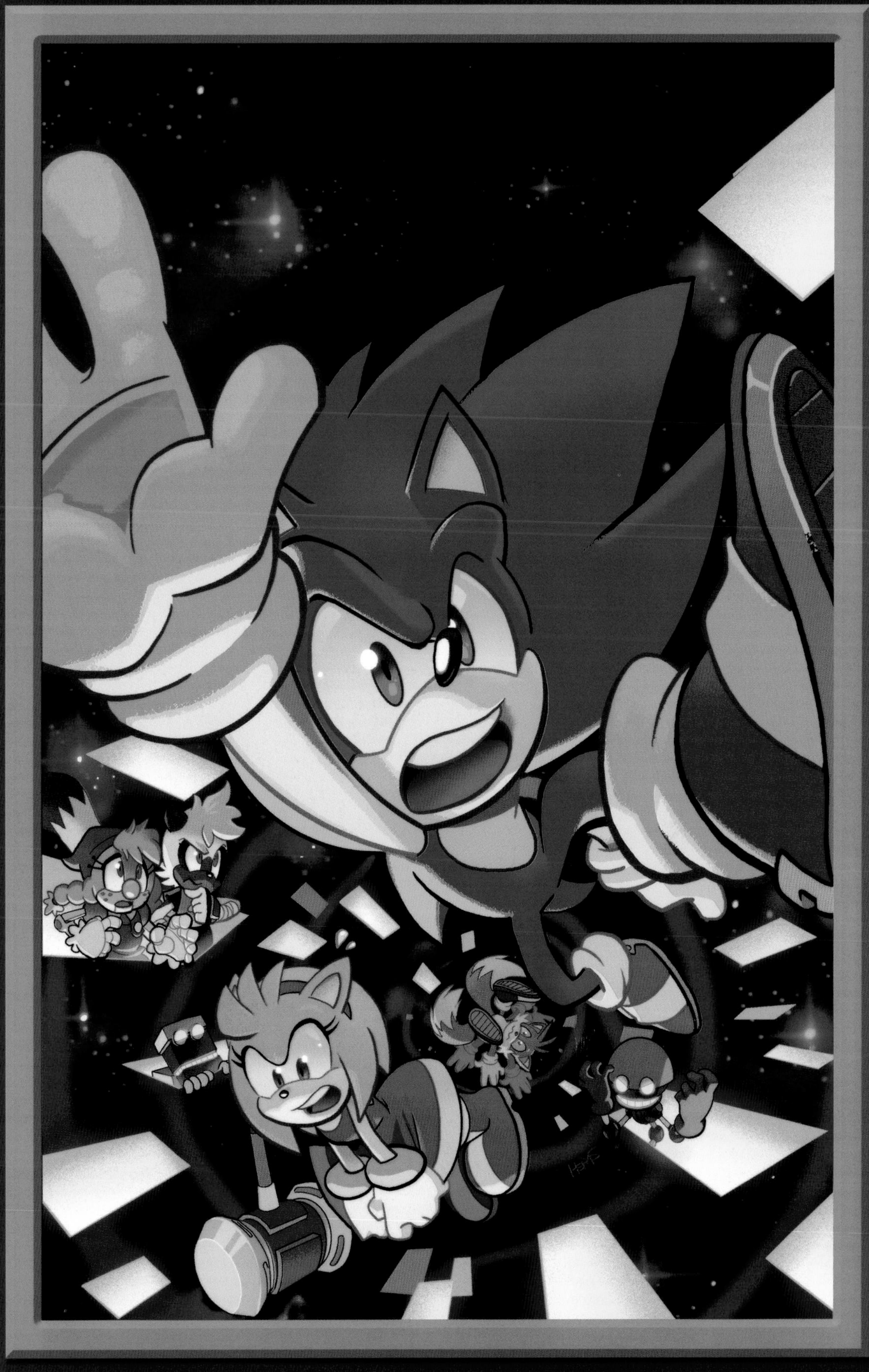

ART BY **MATT HERMS**

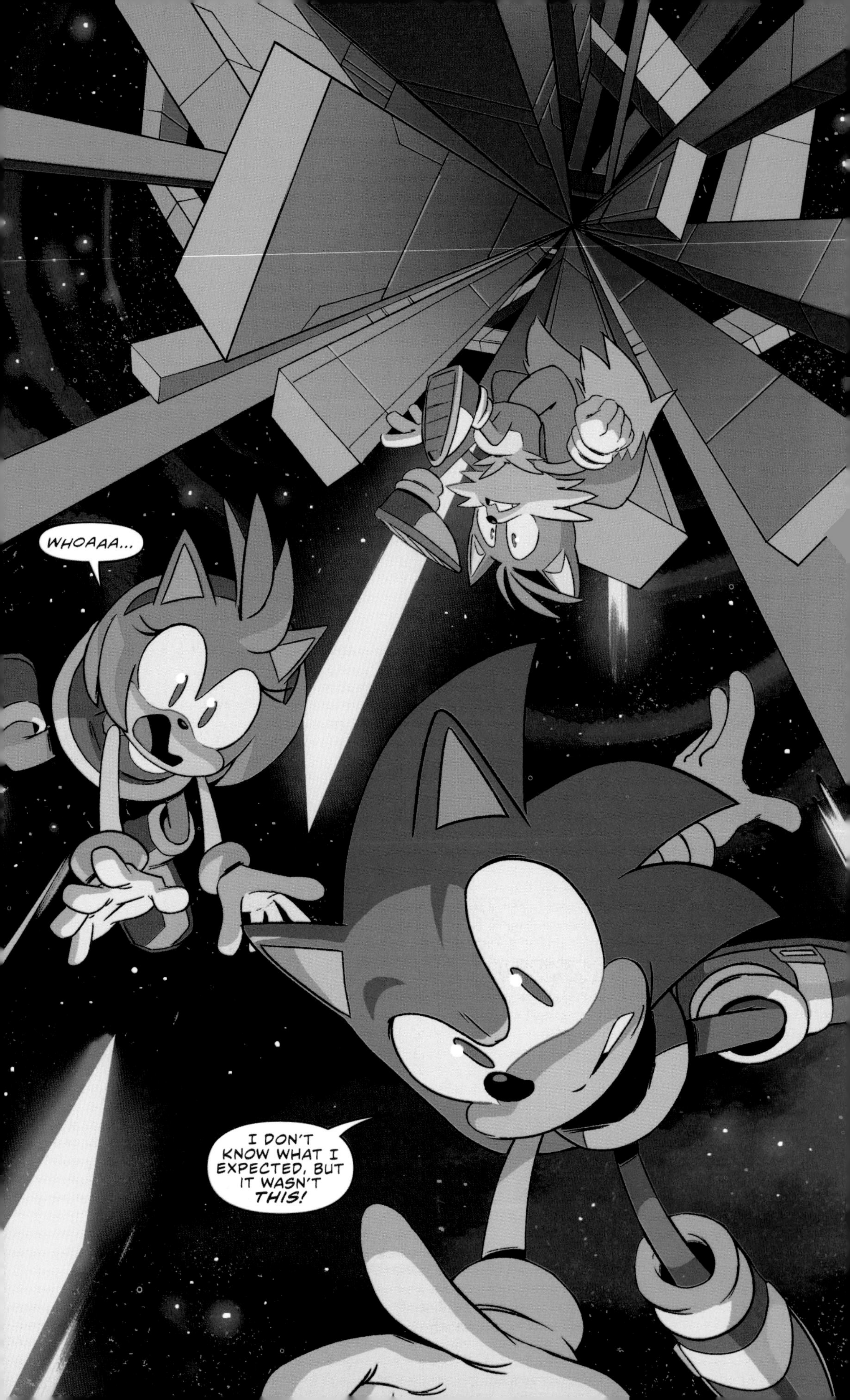
WHOAAA...
I DON'T KNOW WHAT I EXPECTED, BUT IT WASN'T *THIS!*

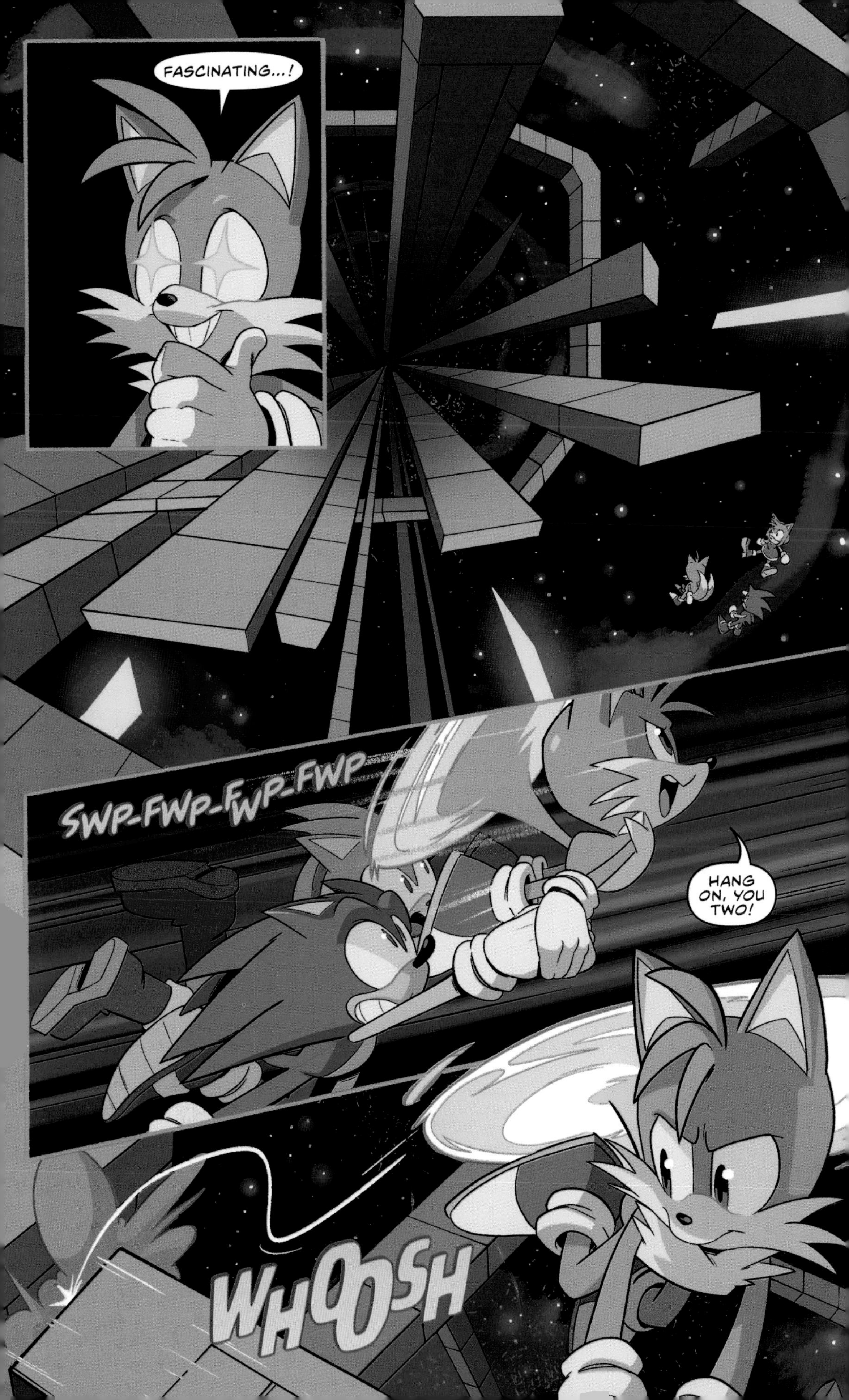
FASCINATING...!
SWP-FWP-FWP-FWP
HANG ON, YOU TWO!
WHOOSH

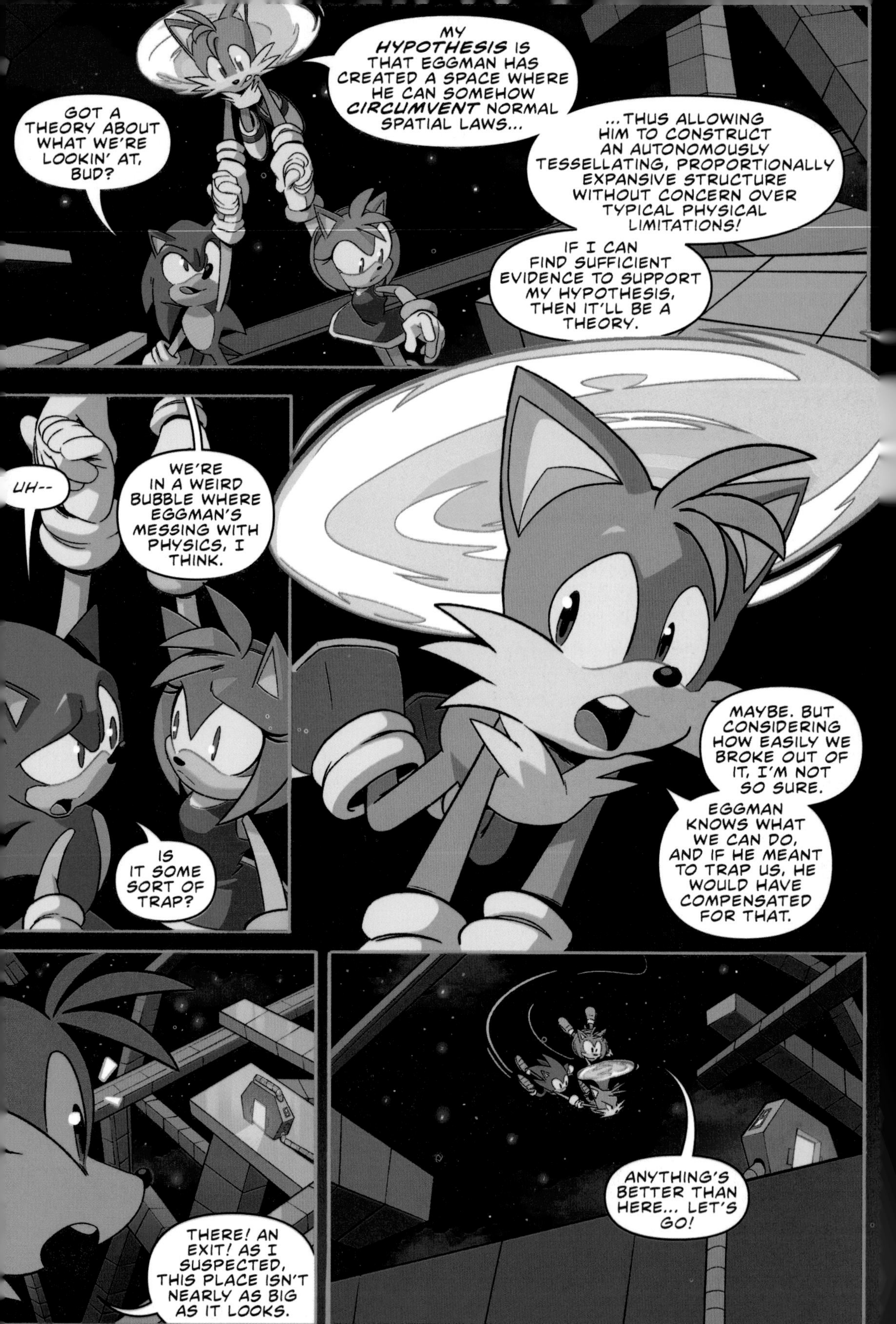
GOT A THEORY ABOUT WHAT WE'RE LOOKIN' AT, BUD?
MY *HYPOTHESIS* IS THAT EGGMAN HAS CREATED A SPACE WHERE HE CAN SOMEHOW *CIRCUMVENT* NORMAL SPATIAL LAWS...
...THUS ALLOWING HIM TO CONSTRUCT AN AUTONOMOUSLY TESSELLATING, PROPORTIONALLY EXPANSIVE STRUCTURE WITHOUT CONCERN OVER TYPICAL PHYSICAL LIMITATIONS!
IF I CAN FIND SUFFICIENT EVIDENCE TO SUPPORT MY HYPOTHESIS, THEN IT'LL BE A THEORY.
UH--
WE'RE IN A WEIRD BUBBLE WHERE EGGMAN'S MESSING WITH PHYSICS, I THINK.
IS IT SOME SORT OF TRAP?
MAYBE. BUT CONSIDERING HOW EASILY WE BROKE OUT OF IT, I'M NOT SO SURE.
EGGMAN KNOWS WHAT WE CAN DO, AND IF HE MEANT TO TRAP US, HE WOULD HAVE COMPENSATED FOR THAT.
THERE! AN EXIT! AS I SUSPECTED, THIS PLACE ISN'T NEARLY AS BIG AS IT LOOKS.
ANYTHING'S BETTER THAN HERE... LET'S GO!

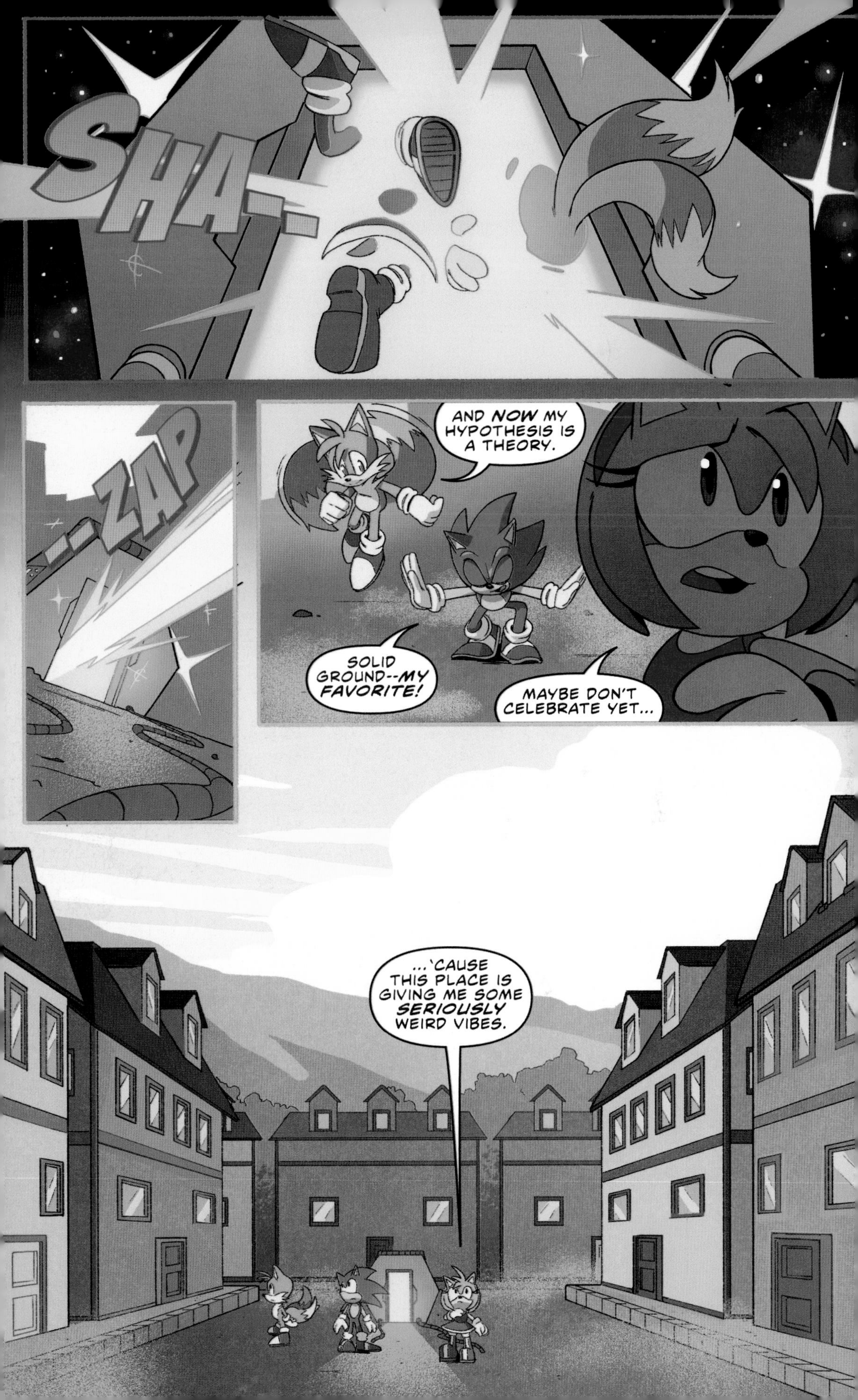
SHA...
...ZAP
AND NOW MY HYPOTHESIS IS A THEORY.
SOLID GROUND--MY FAVORITE!
MAYBE DON'T CELEBRATE YET...
...'CAUSE THIS PLACE IS GIVING ME SOME SERIOUSLY WEIRD VIBES.

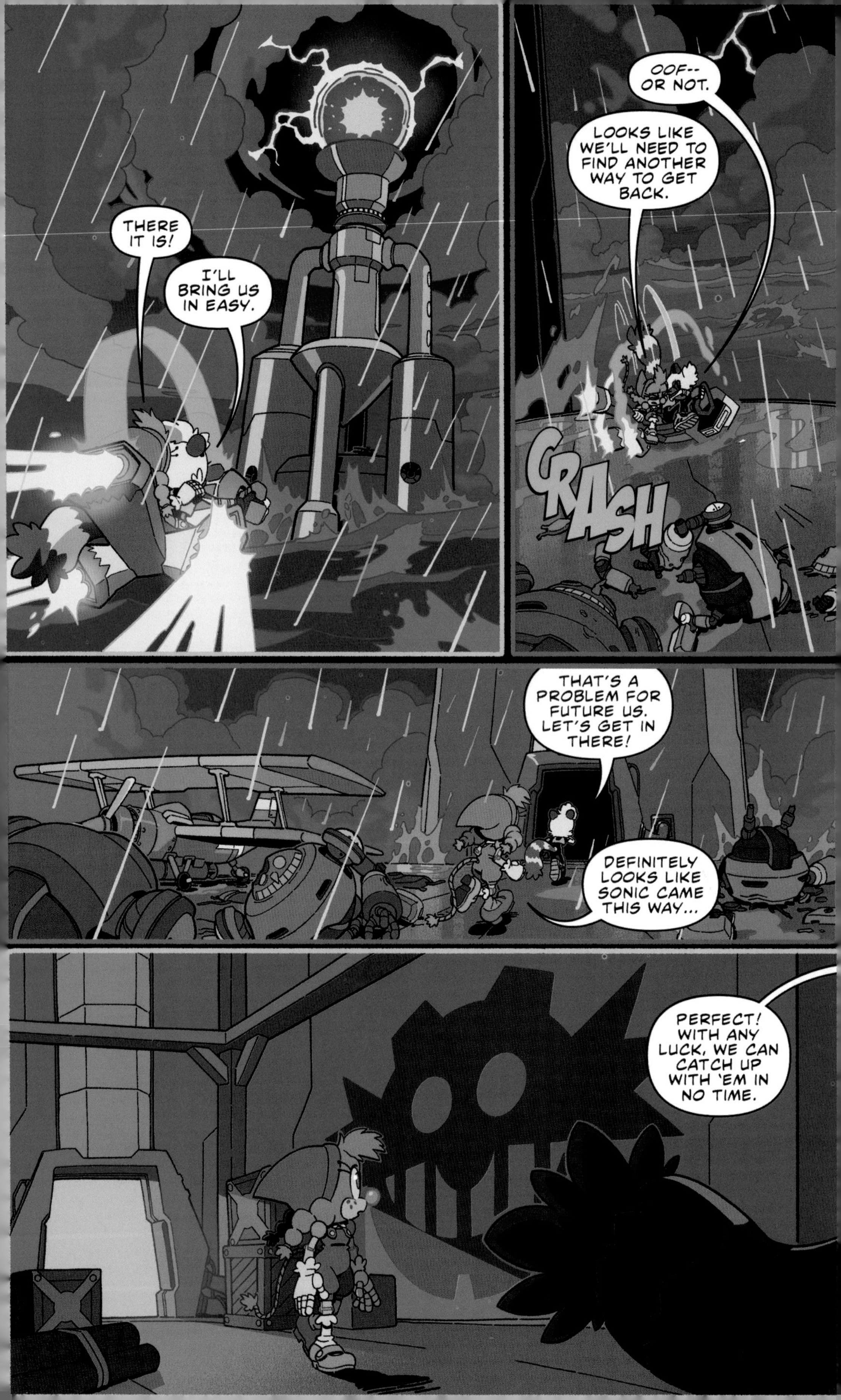
THERE IT IS!
I'LL BRING US IN EASY.
CRASH
OOF-- OR NOT.
LOOKS LIKE WE'LL NEED TO FIND ANOTHER WAY TO GET BACK.
THAT'S A PROBLEM FOR FUTURE US. LET'S GET IN THERE!
DEFINITELY LOOKS LIKE SONIC CAME THIS WAY...
PERFECT! WITH ANY LUCK, WE CAN CATCH UP WITH 'EM IN NO TIME.

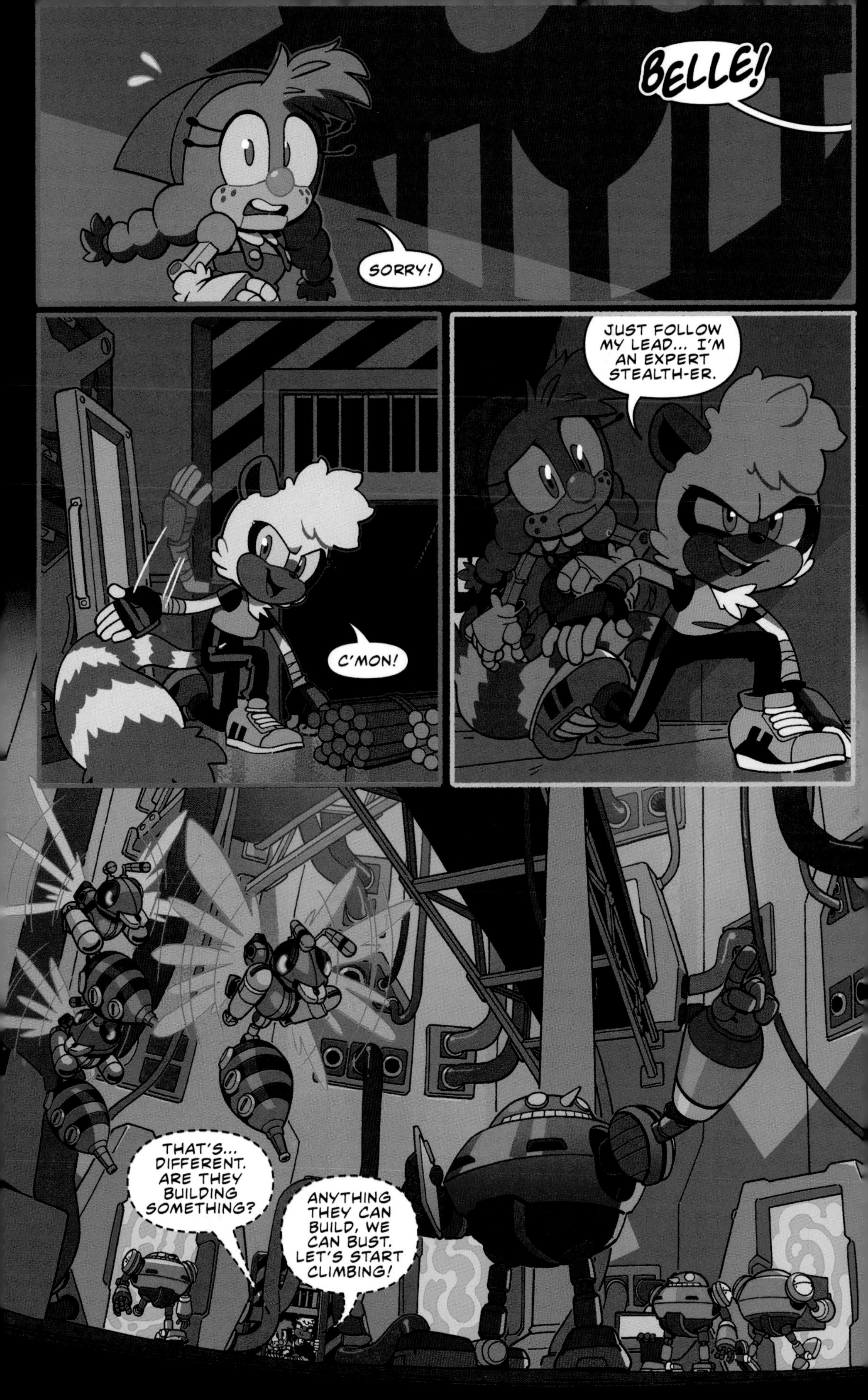
BELLE!
SORRY!
C'MON!
JUST FOLLOW MY LEAD... I'M AN EXPERT STEALTH-ER.
THAT'S... DIFFERENT. ARE THEY BUILDING SOMETHING?
ANYTHING THEY CAN BUILD, WE CAN BUST. LET'S START CLIMBING!

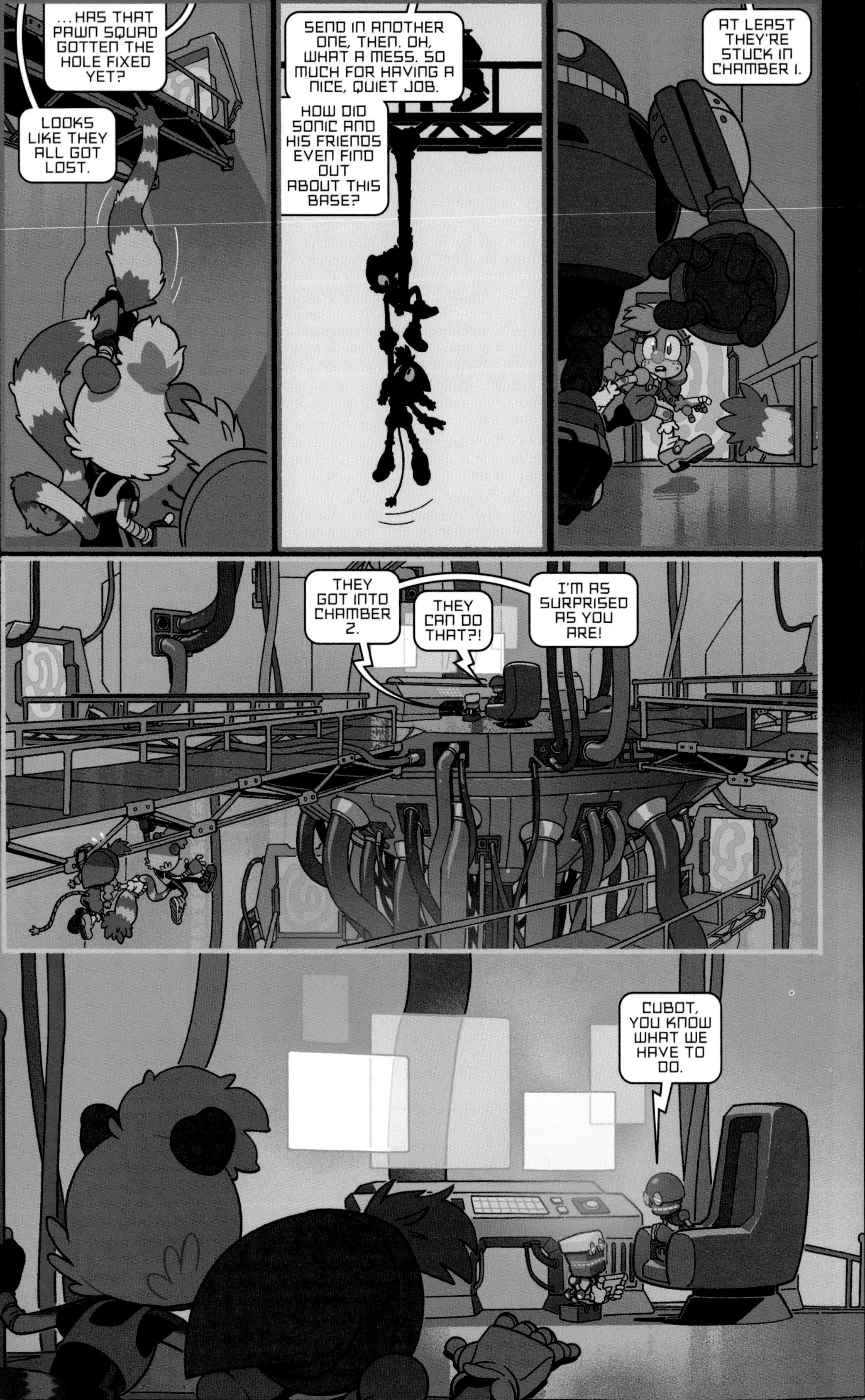
...HAS THAT PAWN SQUAD GOTTEN THE HOLE FIXED YET?
LOOKS LIKE THEY ALL GOT LOST.
SEND IN ANOTHER ONE, THEN. OH, WHAT A MESS. SO MUCH FOR HAVING A NICE, QUIET JOB.
HOW DID SONIC AND HIS FRIENDS EVEN FIND OUT ABOUT THIS BASE?
AT LEAST THEY'RE STUCK IN CHAMBER 1.
THEY GOT INTO CHAMBER 2.
THEY CAN DO THAT?!
I'M AS SURPRISED AS YOU ARE!
CUBOT, YOU KNOW WHAT WE HAVE TO DO.

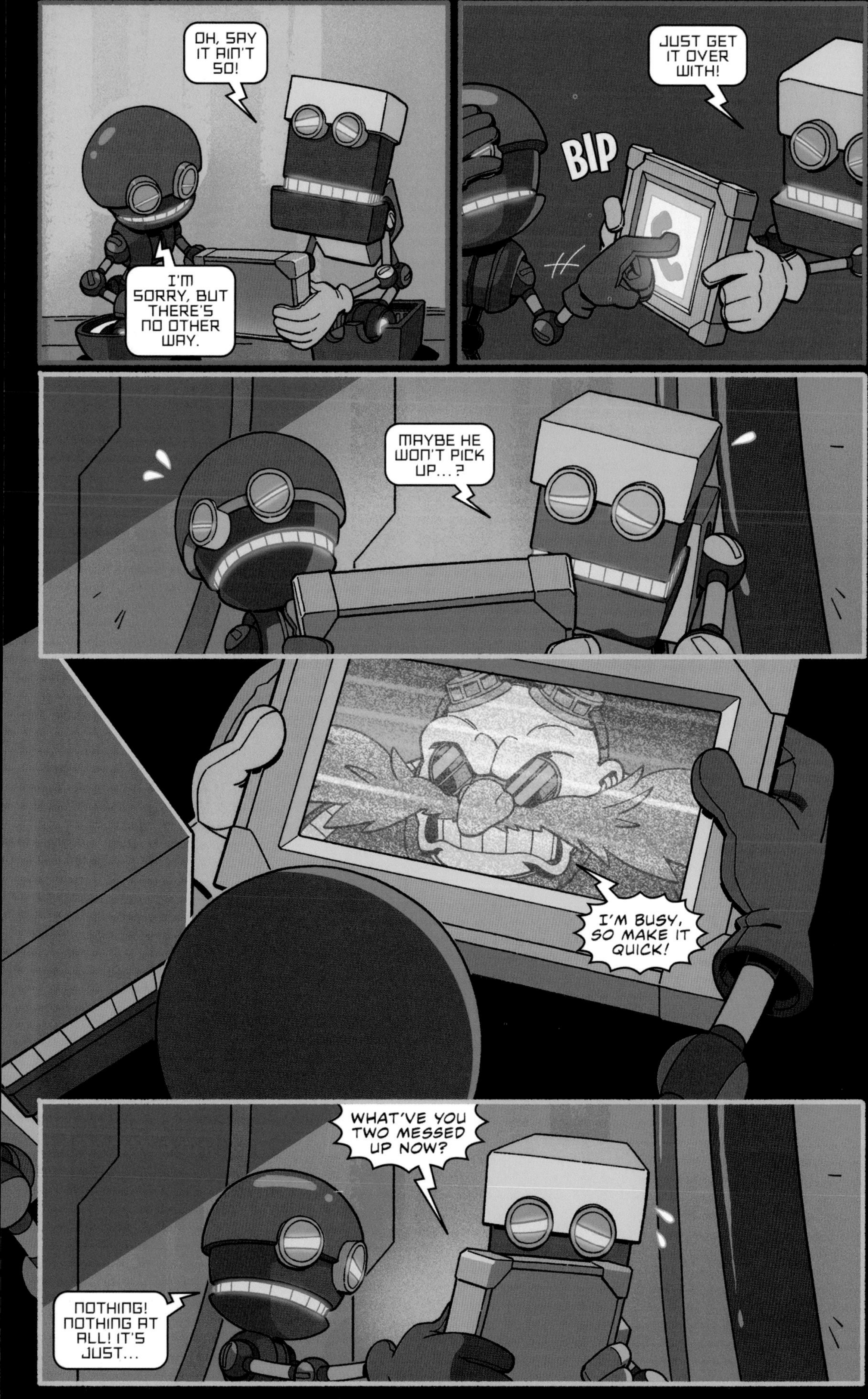
OH, SAY IT AIN'T SO!
I'M SORRY, BUT THERE'S NO OTHER WAY.
JUST GET IT OVER WITH!
BIP
MAYBE HE WON'T PICK UP...?
I'M BUSY, SO MAKE IT QUICK!
WHAT'VE YOU TWO MESSED UP NOW?
NOTHING! NOTHING AT ALL! IT'S JUST...

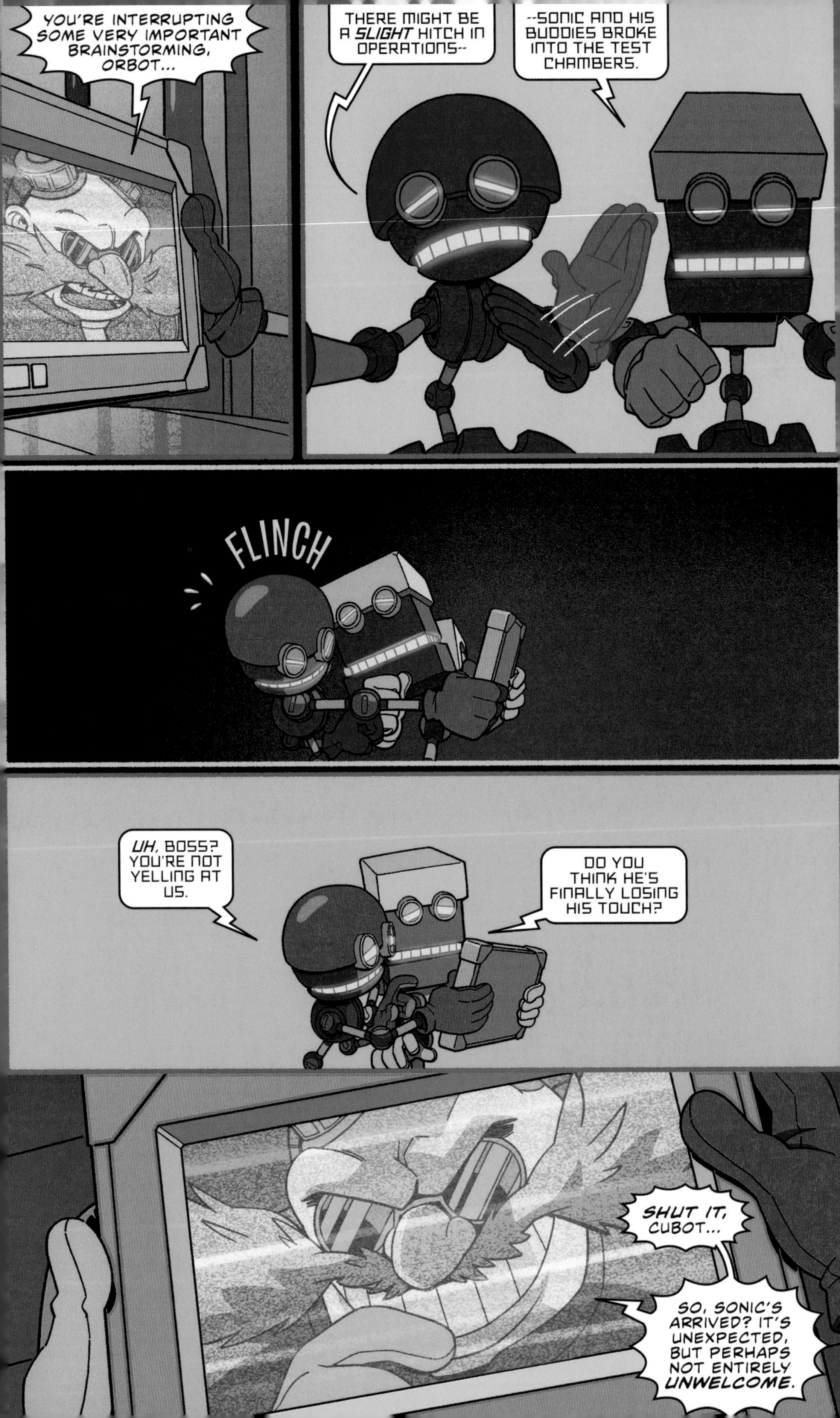
YOU'RE INTERRUPTING SOME VERY IMPORTANT BRAINSTORMING, ORBOT...
THERE MIGHT BE A *SLIGHT* HITCH IN OPERATIONS--
--SONIC AND HIS BUDDIES BROKE INTO THE TEST CHAMBERS.
FLINCH
UH, BOSS? YOU'RE NOT YELLING AT US.
DO YOU THINK HE'S FINALLY LOSING HIS TOUCH?
SHUT IT, CUBOT...
SO, SONIC'S ARRIVED? IT'S UNEXPECTED, BUT PERHAPS NOT ENTIRELY *UNWELCOME.*

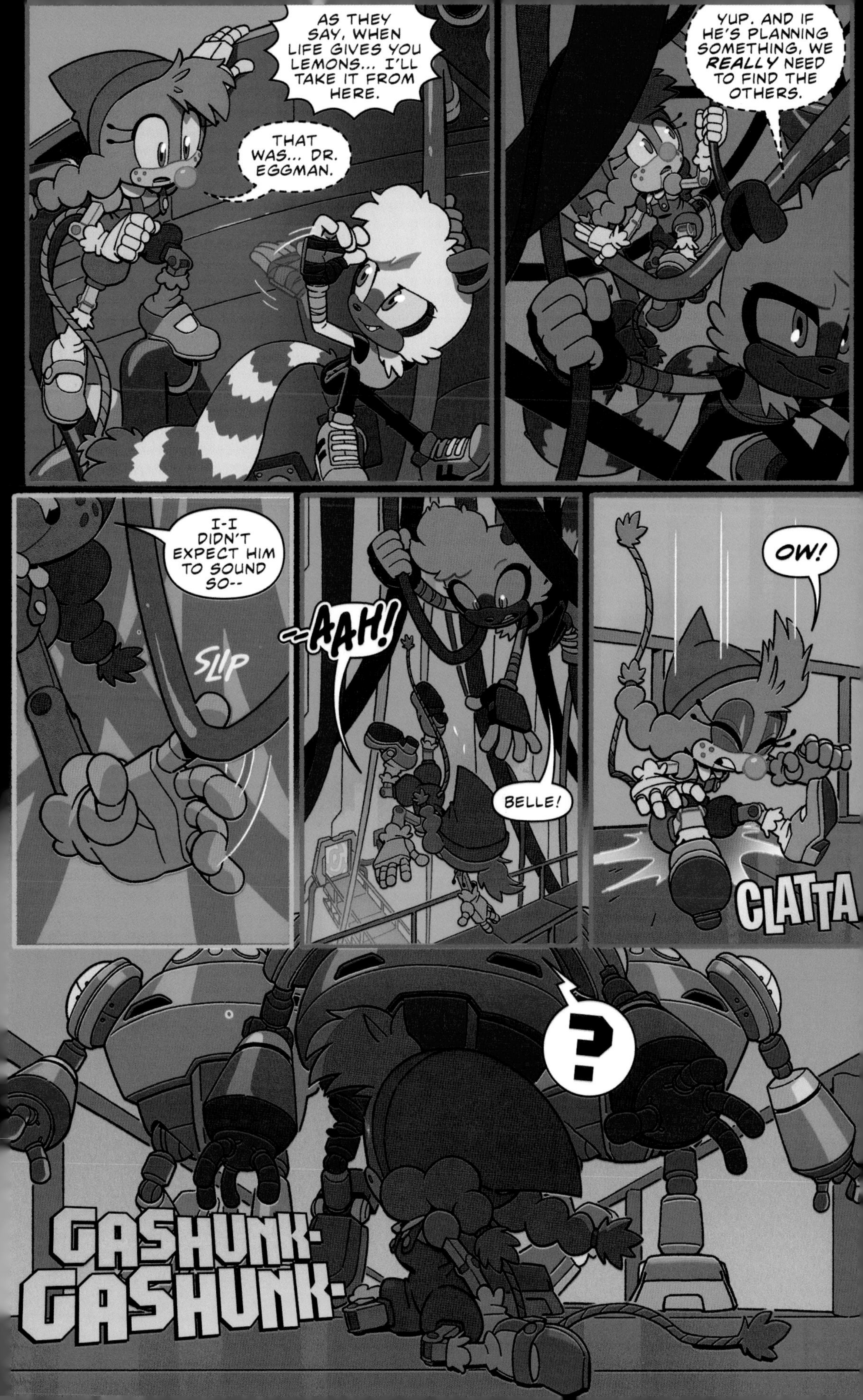
AS THEY SAY, WHEN LIFE GIVES YOU LEMONS... I'LL TAKE IT FROM HERE.
THAT WAS... DR. EGGMAN.
YUP. AND IF HE'S PLANNING SOMETHING, WE REALLY NEED TO FIND THE OTHERS.
I-I DIDN'T EXPECT HIM TO SOUND SO--
SLIP
--AAH!
BELLE!
OW!
CLATTA
?
GASHUNK-
GASHUNK-

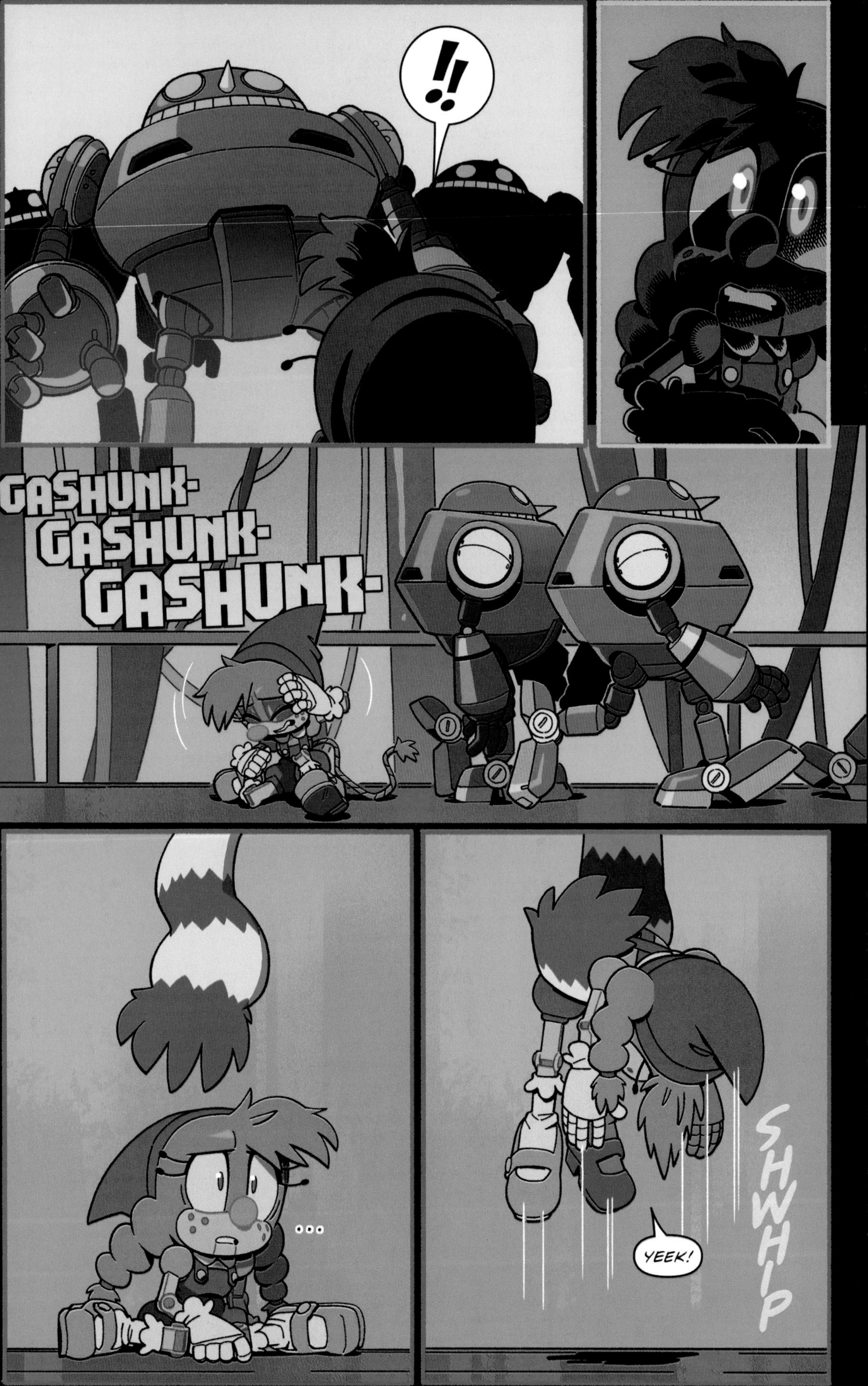
!!
GASHUNK-
GASHUNK-
GASHUNK-
...
YEEK!
SHWHIP

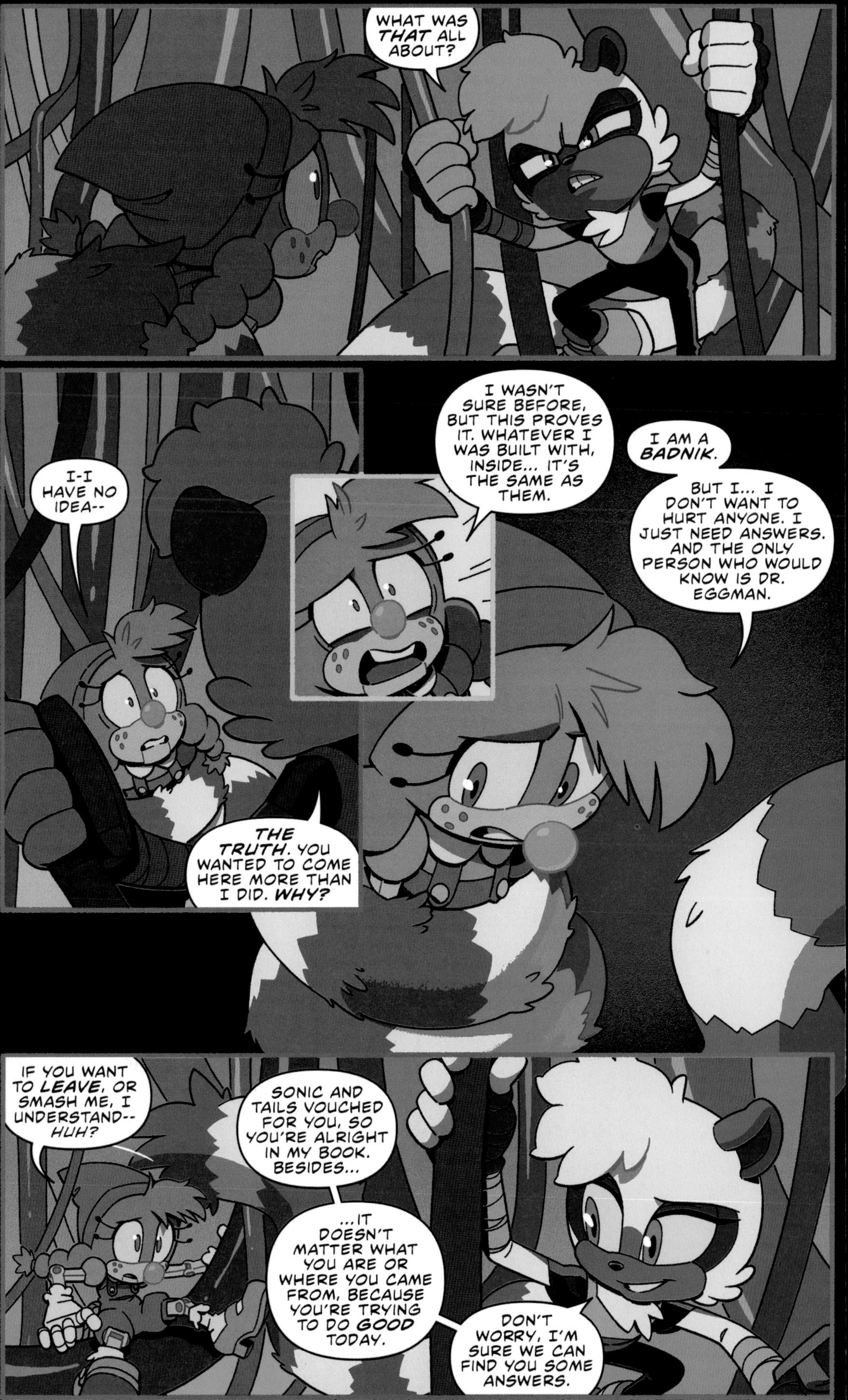
WHAT WAS THAT ALL ABOUT?
I-I HAVE NO IDEA--
THE TRUTH. YOU WANTED TO COME HERE MORE THAN I DID. WHY?
I WASN'T SURE BEFORE, BUT THIS PROVES IT. WHATEVER I WAS BUILT WITH, INSIDE... IT'S THE SAME AS THEM.
I AM A BADNIK.
BUT I... I DON'T WANT TO HURT ANYONE. I JUST NEED ANSWERS. AND THE ONLY PERSON WHO WOULD KNOW IS DR. EGGMAN.
IF YOU WANT TO LEAVE, OR SMASH ME, I UNDERSTAND-- HUH?
SONIC AND TAILS VOUCHED FOR YOU, SO YOU'RE ALRIGHT IN MY BOOK. BESIDES...
...IT DOESN'T MATTER WHAT YOU ARE OR WHERE YOU CAME FROM, BECAUSE YOU'RE TRYING TO DO GOOD TODAY.
DON'T WORRY, I'M SURE WE CAN FIND YOU SOME ANSWERS.

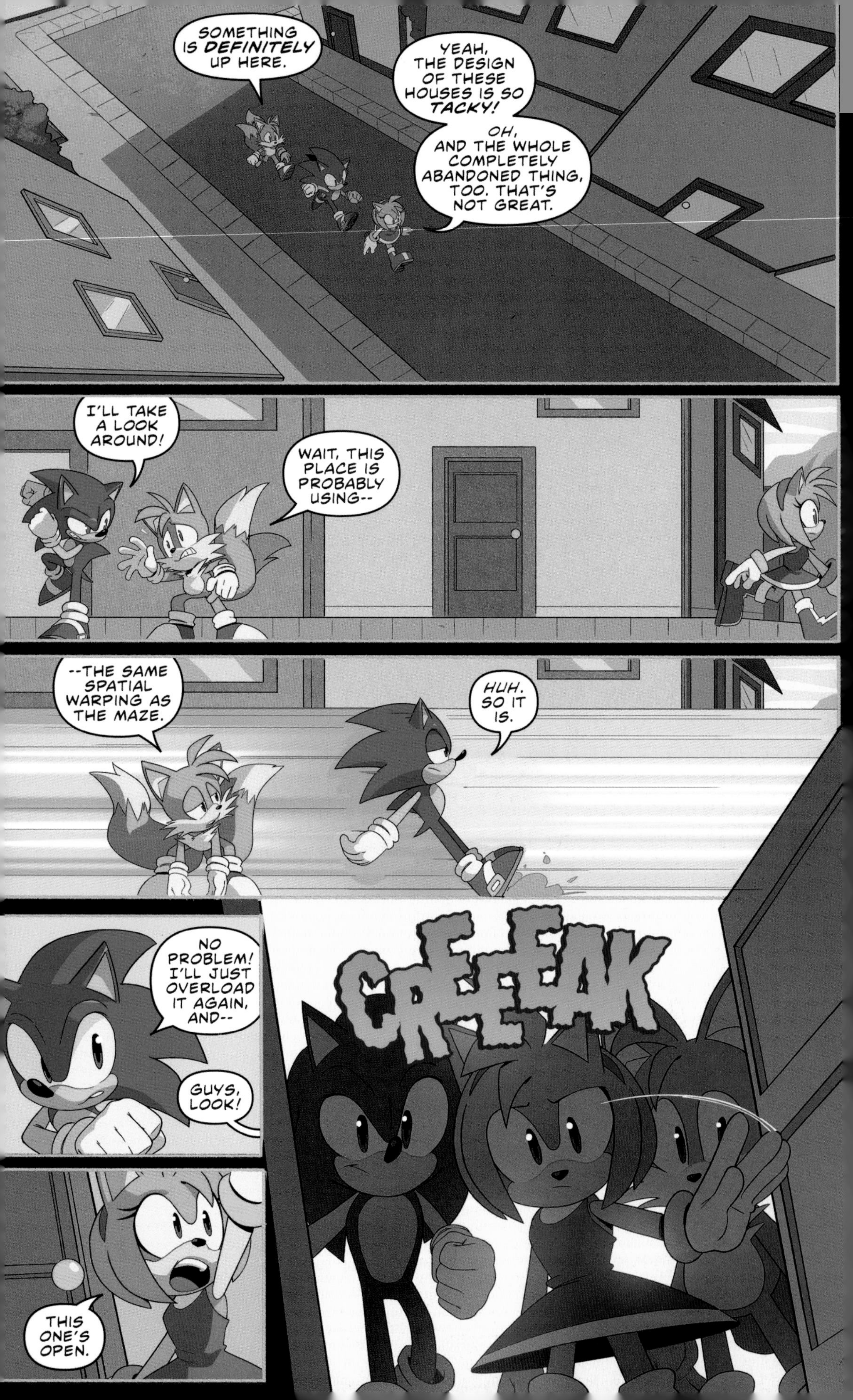
SOMETHING IS DEFINITELY UP HERE.
YEAH, THE DESIGN OF THESE HOUSES IS SO TACKY!
OH, AND THE WHOLE COMPLETELY ABANDONED THING, TOO. THAT'S NOT GREAT.
I'LL TAKE A LOOK AROUND!
WAIT, THIS PLACE IS PROBABLY USING--
--THE SAME SPATIAL WARPING AS THE MAZE.
HUH. SO IT IS.
NO PROBLEM! I'LL JUST OVERLOAD IT AGAIN, AND--
GUYS, LOOK!
THIS ONE'S OPEN.
CREEEAK

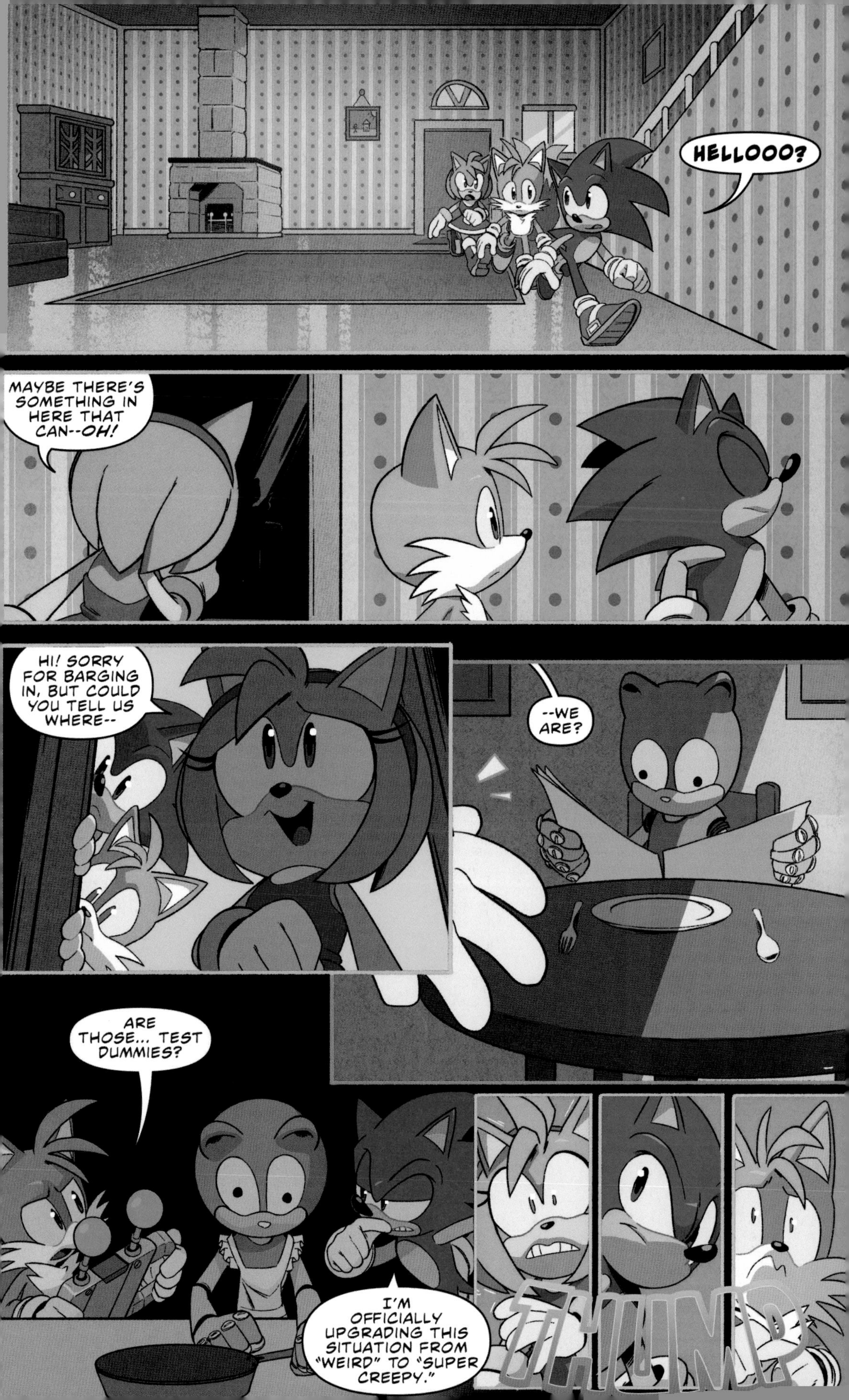
HELLOOO?
MAYBE THERE'S SOMETHING IN HERE THAT CAN--OH!
HI! SORRY FOR BARGING IN, BUT COULD YOU TELL US WHERE--
--WE ARE?
ARE THOSE... TEST DUMMIES?
I'M OFFICIALLY UPGRADING THIS SITUATION FROM "WEIRD" TO "SUPER CREEPY."
THUMP

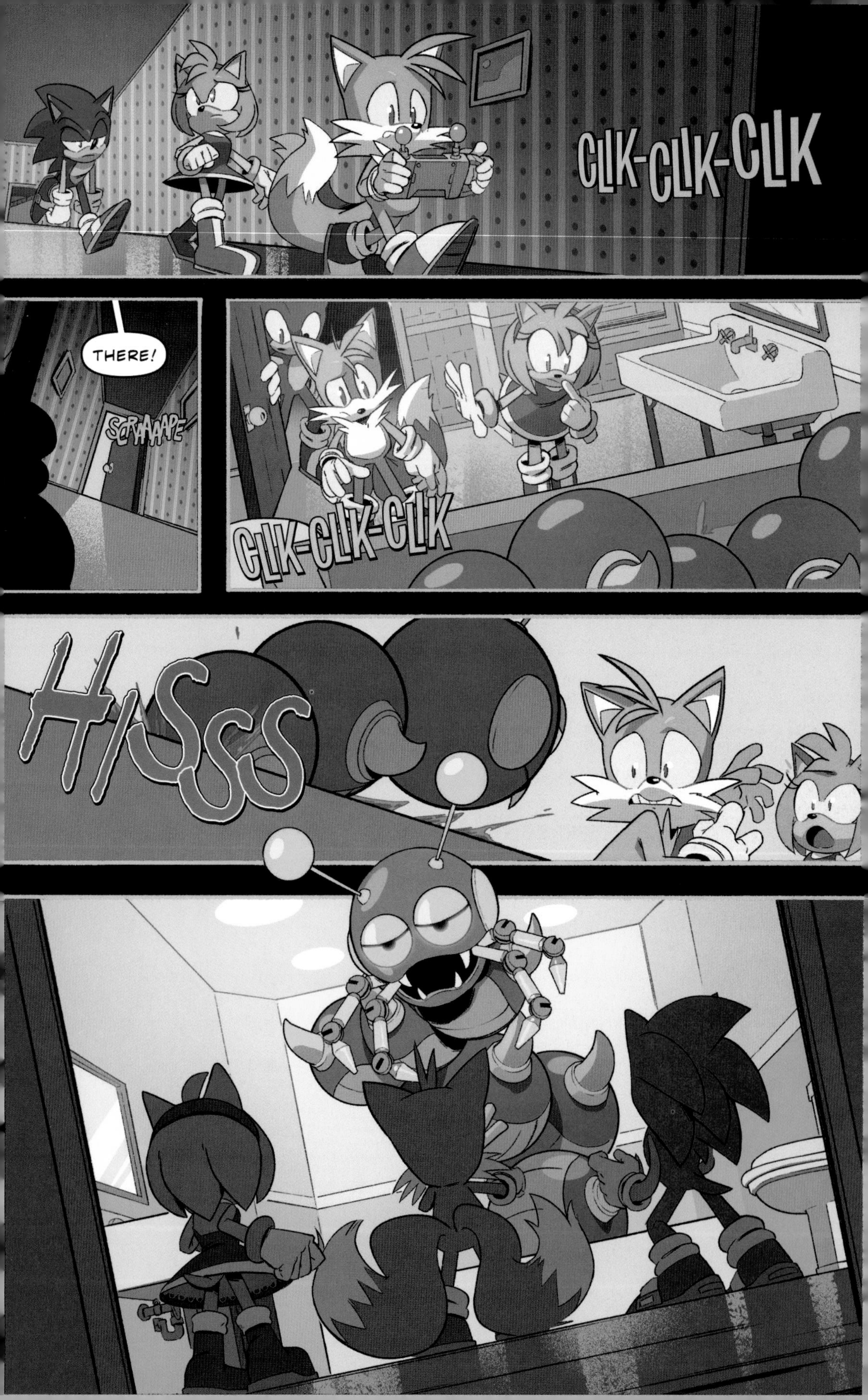
CLIK-CLIK-CLIK
THERE!
SCRAAAAPE
CLIK-CLIK-CLIK
HISSS

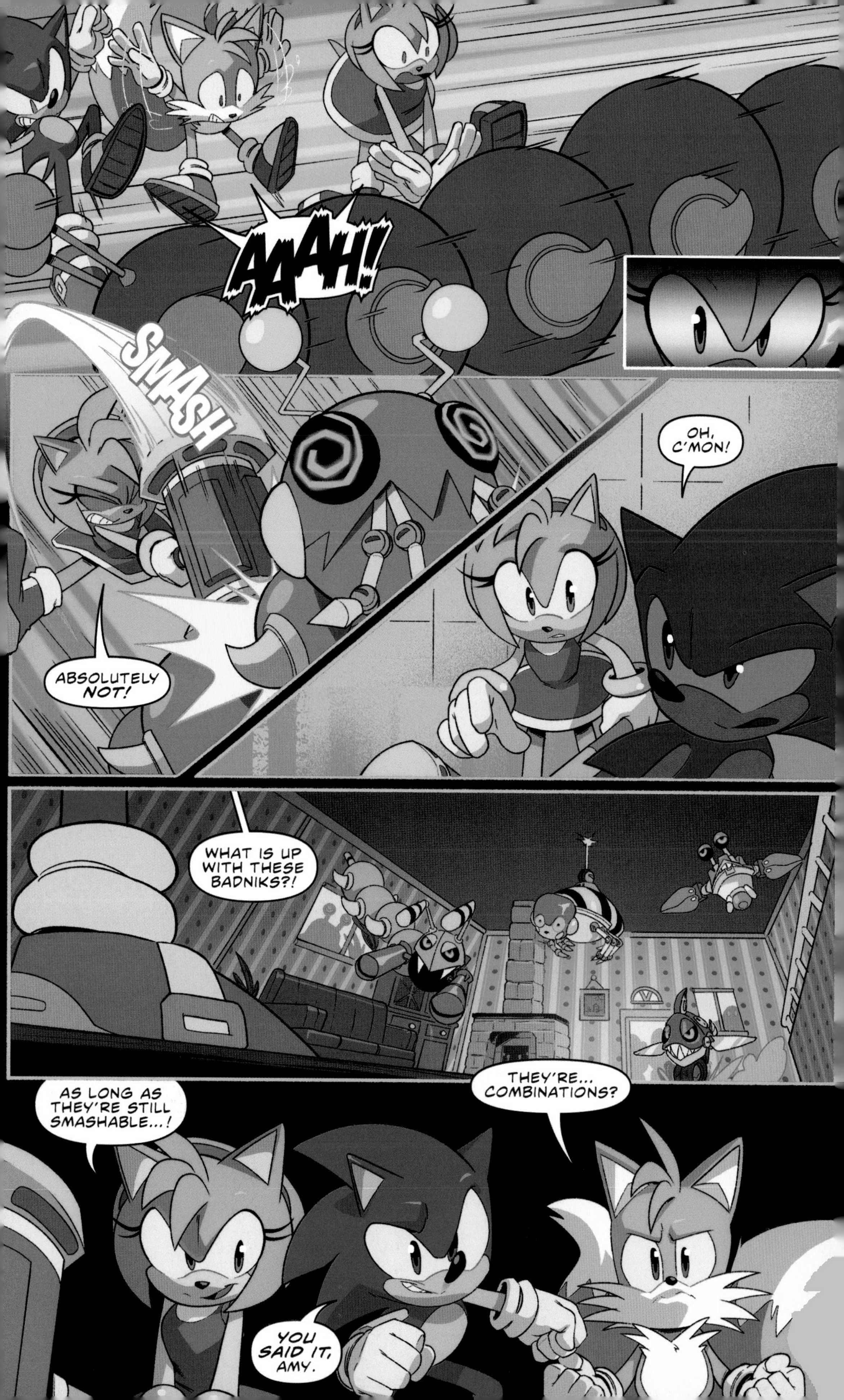

AAAH!
SMASH
ABSOLUTELY NOT!
OH, C'MON!
WHAT IS UP WITH THESE BADNIKS?!
AS LONG AS THEY'RE STILL SMASHABLE...!
THEY'RE... COMBINATIONS?
YOU SAID IT, AMY.

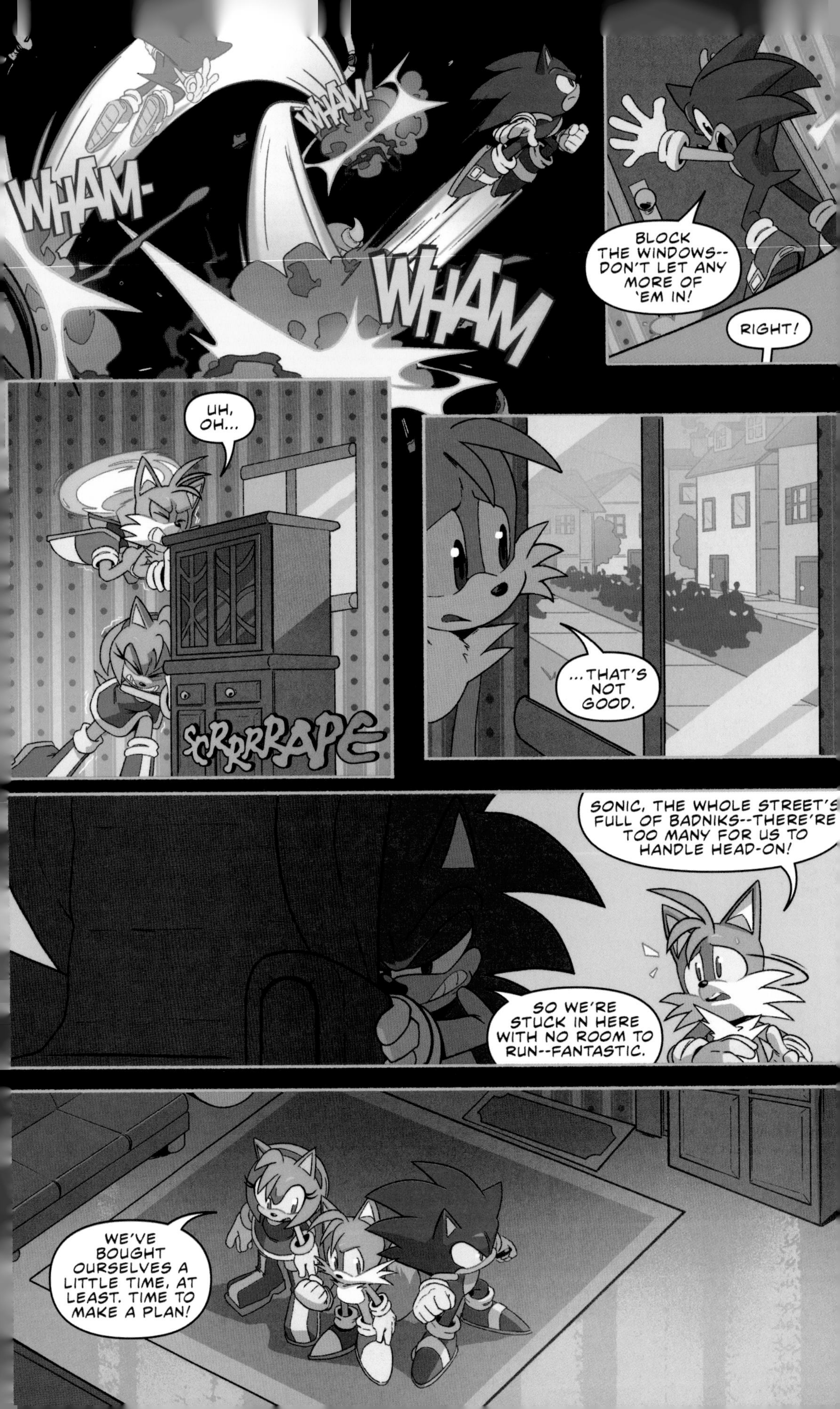
WHAM-
WHAM-
WHAM
BLOCK THE WINDOWS--DON'T LET ANY MORE OF 'EM IN!
RIGHT!
UH, OH...
SCRRRRAPE
...THAT'S NOT GOOD.
SONIC, THE WHOLE STREET'S FULL OF BADNIKS--THERE'RE TOO MANY FOR US TO HANDLE HEAD-ON!
SO WE'RE STUCK IN HERE WITH NO ROOM TO RUN--FANTASTIC.
WE'VE BOUGHT OURSELVES A LITTLE TIME, AT LEAST. TIME TO MAKE A PLAN!

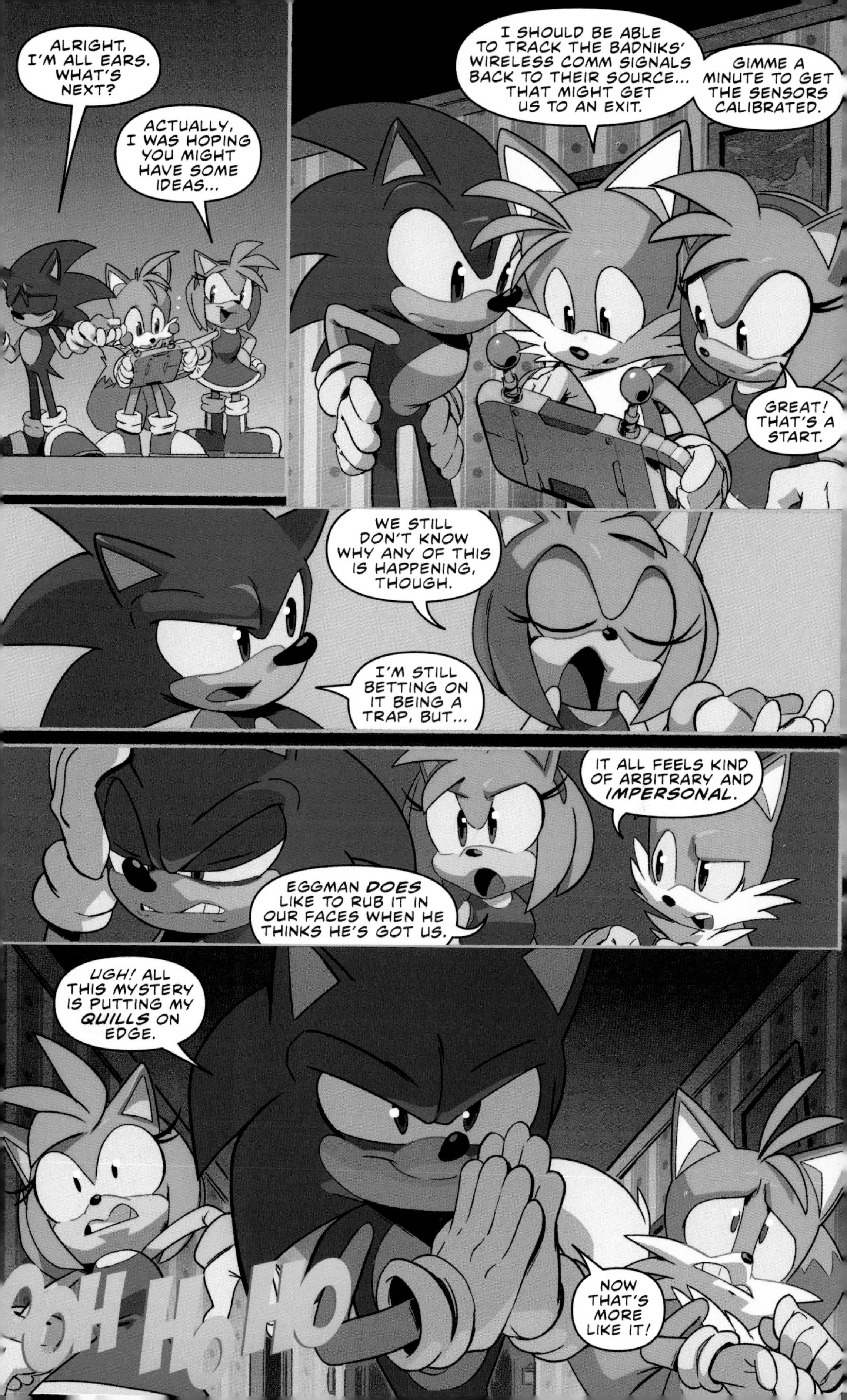
ALRIGHT, I'M ALL EARS. WHAT'S NEXT?
ACTUALLY, I WAS HOPING YOU MIGHT HAVE SOME IDEAS...
I SHOULD BE ABLE TO TRACK THE BADNIKS' WIRELESS COMM SIGNALS BACK TO THEIR SOURCE... THAT MIGHT GET US TO AN EXIT.
GIMME A MINUTE TO GET THE SENSORS CALIBRATED.
GREAT! THAT'S A START.
WE STILL DON'T KNOW WHY ANY OF THIS IS HAPPENING, THOUGH.
I'M STILL BETTING ON IT BEING A TRAP, BUT...
IT ALL FEELS KIND OF ARBITRARY AND *IMPERSONAL*.
EGGMAN *DOES* LIKE TO RUB IT IN OUR FACES WHEN HE THINKS HE'S GOT US.
UGH! ALL THIS MYSTERY IS PUTTING MY *QUILLS* ON EDGE.
OOH HO HO
NOW THAT'S MORE LIKE IT!

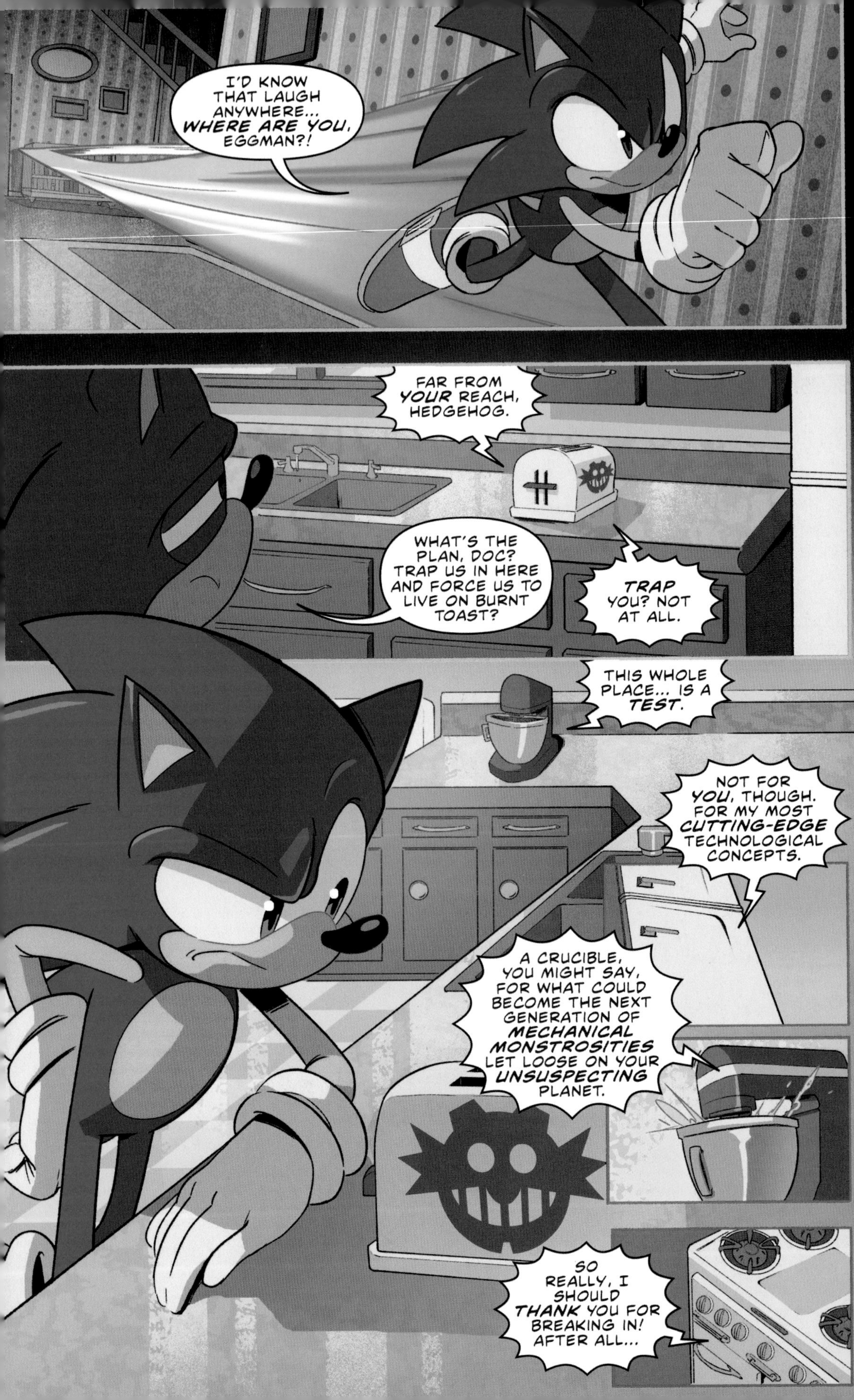

I'D KNOW THAT LAUGH ANYWHERE... WHERE ARE YOU, EGGMAN?!
FAR FROM YOUR REACH, HEDGEHOG.
WHAT'S THE PLAN, DOC? TRAP US IN HERE AND FORCE US TO LIVE ON BURNT TOAST?
TRAP YOU? NOT AT ALL.
THIS WHOLE PLACE... IS A TEST.
NOT FOR YOU, THOUGH. FOR MY MOST CUTTING-EDGE TECHNOLOGICAL CONCEPTS.
A CRUCIBLE, YOU MIGHT SAY, FOR WHAT COULD BECOME THE NEXT GENERATION OF MECHANICAL MONSTROSITIES LET LOOSE ON YOUR UNSUSPECTING PLANET.
SO REALLY, I SHOULD THANK YOU FOR BREAKING IN! AFTER ALL...

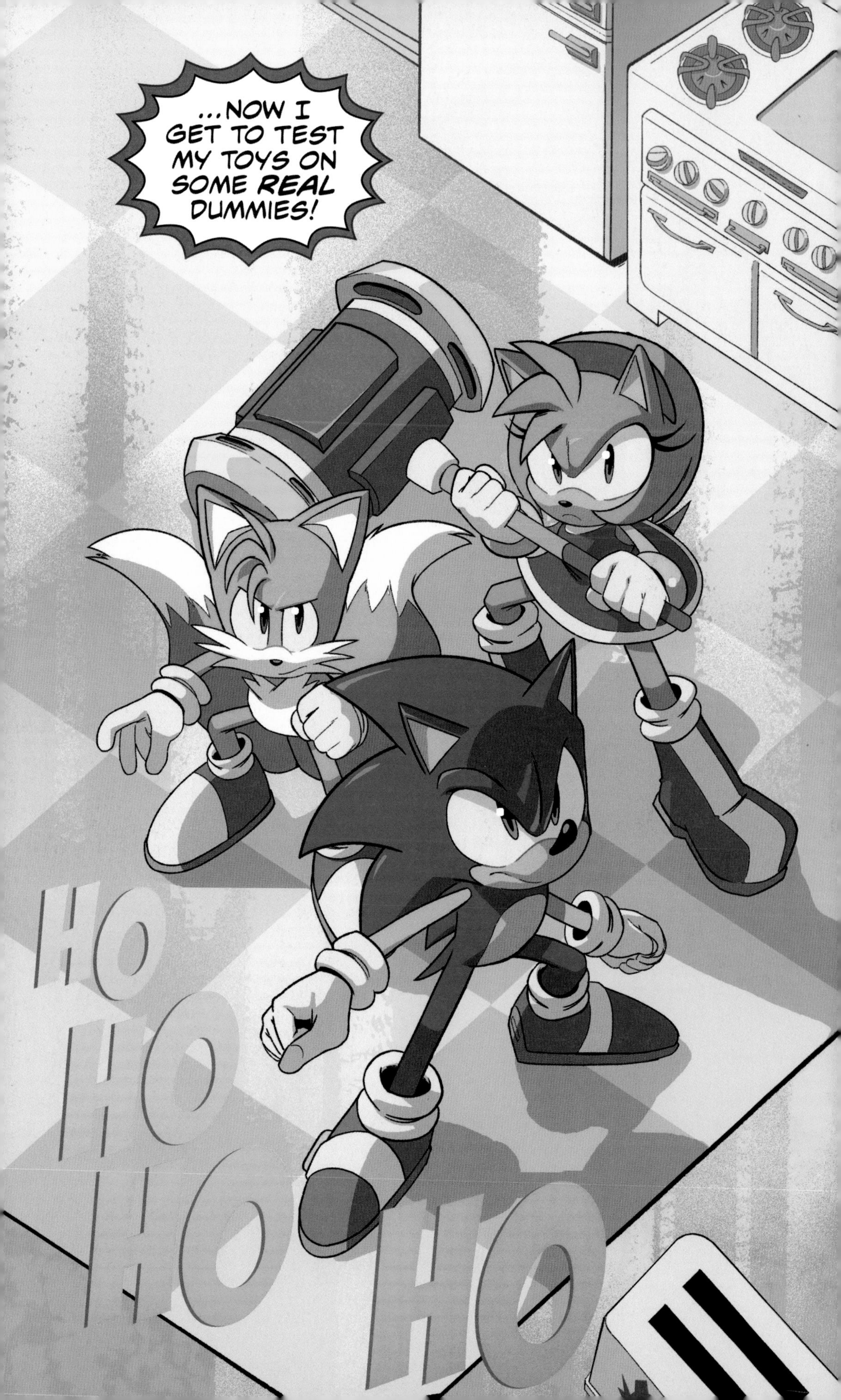
...NOW I GET TO TEST MY TOYS ON SOME REAL DUMMIES!
HO HO HO HO

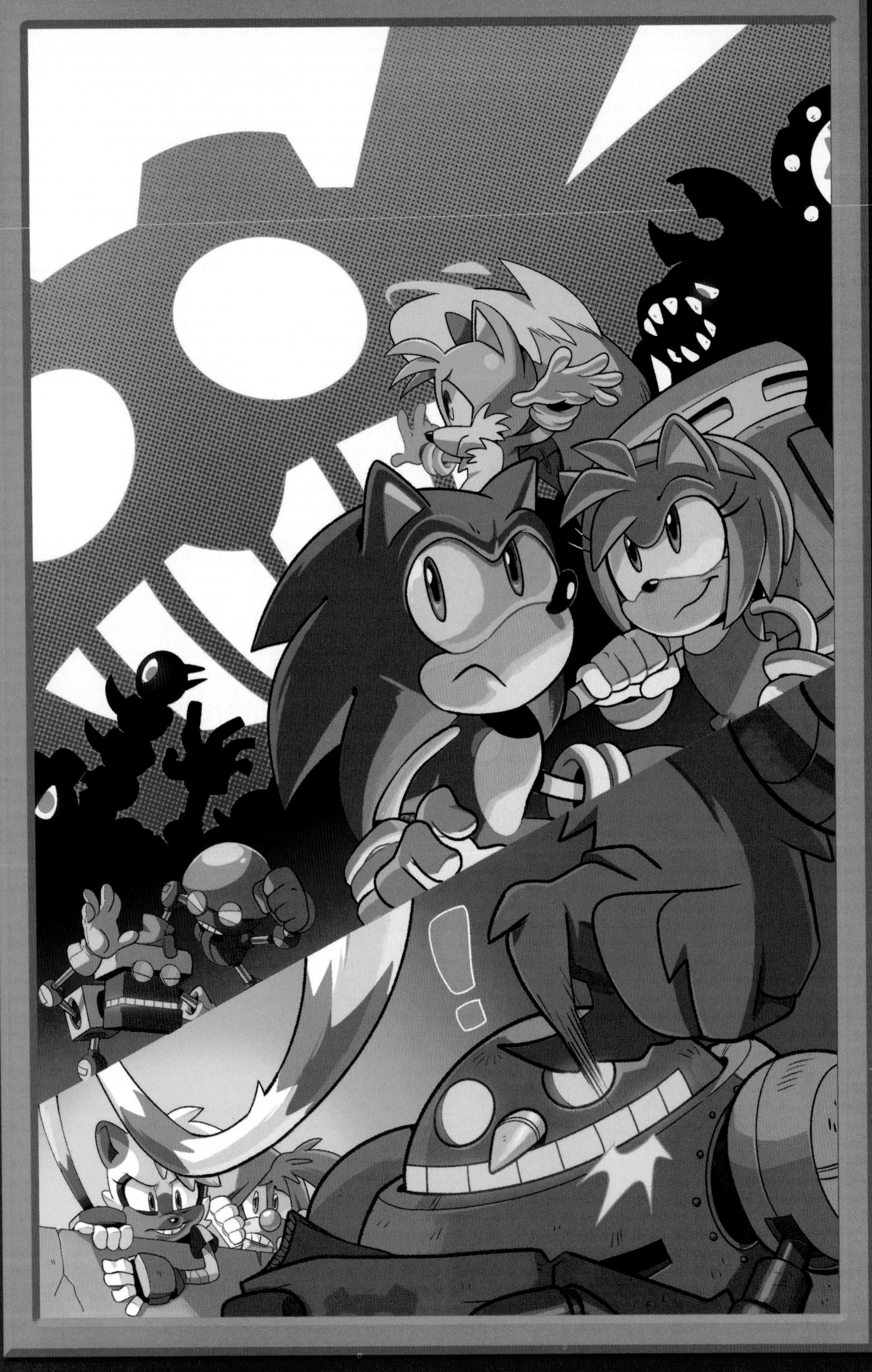
!

ART BY **THOMAS ROTHLISBERGER** COLORS BY **BRACARDI CURRY**

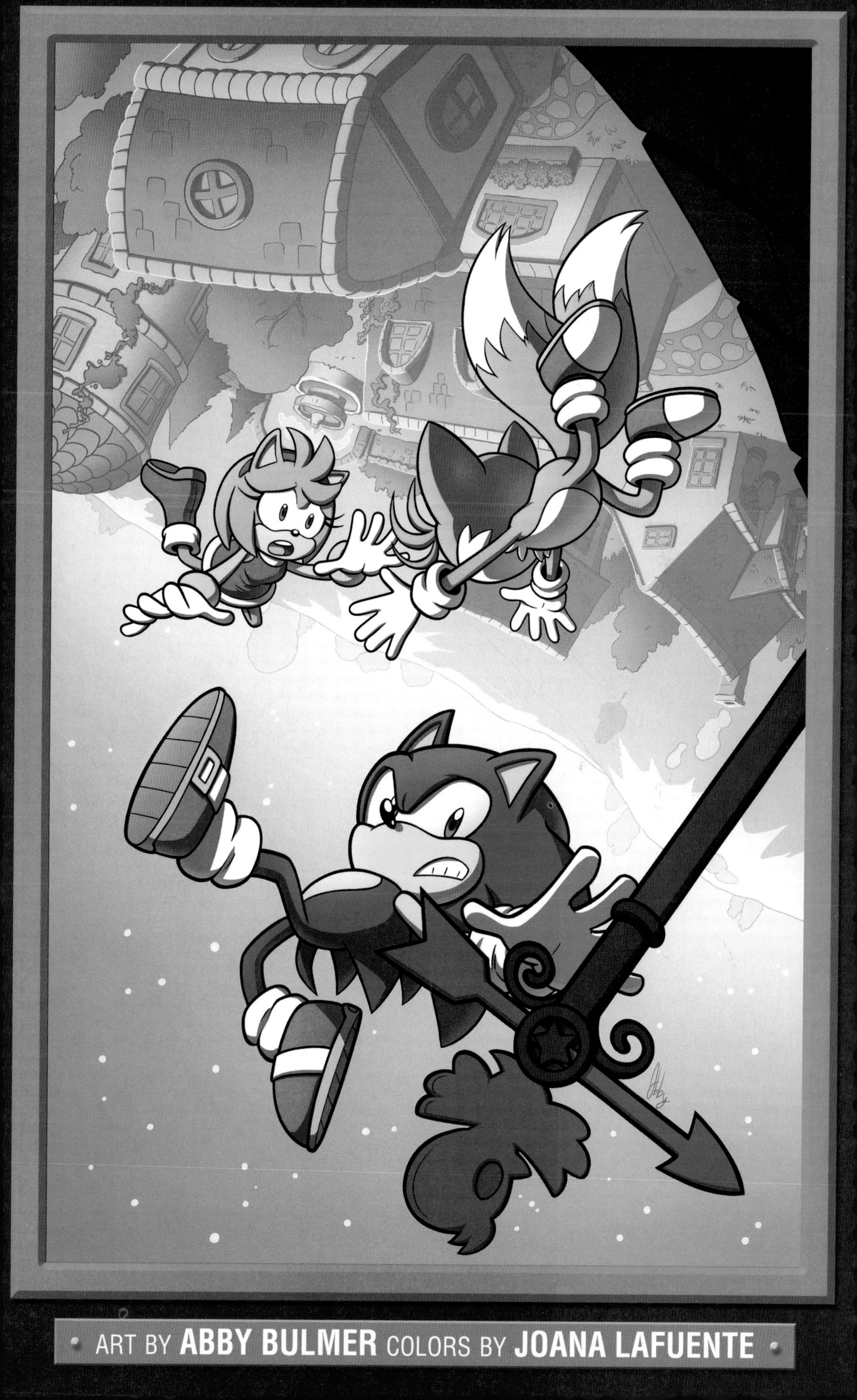

ART BY **ABBY BULMER** COLORS BY **JOANA LAFUENTE**

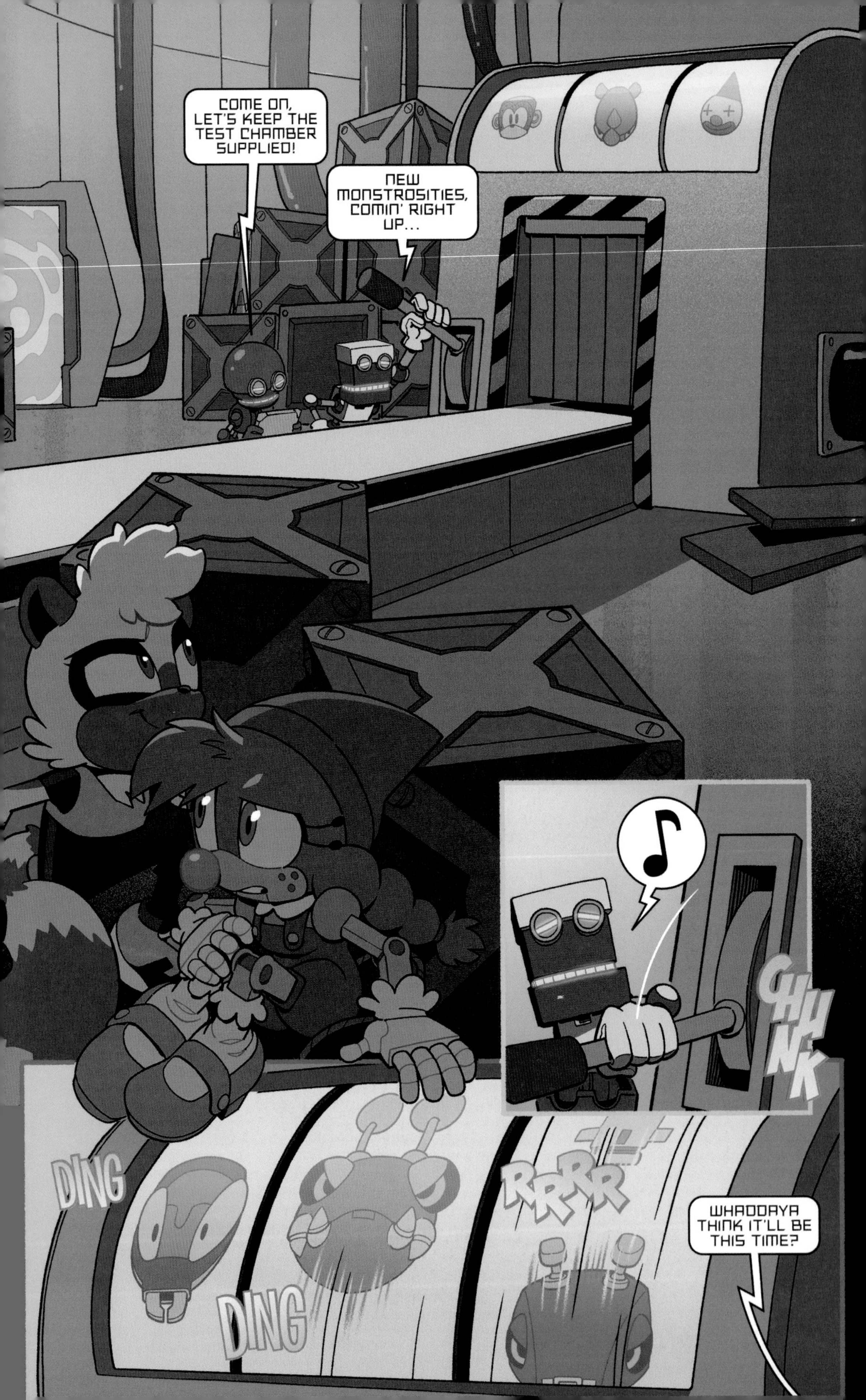
COME ON, LET'S KEEP THE TEST CHAMBER SUPPLIED!
NEW MONSTROSITIES, COMIN' RIGHT UP...
♪
CHUNK
DING
DING
RRRR
WHADDAYA THINK IT'LL BE THIS TIME?

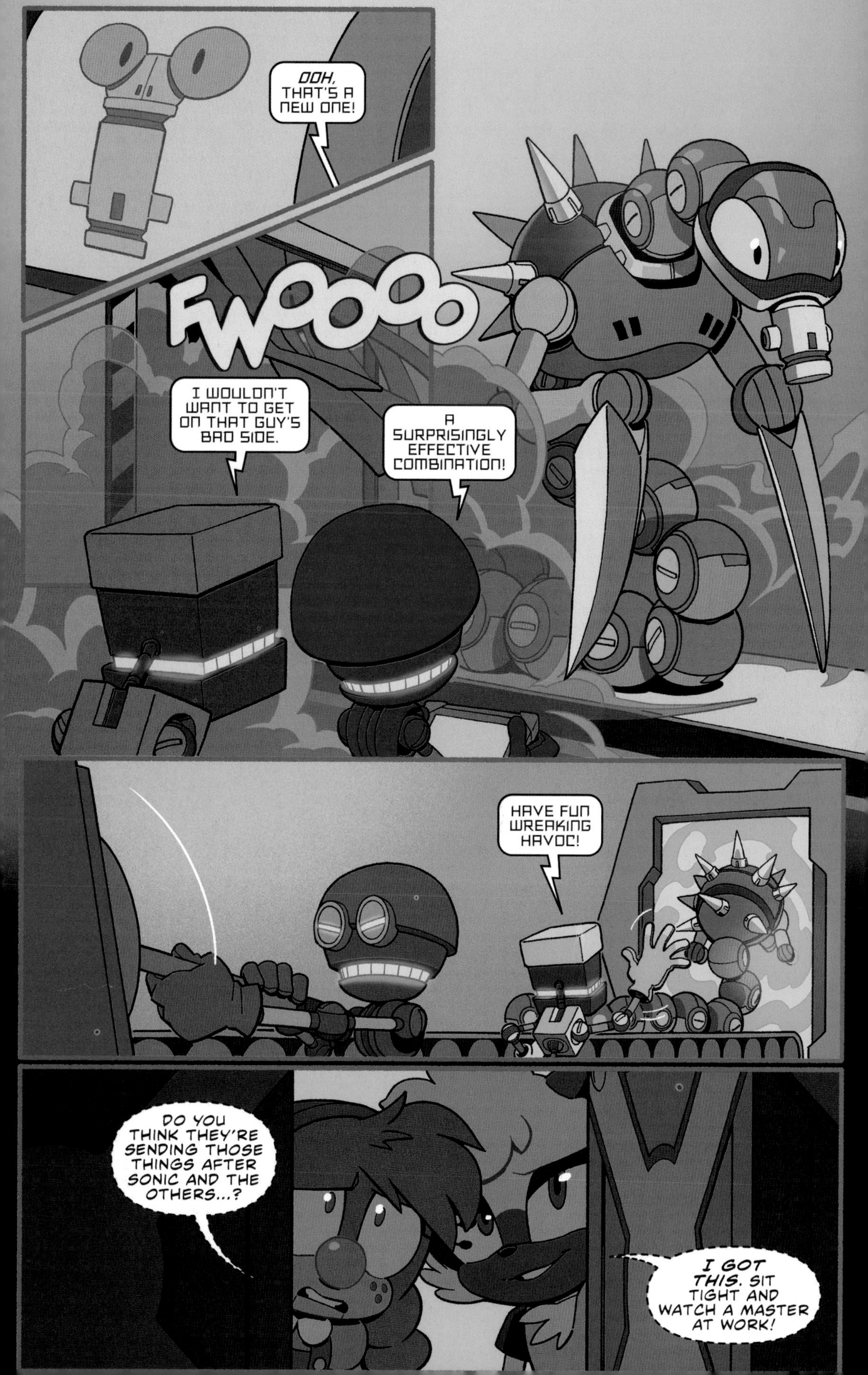
OOH, THAT'S A NEW ONE!
FWOOOO
I WOULDN'T WANT TO GET ON THAT GUY'S BAD SIDE.
A SURPRISINGLY EFFECTIVE COMBINATION!
HAVE FUN WREAKING HAVOC!
DO YOU THINK THEY'RE SENDING THOSE THINGS AFTER SONIC AND THE OTHERS...?
I GOT THIS. SIT TIGHT AND WATCH A MASTER AT WORK!

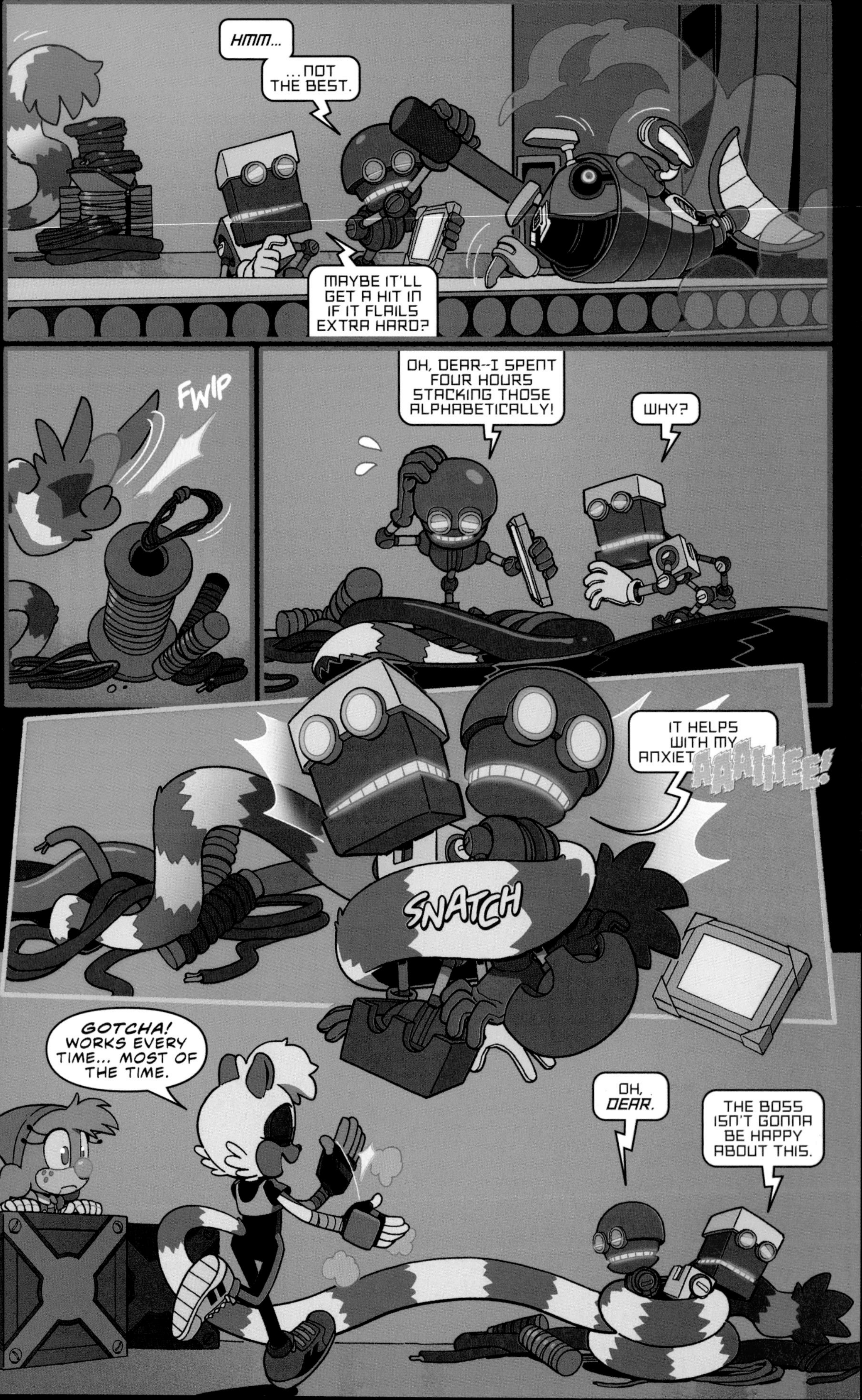
HMM...
...NOT THE BEST.
MAYBE IT'LL GET A HIT IN IF IT FLAILS EXTRA HARD?
FWIP
OH, DEAR--I SPENT FOUR HOURS STACKING THOSE ALPHABETICALLY!
WHY?
IT HELPS WITH MY ANXIET
AAAIIIEE!
SNATCH
GOTCHA! WORKS EVERY TIME... MOST OF THE TIME.
OH, DEAR.
THE BOSS ISN'T GONNA BE HAPPY ABOUT THIS.

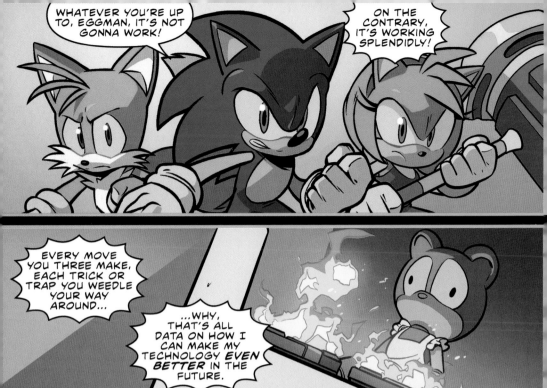

WHATEVER YOU'RE UP TO, EGGMAN, IT'S NOT GONNA WORK!

ON THE CONTRARY, IT'S WORKING SPLENDIDLY!

EVERY MOVE YOU THREE MAKE, EACH TRICK OR TRAP YOU WEEDLE YOUR WAY AROUND...

...WHY, THAT'S ALL DATA ON HOW I CAN MAKE MY TECHNOLOGY *EVEN BETTER* IN THE FUTURE.

AND OH, I CAN'T WAIT TO SEE HOW YOU HANDLE WHAT I'VE BEEN COOKING UP NEXT!

WHAM

WHY DON'T YOU COME OUT, SO I CAN SHOW YOU?

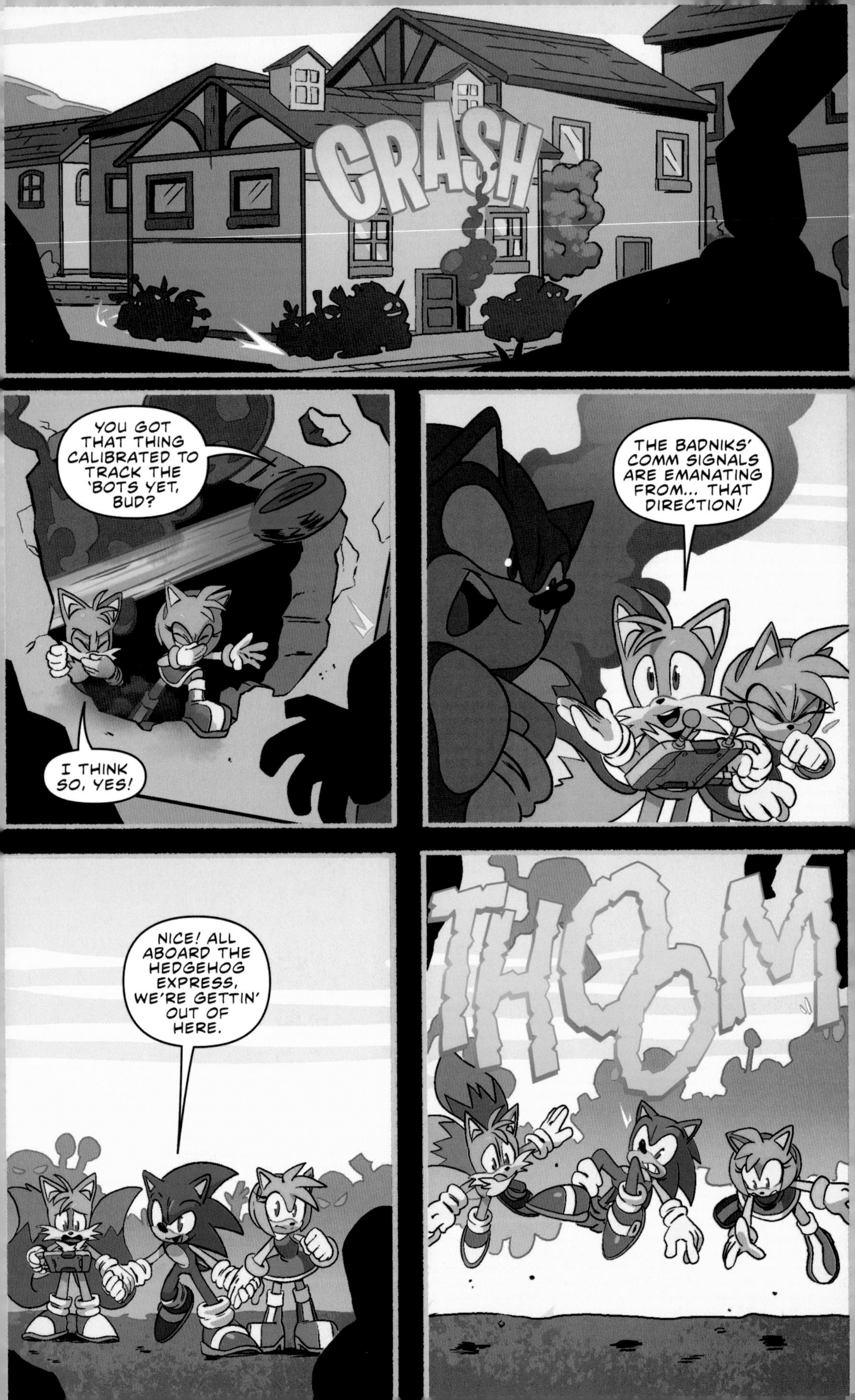
CRASH
YOU GOT THAT THING CALIBRATED TO TRACK THE 'BOTS YET, BUD?
I THINK SO, YES!
THE BADNIKS' COMM SIGNALS ARE EMANATING FROM... THAT DIRECTION!
NICE! ALL ABOARD THE HEDGEHOG EXPRESS, WE'RE GETTIN' OUT OF HERE.
THOOM

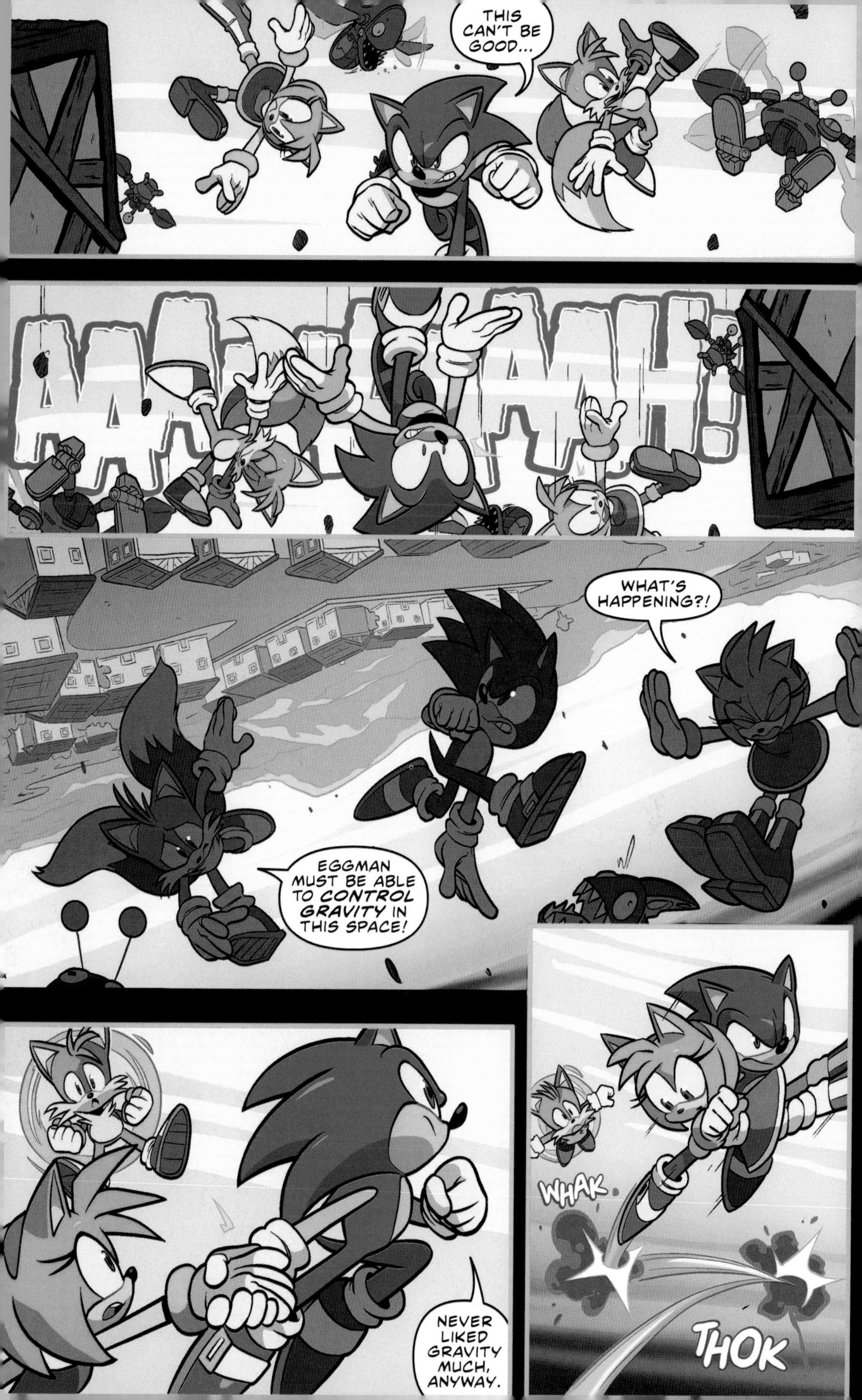
THIS CAN'T BE GOOD...
WHAT'S HAPPENING?!
EGGMAN MUST BE ABLE TO CONTROL GRAVITY IN THIS SPACE!
NEVER LIKED GRAVITY MUCH, ANYWAY.
WHAK
THOK

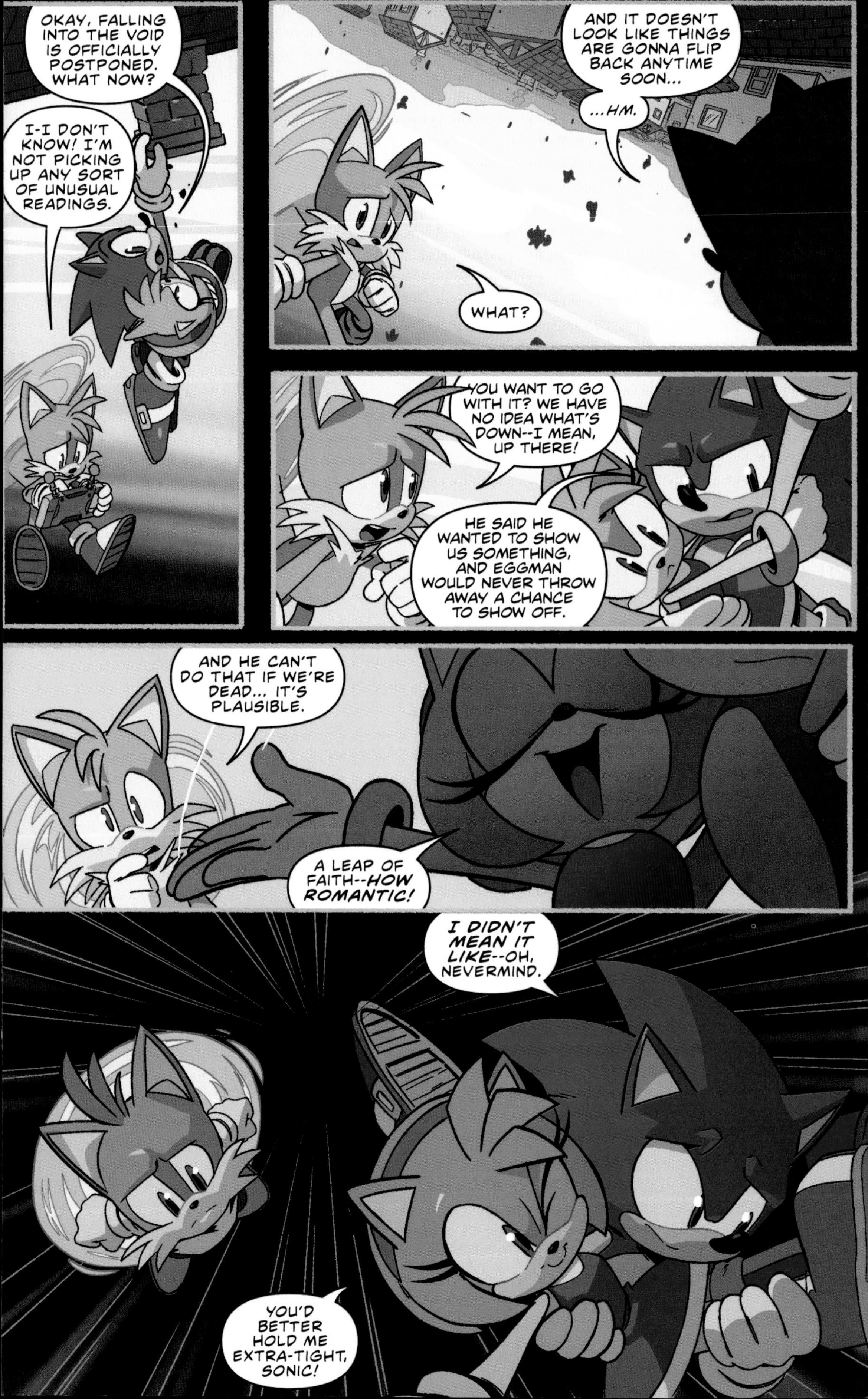
OKAY, FALLING INTO THE VOID IS OFFICIALLY POSTPONED. WHAT NOW?
I-I DON'T KNOW! I'M NOT PICKING UP ANY SORT OF UNUSUAL READINGS.
AND IT DOESN'T LOOK LIKE THINGS ARE GONNA FLIP BACK ANYTIME SOON...
...HM.
WHAT?
YOU WANT TO GO WITH IT? WE HAVE NO IDEA WHAT'S DOWN--I MEAN, UP THERE!
HE SAID HE WANTED TO SHOW US SOMETHING, AND EGGMAN WOULD NEVER THROW AWAY A CHANCE TO SHOW OFF.
AND HE CAN'T DO THAT IF WE'RE DEAD... IT'S PLAUSIBLE.
A LEAP OF FAITH--*HOW ROMANTIC!*
I DIDN'T MEAN IT LIKE--OH, NEVERMIND.
YOU'D BETTER HOLD ME EXTRA-TIGHT, SONIC!

WE SHOULD'VE TRIED TO GATHER MORE EVIDENCE, OR--

STAY COOL. ANY SECOND NOW...

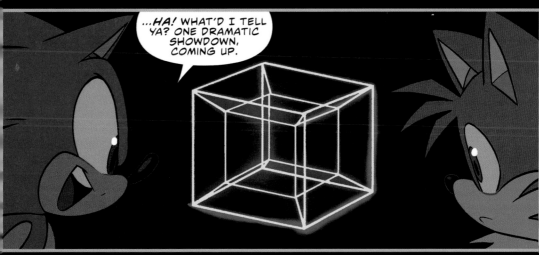

...HA! WHAT'D I TELL YA? ONE DRAMATIC SHOWDOWN, COMING UP.

WHAM

ALRIGHT EGGMAN, WE'RE HERE! COME ON OUT, AND LET'S GET THIS DONE.

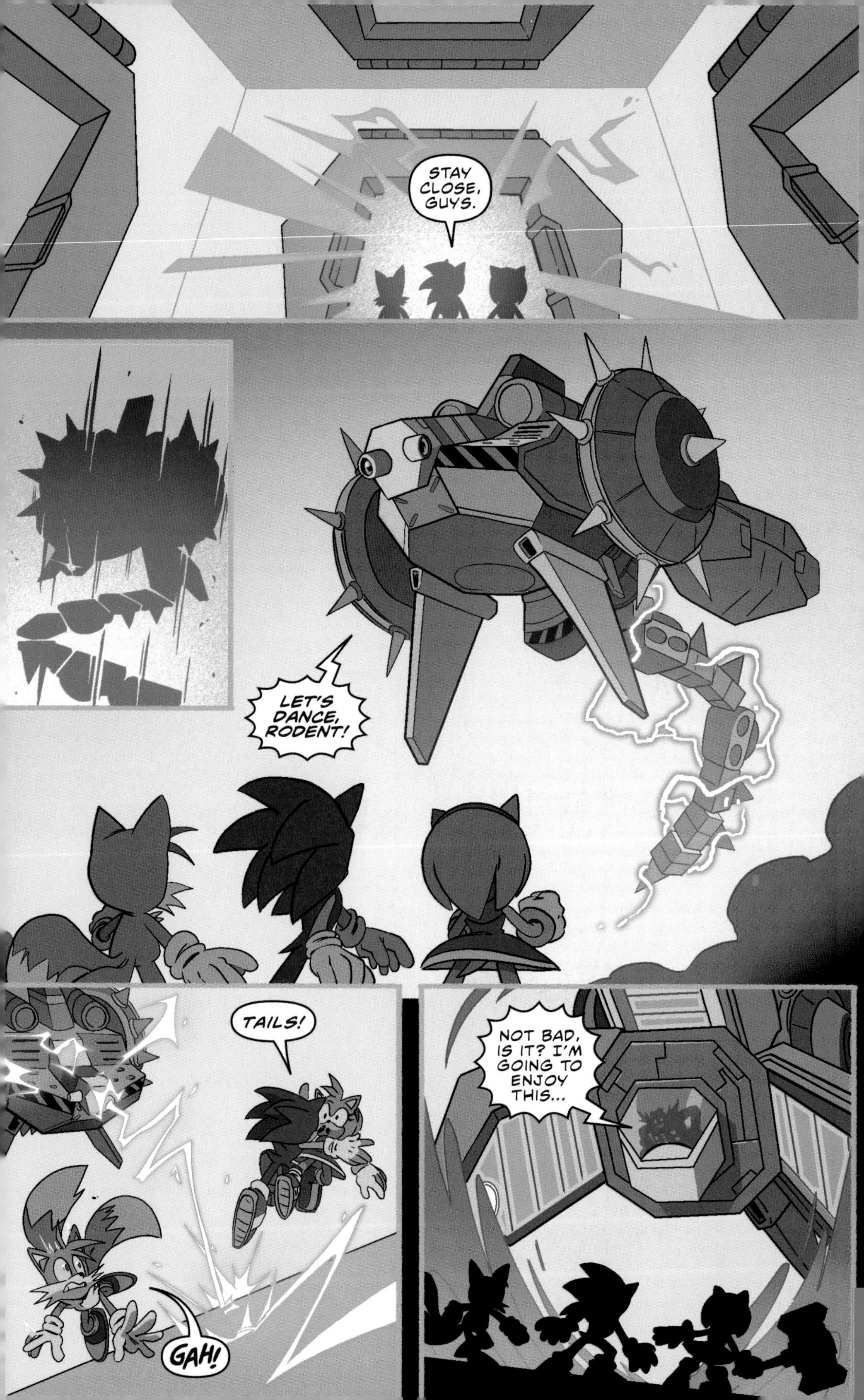
STAY CLOSE, GUYS.
LET'S DANCE, RODENT!
TAILS!
GAH!
NOT BAD, IS IT? I'M GOING TO ENJOY THIS...

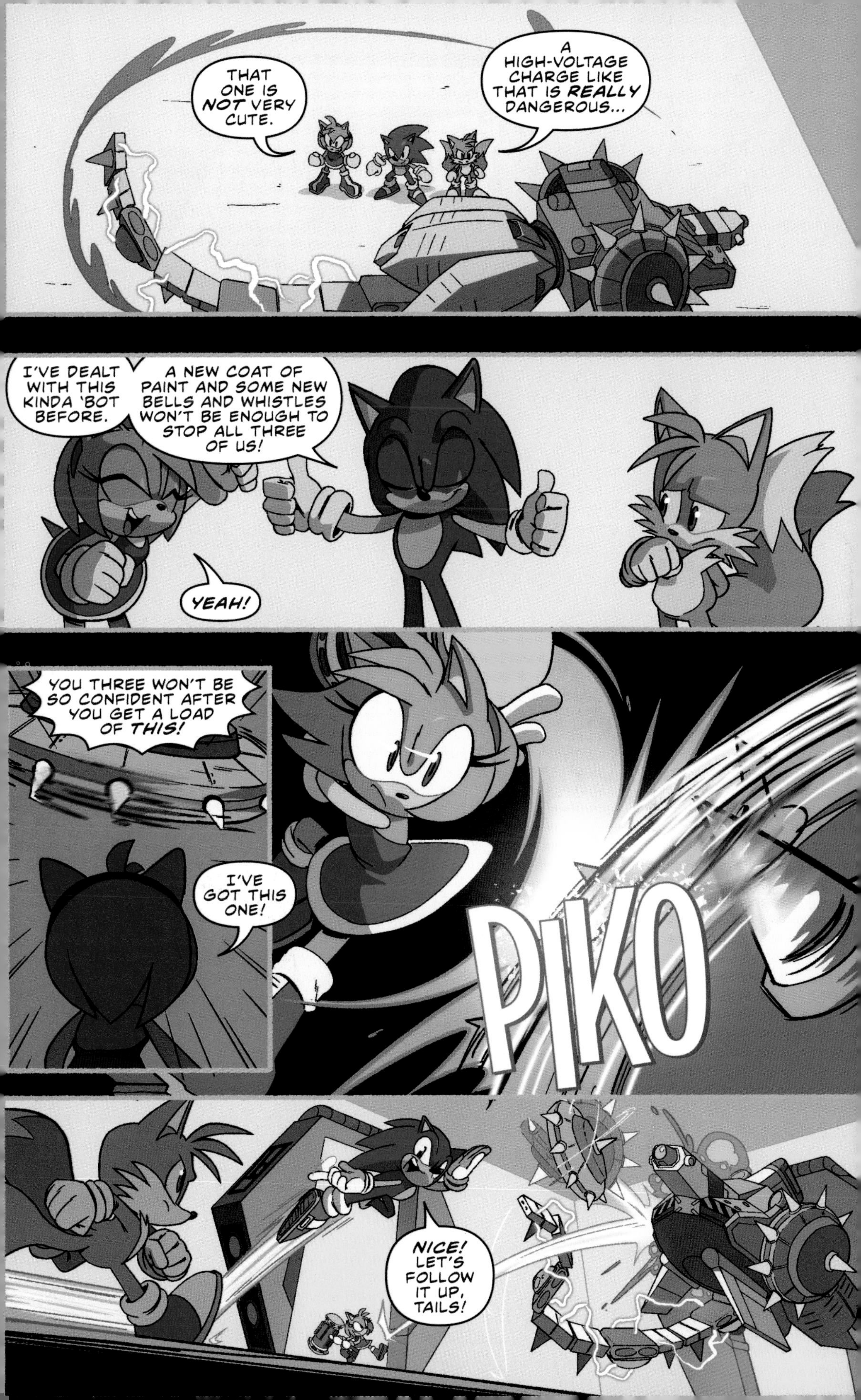
THAT ONE IS NOT VERY CUTE.
A HIGH-VOLTAGE CHARGE LIKE THAT IS REALLY DANGEROUS...
I'VE DEALT WITH THIS KINDA 'BOT BEFORE.
A NEW COAT OF PAINT AND SOME NEW BELLS AND WHISTLES WON'T BE ENOUGH TO STOP ALL THREE OF US!
YEAH!
YOU THREE WON'T BE SO CONFIDENT AFTER YOU GET A LOAD OF THIS!
I'VE GOT THIS ONE!
PIKO
NICE! LET'S FOLLOW IT UP, TAILS!

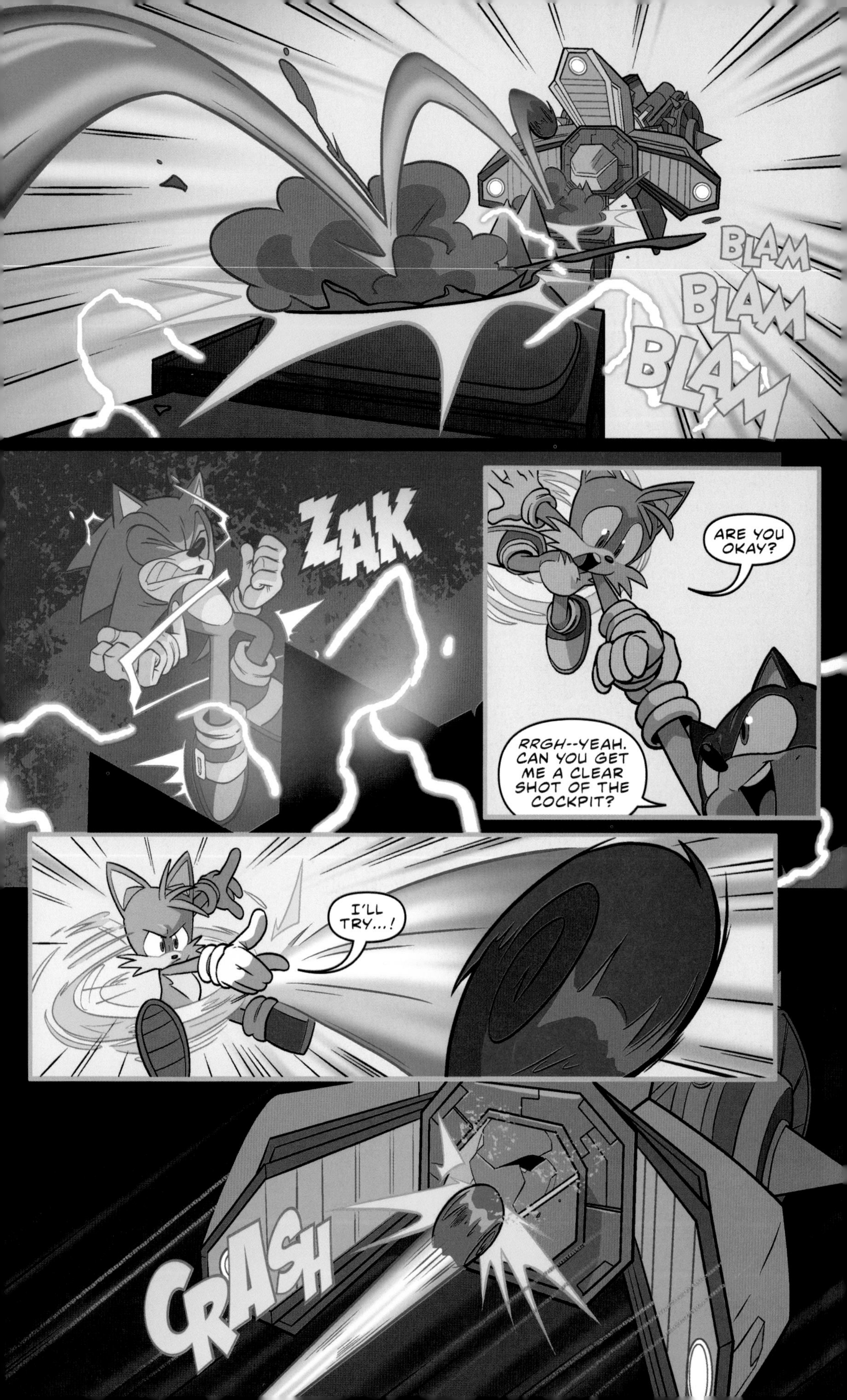
BLAM
BLAM
BLAM
ZAK
ARE YOU OKAY?
RRGH--YEAH. CAN YOU GET ME A CLEAR SHOT OF THE COCKPIT?
I'LL TRY...!
CRASH

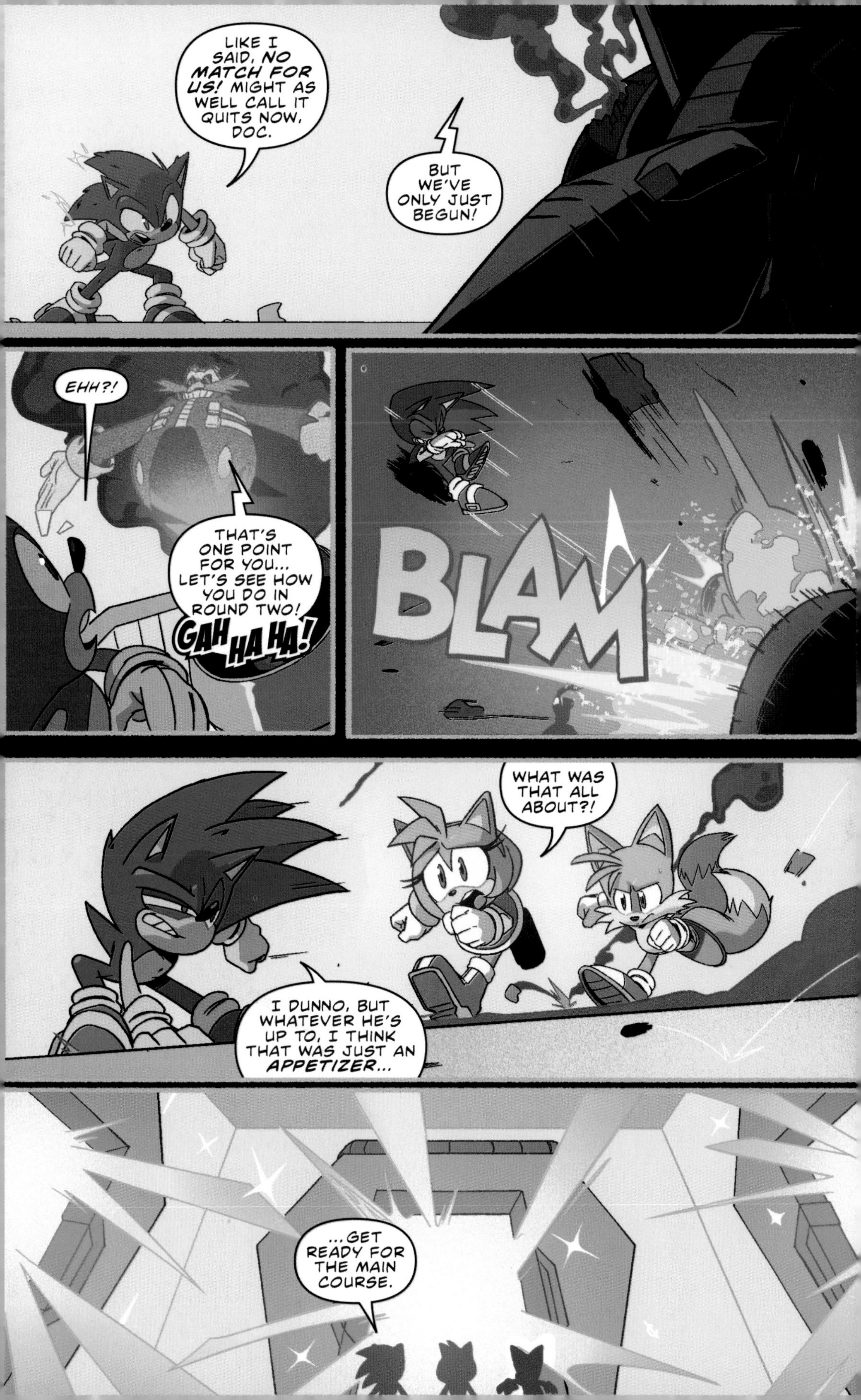
LIKE I SAID, NO MATCH FOR US! MIGHT AS WELL CALL IT QUITS NOW, DOC.
BUT WE'VE ONLY JUST BEGUN!
EHH?!
THAT'S ONE POINT FOR YOU... LET'S SEE HOW YOU DO IN ROUND TWO!
GAH HA HA!
BLAM
WHAT WAS THAT ALL ABOUT?!
I DUNNO, BUT WHATEVER HE'S UP TO, I THINK THAT WAS JUST AN APPETIZER...
...GET READY FOR THE MAIN COURSE.

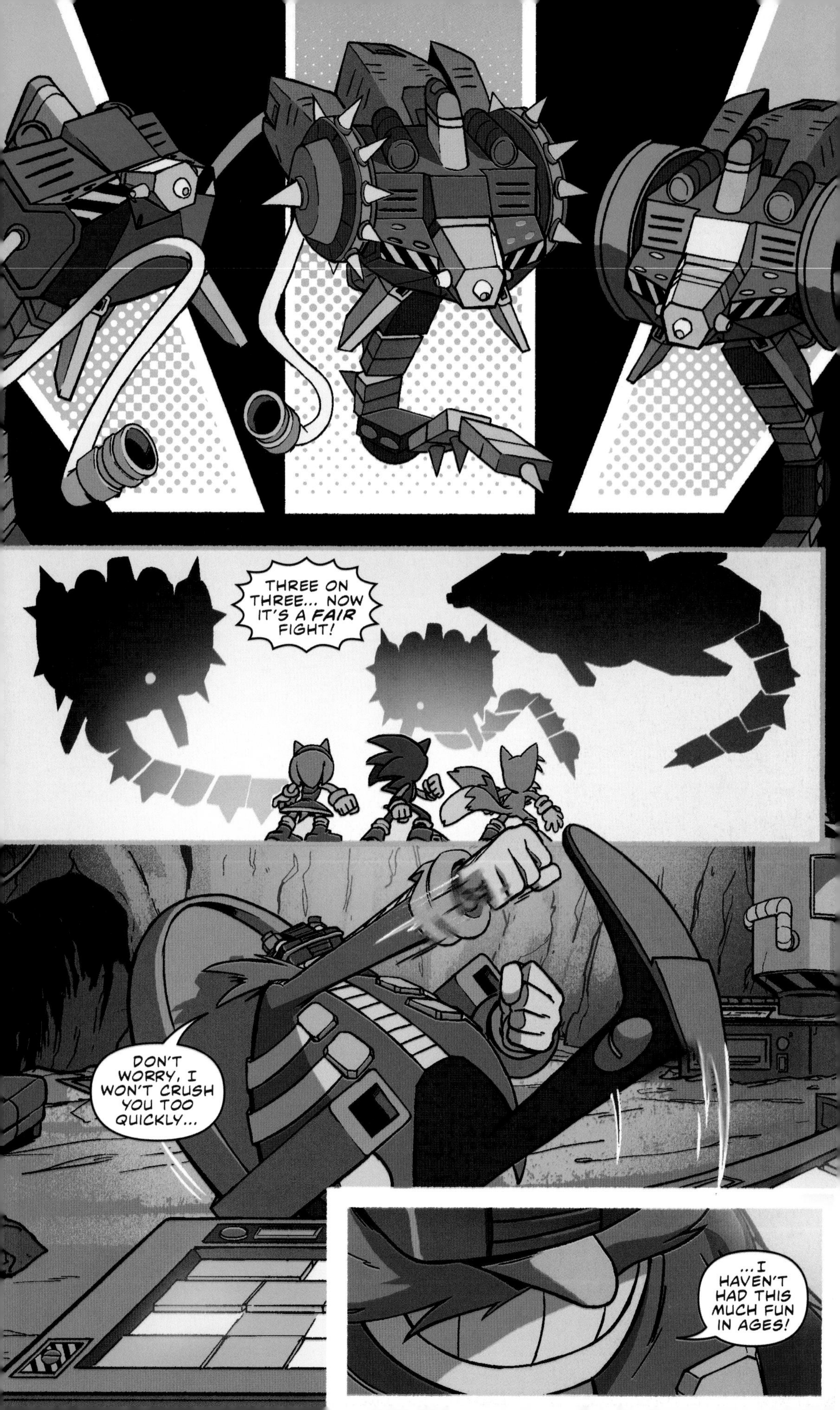
THREE ON THREE... NOW IT'S A FAIR FIGHT!
DON'T WORRY, I WON'T CRUSH YOU TOO QUICKLY...
...I HAVEN'T HAD THIS MUCH FUN IN AGES!

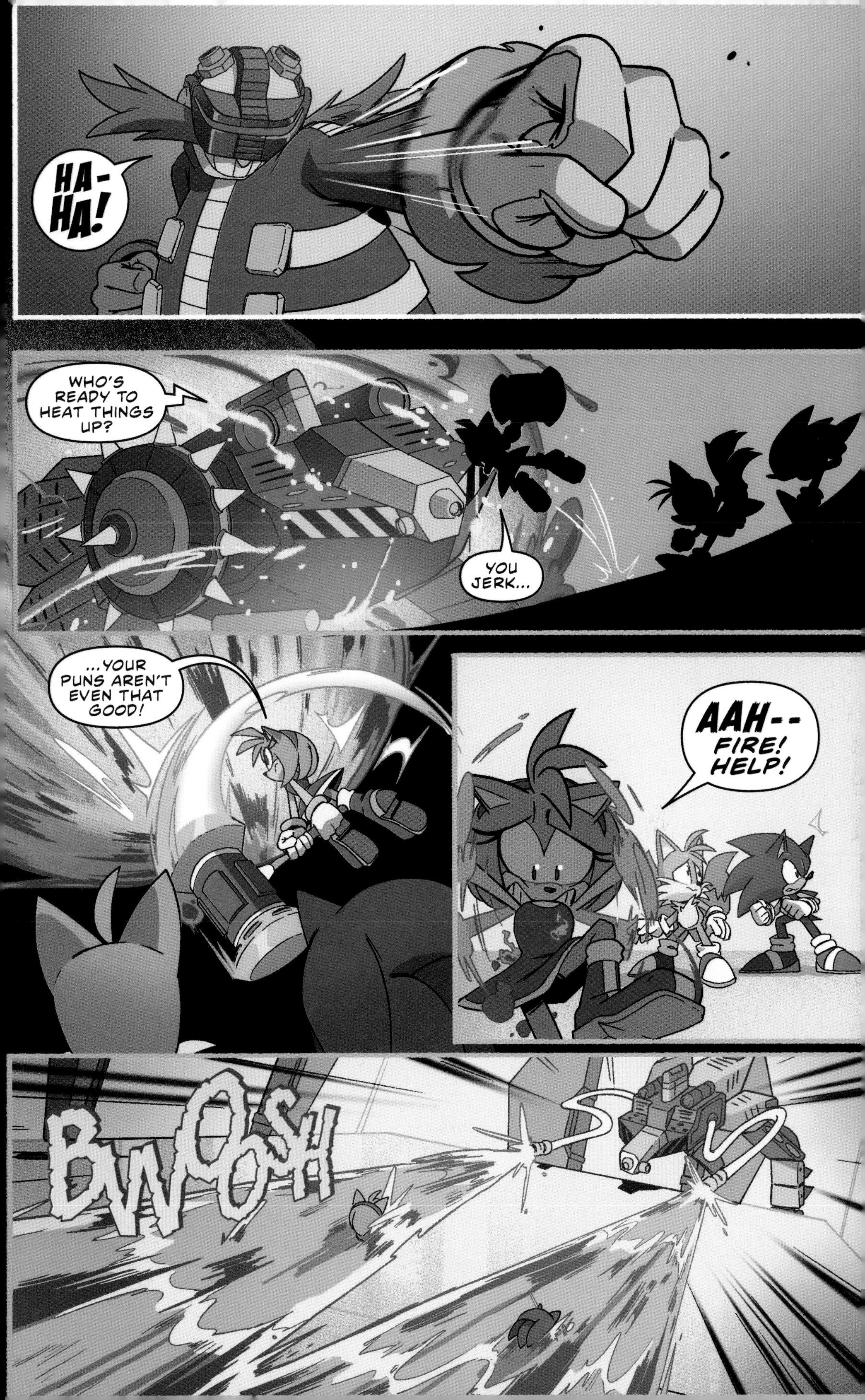
HA-HA!
WHO'S READY TO HEAT THINGS UP?
YOU JERK...
...YOUR PUNS AREN'T EVEN THAT GOOD!
AAH-- FIRE! HELP!
BWOOSH

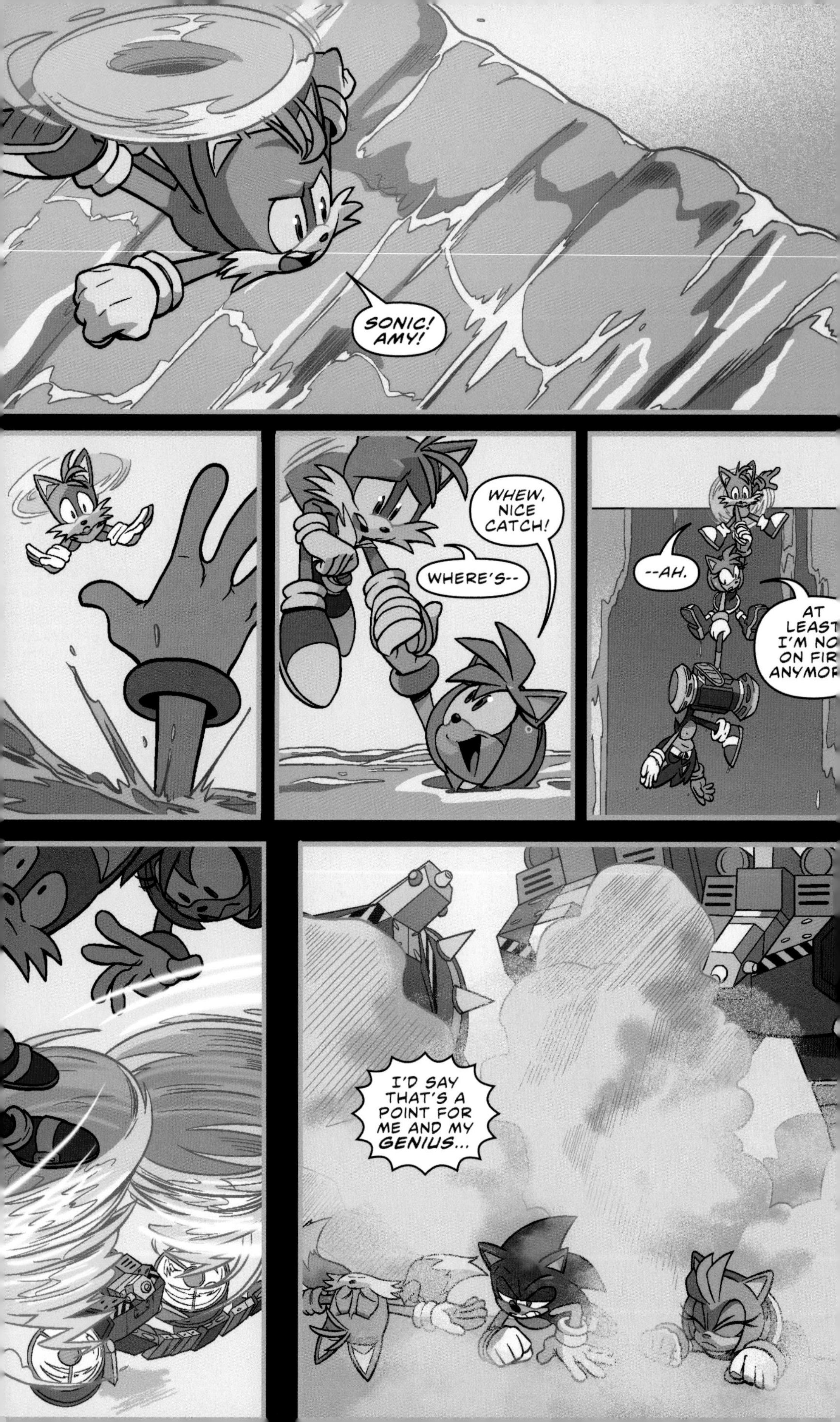
SONIC! AMY!
WHEW, NICE CATCH!
WHERE'S--
--AH.
AT LEAST I'M NO ON FIR ANYMOR
I'D SAY THAT'S A POINT FOR ME AND MY GENIUS...

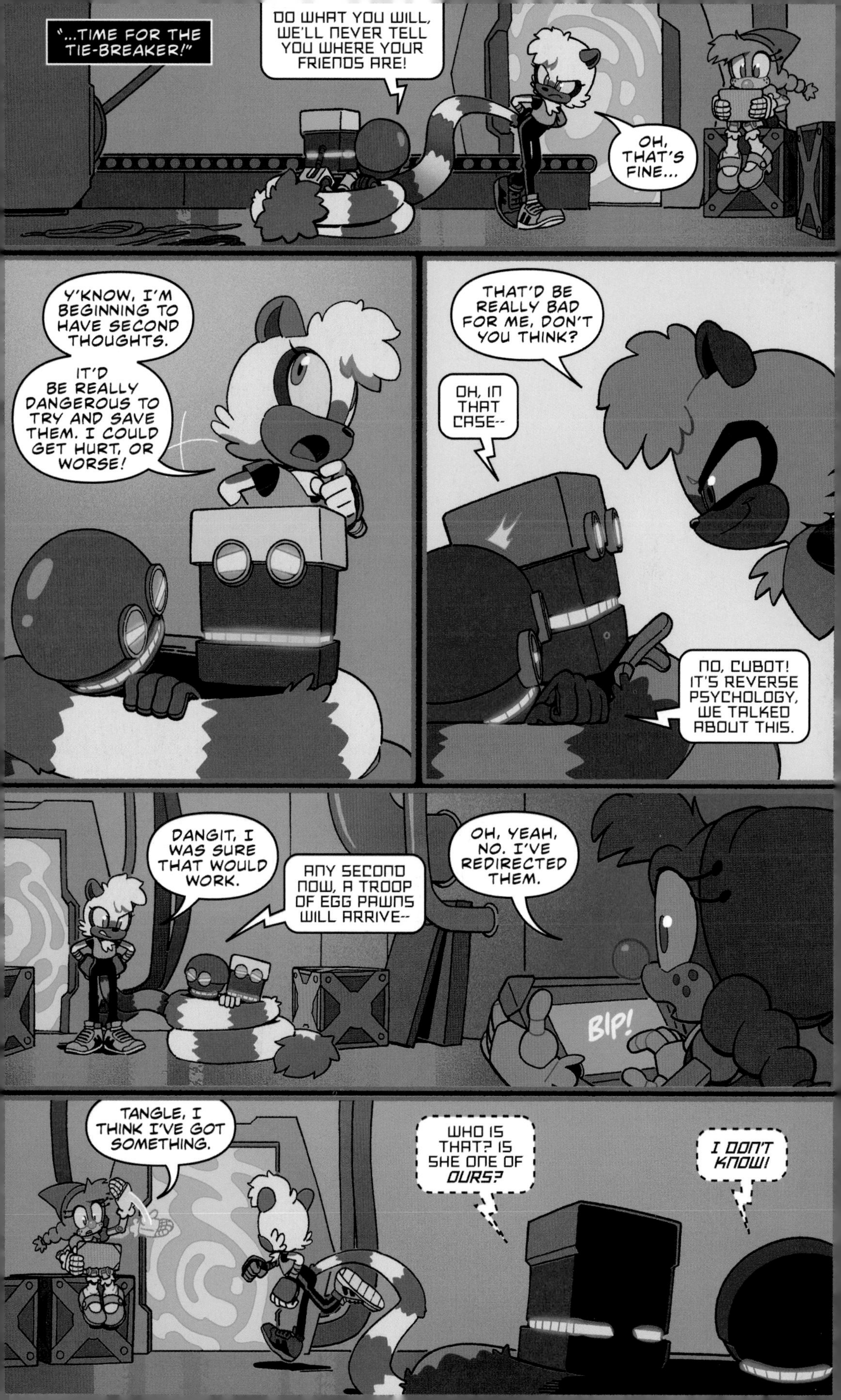
"...TIME FOR THE TIE-BREAKER!"
DO WHAT YOU WILL, WE'LL NEVER TELL YOU WHERE YOUR FRIENDS ARE!
OH, THAT'S FINE...
Y'KNOW, I'M BEGINNING TO HAVE SECOND THOUGHTS.
IT'D BE REALLY DANGEROUS TO TRY AND SAVE THEM. I COULD GET HURT, OR WORSE!
THAT'D BE REALLY BAD FOR ME, DON'T YOU THINK?
OH, IN THAT CASE--
NO, CUBOT! IT'S REVERSE PSYCHOLOGY, WE TALKED ABOUT THIS.
DANGIT, I WAS SURE THAT WOULD WORK.
ANY SECOND NOW, A TROOP OF EGG PAWNS WILL ARRIVE--
OH, YEAH, NO. I'VE REDIRECTED THEM.
BIP!
TANGLE, I THINK I'VE GOT SOMETHING.
WHO IS THAT? IS SHE ONE OF *OURS?*
I DON'T KNOW!

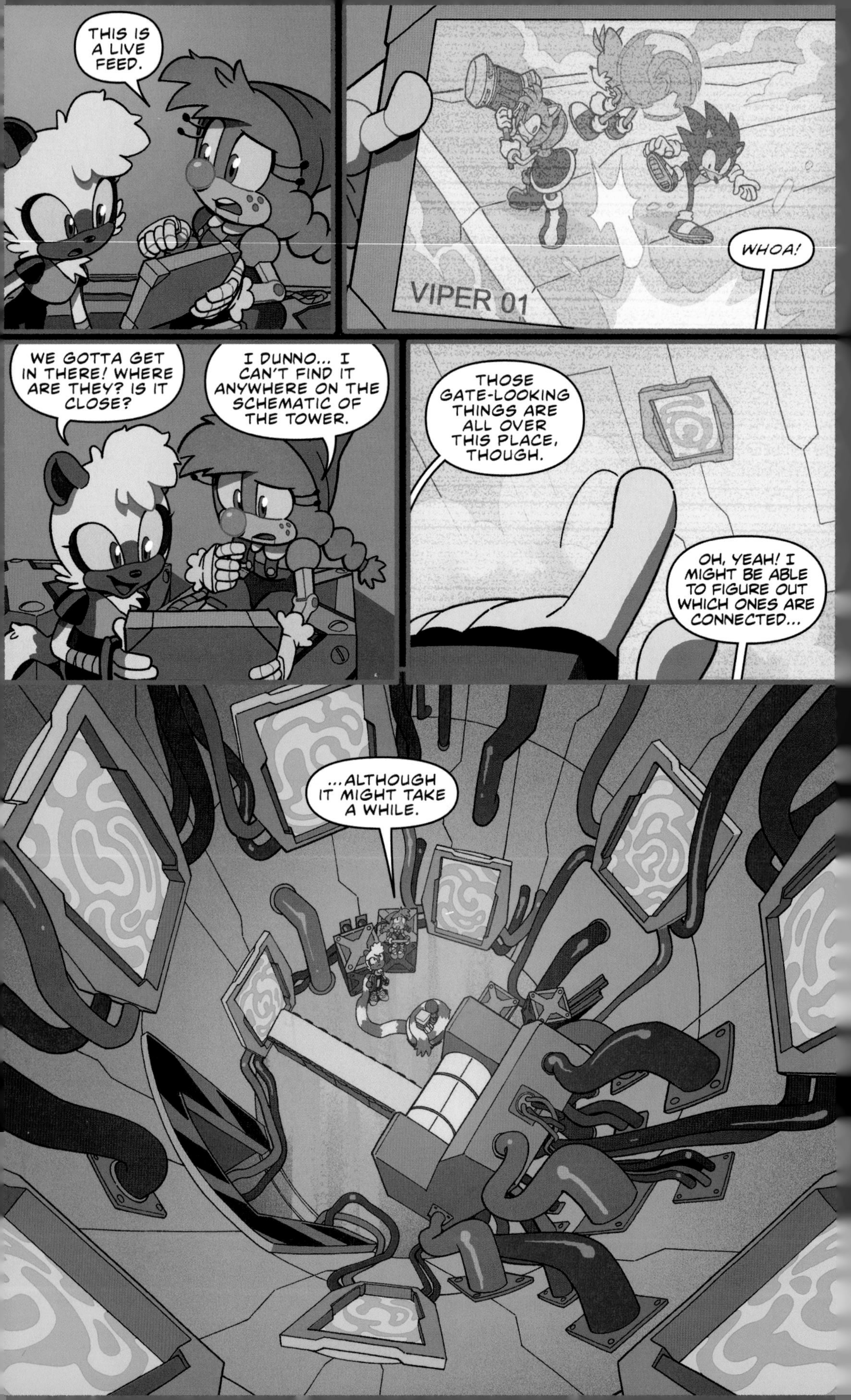
THIS IS A LIVE FEED.
VIPER 01
WHOA!
WE GOTTA GET IN THERE! WHERE ARE THEY? IS IT CLOSE?
I DUNNO... I CAN'T FIND IT ANYWHERE ON THE SCHEMATIC OF THE TOWER.
THOSE GATE-LOOKING THINGS ARE ALL OVER THIS PLACE, THOUGH.
OH, YEAH! I MIGHT BE ABLE TO FIGURE OUT WHICH ONES ARE CONNECTED...
...ALTHOUGH IT MIGHT TAKE A WHILE.

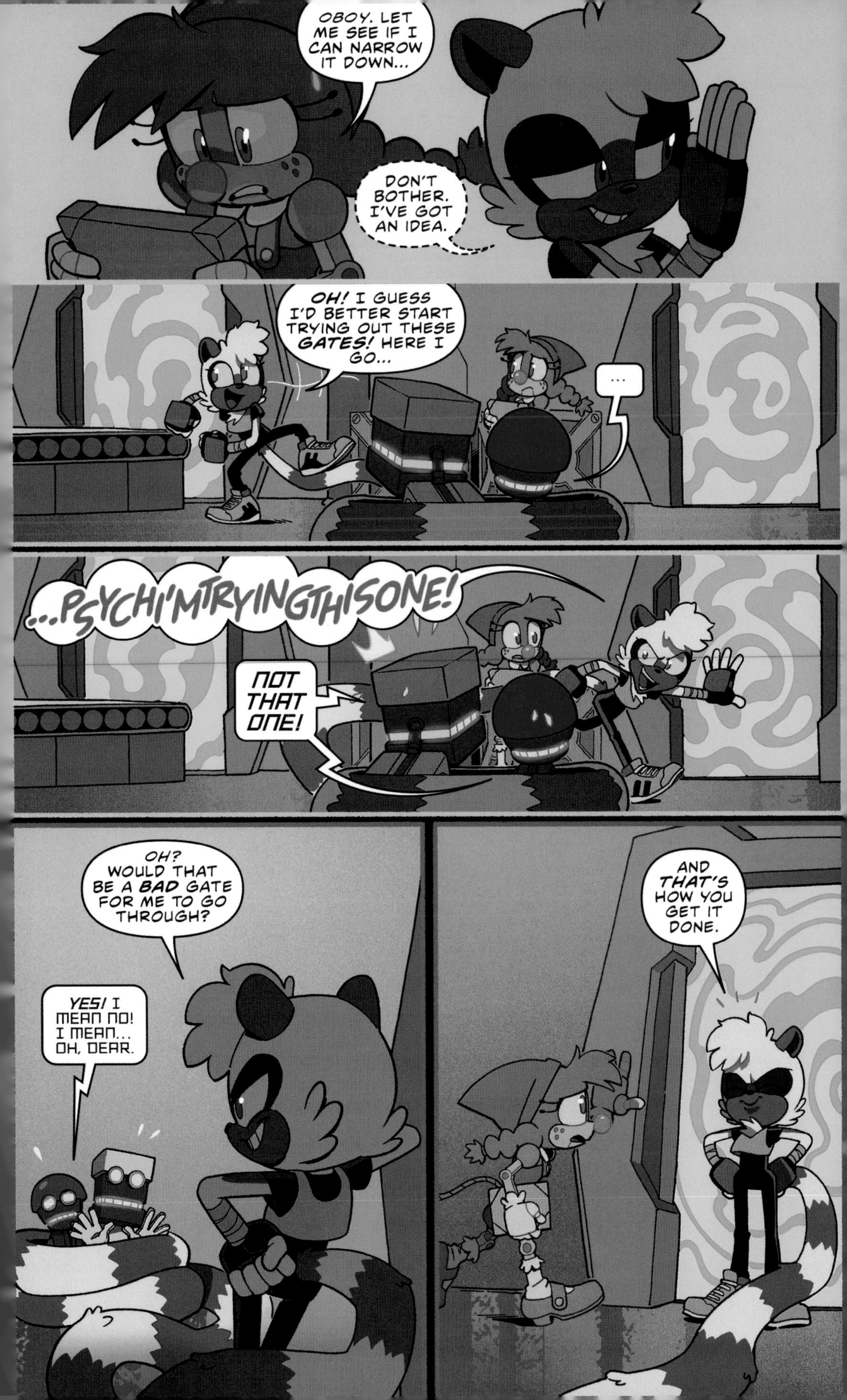
OBOY. LET ME SEE IF I CAN NARROW IT DOWN...
DON'T BOTHER. I'VE GOT AN IDEA.
OH! I GUESS I'D BETTER START TRYING OUT THESE GATES! HERE I GO...
...
...PSYCHI'MTRYINGTHISONE!
NOT THAT ONE!
OH? WOULD THAT BE A BAD GATE FOR ME TO GO THROUGH?
YES! I MEAN NO! I MEAN... OH, DEAR.
AND THAT'S HOW YOU GET IT DONE.

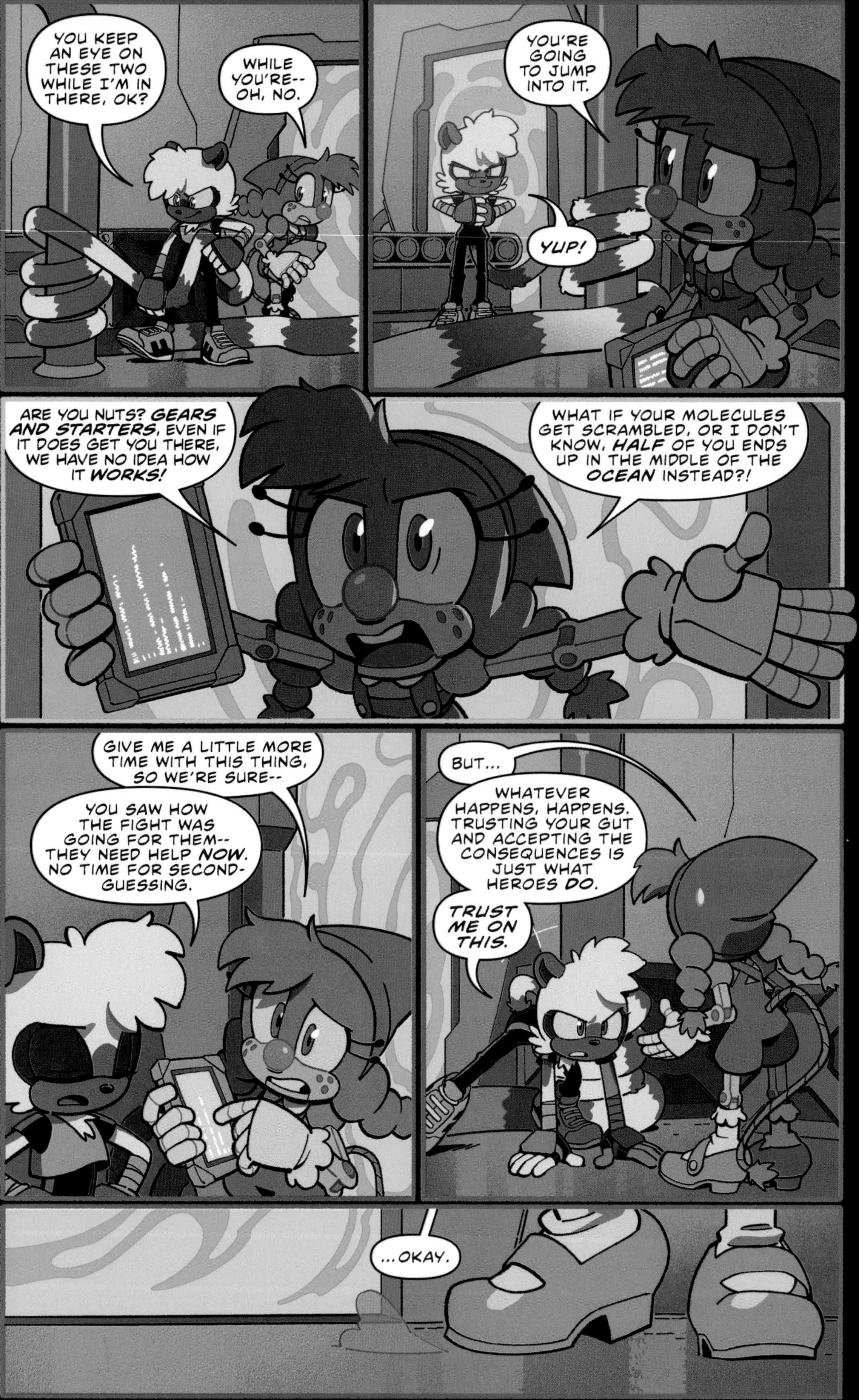
YOU KEEP AN EYE ON THESE TWO WHILE I'M IN THERE, OK?
WHILE YOU'RE-- OH, NO.
YOU'RE GOING TO JUMP INTO IT.
YUP!
ARE YOU NUTS? GEARS AND STARTERS, EVEN IF IT DOES GET YOU THERE, WE HAVE NO IDEA HOW IT WORKS!
WHAT IF YOUR MOLECULES GET SCRAMBLED, OR I DON'T KNOW, HALF OF YOU ENDS UP IN THE MIDDLE OF THE OCEAN INSTEAD?!
GIVE ME A LITTLE MORE TIME WITH THIS THING, SO WE'RE SURE--
YOU SAW HOW THE FIGHT WAS GOING FOR THEM-- THEY NEED HELP NOW. NO TIME FOR SECOND-GUESSING.
BUT...
WHATEVER HAPPENS, HAPPENS. TRUSTING YOUR GUT AND ACCEPTING THE CONSEQUENCES IS JUST WHAT HEROES DO.
TRUST ME ON THIS.
...OKAY.

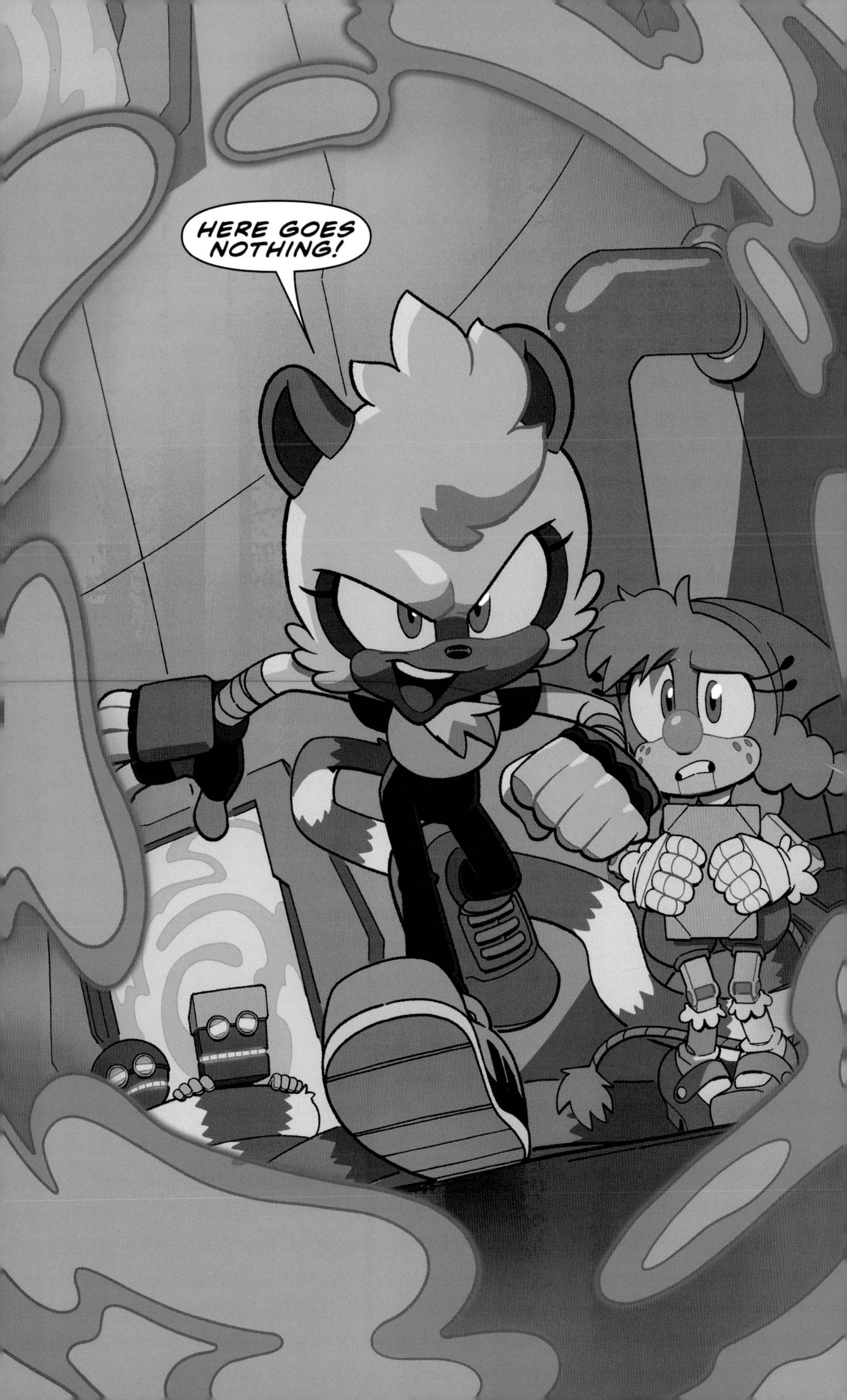
HERE GOES NOTHING!

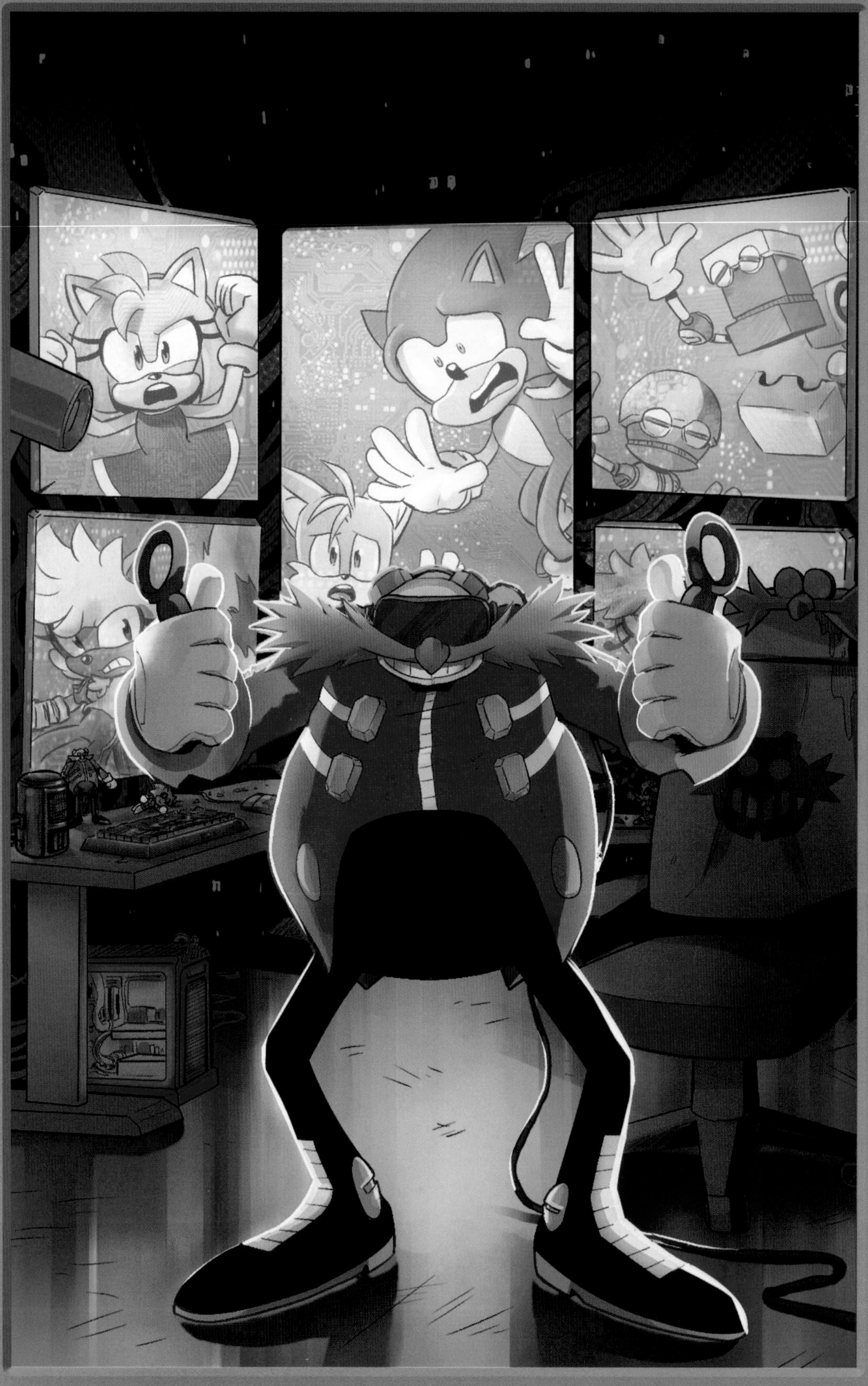

ART BY **GIGI DUTREIX**

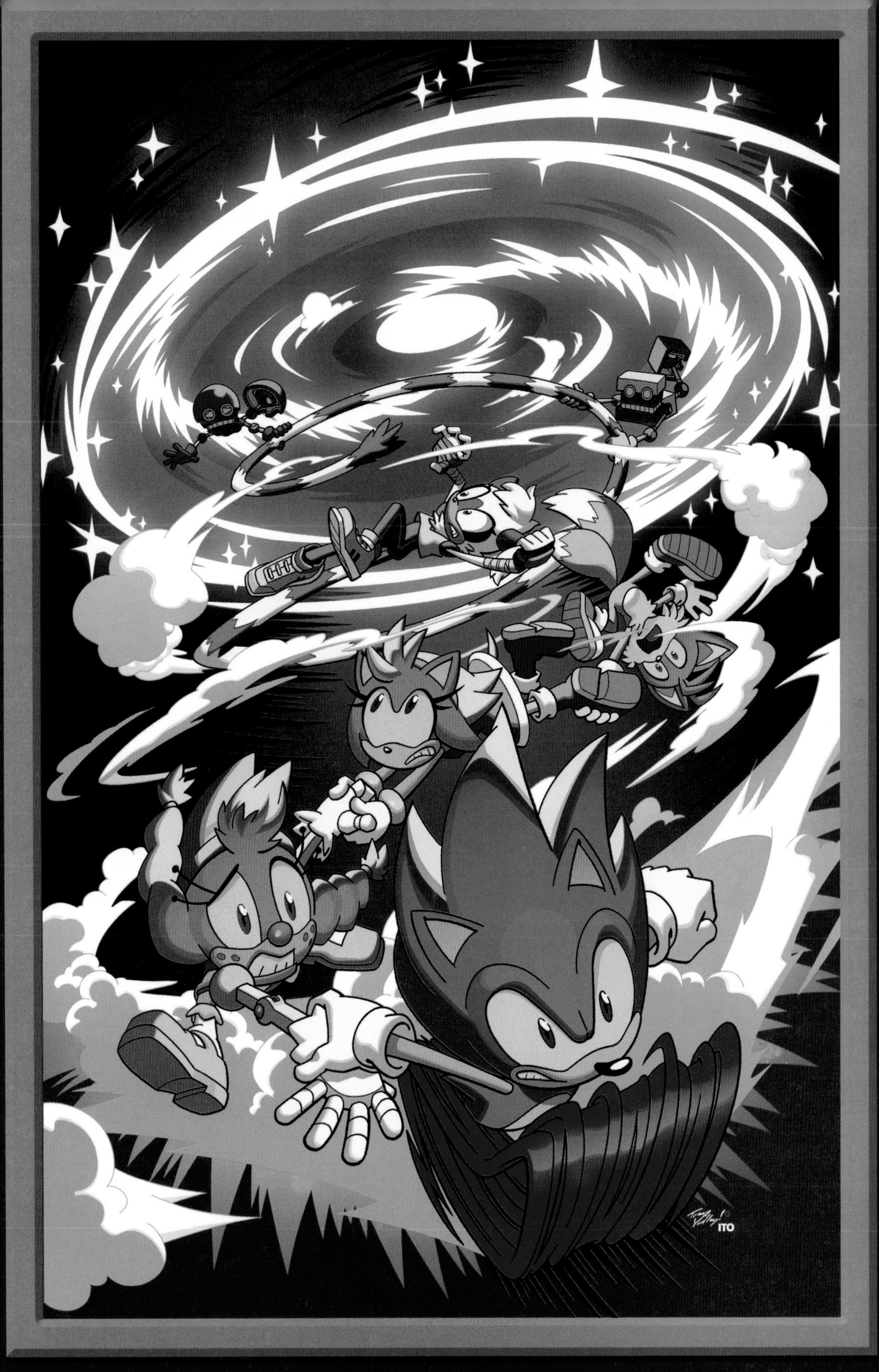

ART BY **TRACY YARDLEY** COLORS BY **LEONARDO ITO**

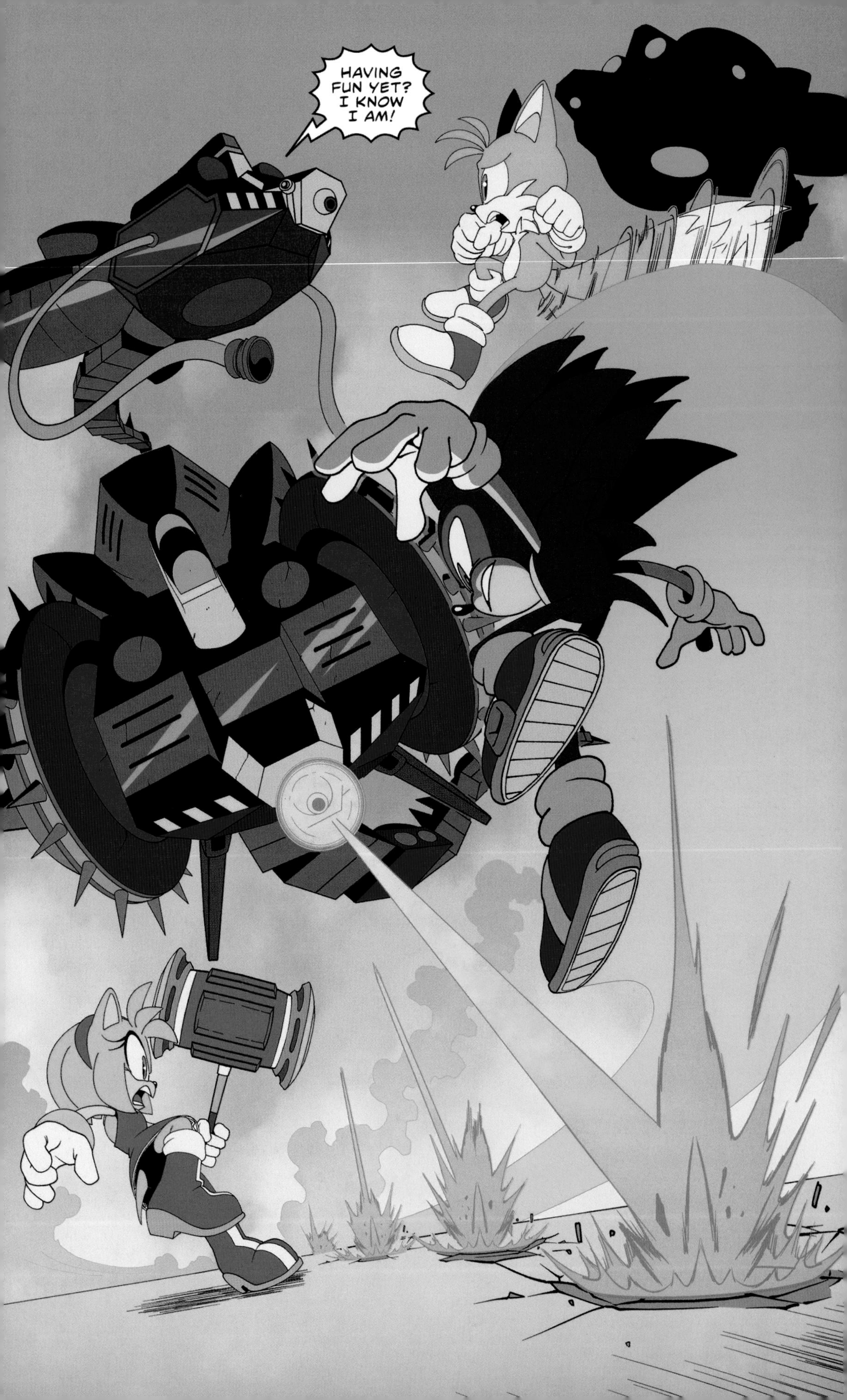
HAVING FUN YET? I KNOW I AM!

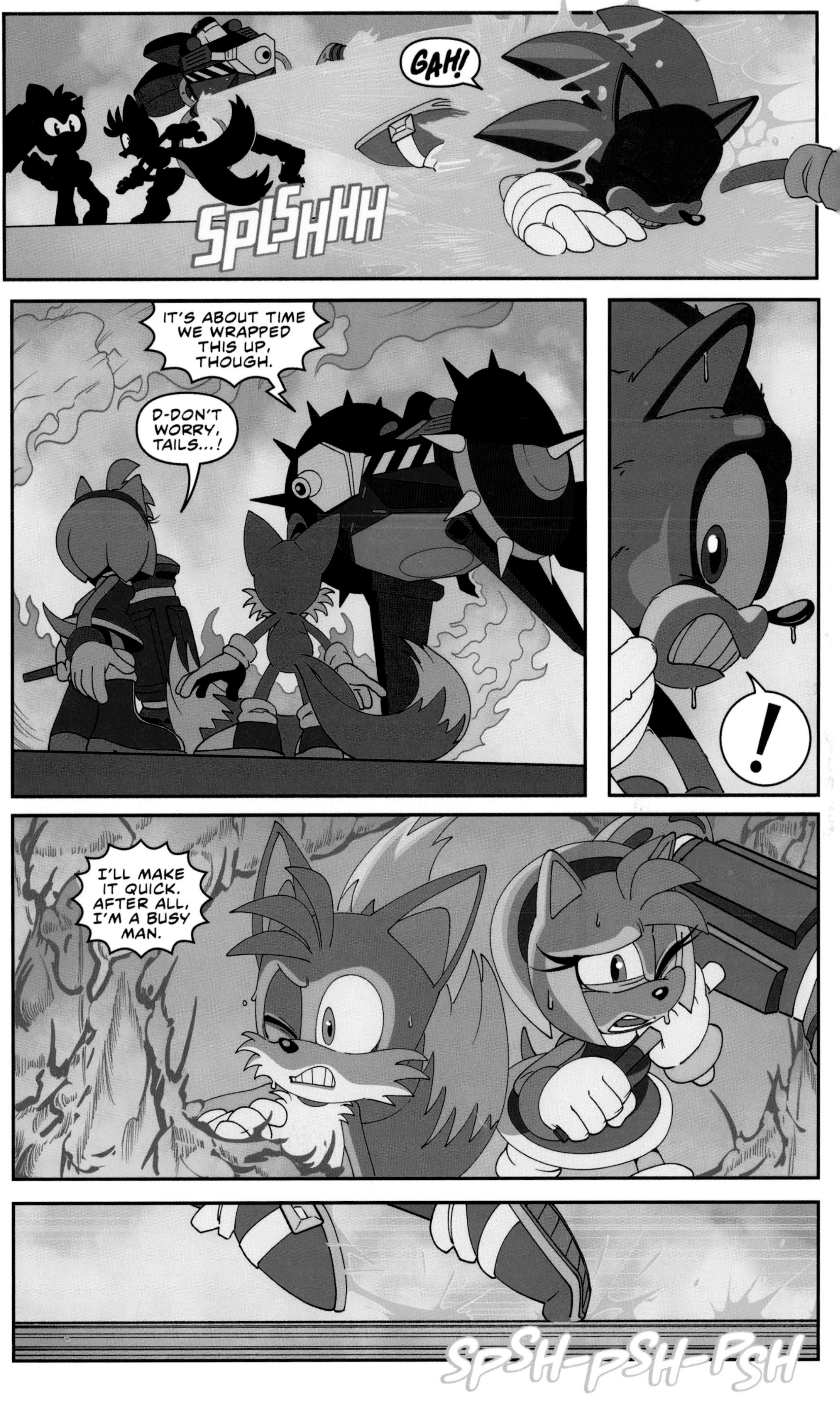
GAH!
SPLSHHH
IT'S ABOUT TIME WE WRAPPED THIS UP, THOUGH.
D-DON'T WORRY, TAILS...!
!
I'LL MAKE IT QUICK. AFTER ALL, I'M A BUSY MAN.
SPSH-PSH-PSH

HEY, DOC!

HEADS DOWN, GUYS!

THANKS FOR THE SHOWER...

...BUT I THINK YOU NEED ONE MORE!

WHA-- NO!

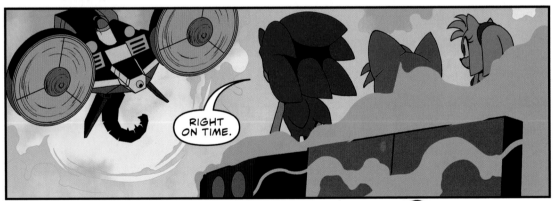

RIGHT ON TIME.

AMY, GIMME A BOOST!

HUH? TAILS CAN--

--NO TIME! GET ME UP THERE!

IF YOU SAY SO...

BOING

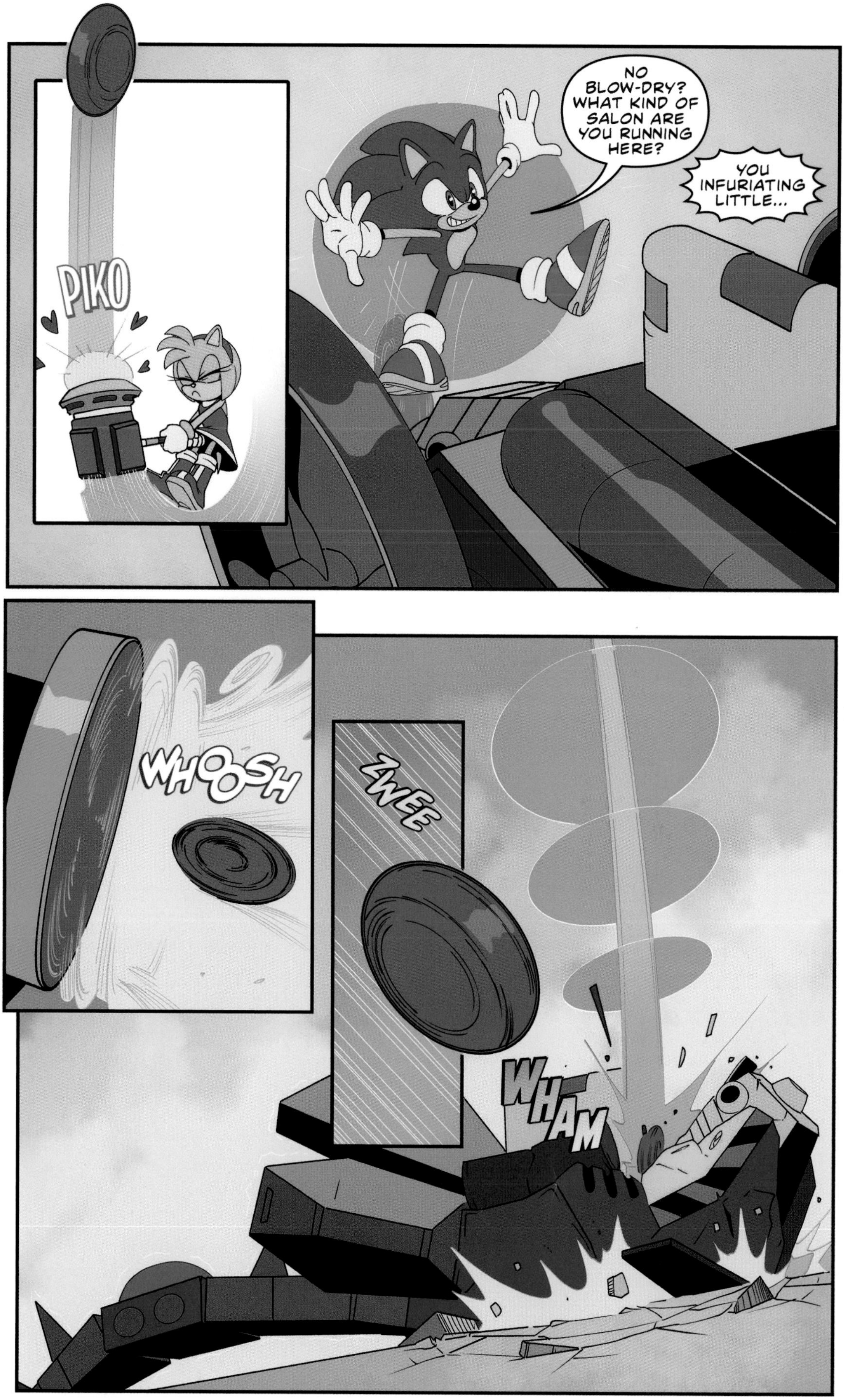
PIKO
NO BLOW-DRY? WHAT KIND OF SALON ARE YOU RUNNING HERE?
YOU INFURIATING LITTLE...
WHOOSH
ZWEE
WHAM

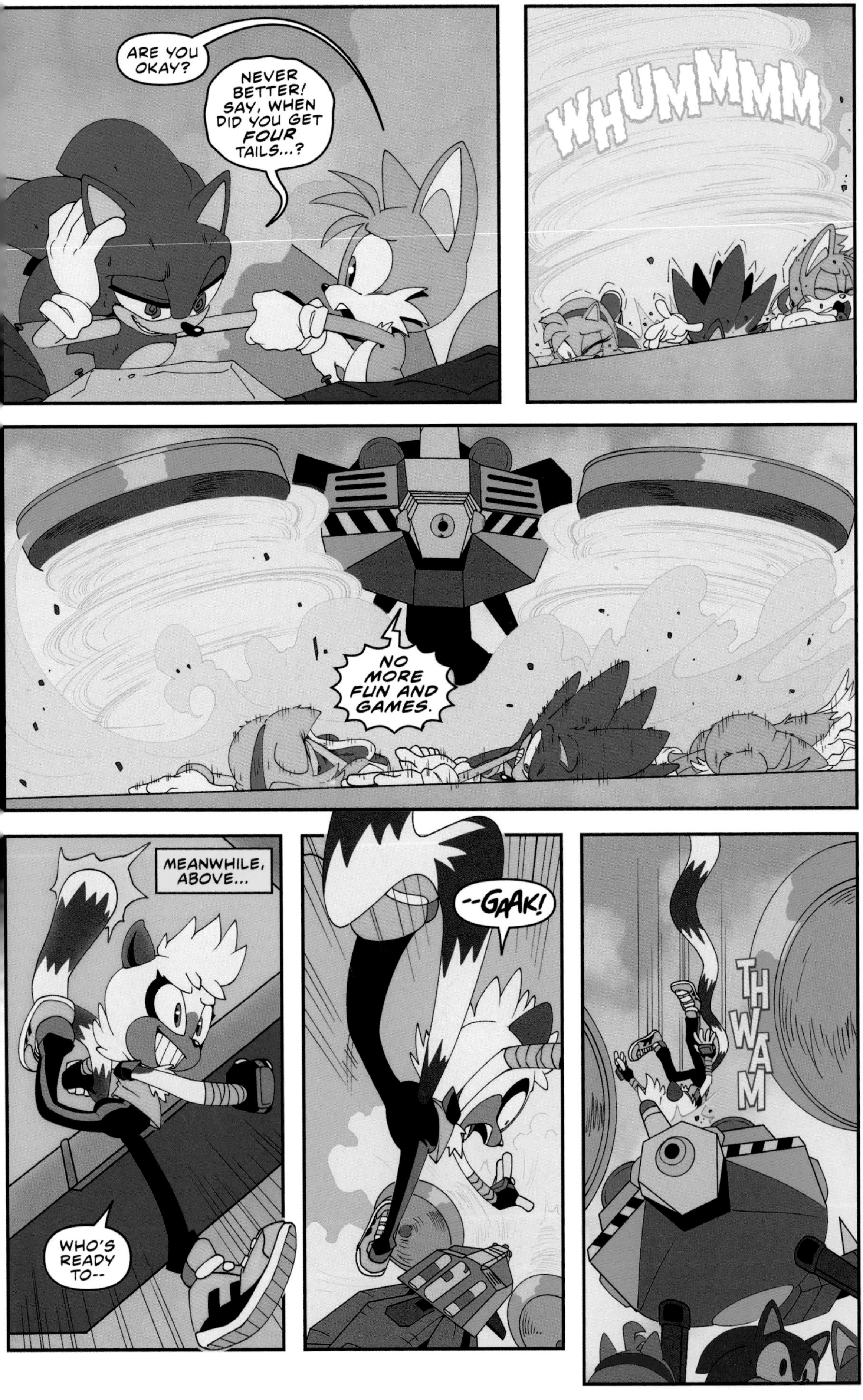
ARE YOU OKAY?
NEVER BETTER! SAY, WHEN DID YOU GET FOUR TAILS...?
WHUMMMM
NO MORE FUN AND GAMES.
MEANWHILE, ABOVE...
WHO'S READY TO--
--GAAK!
THWAM

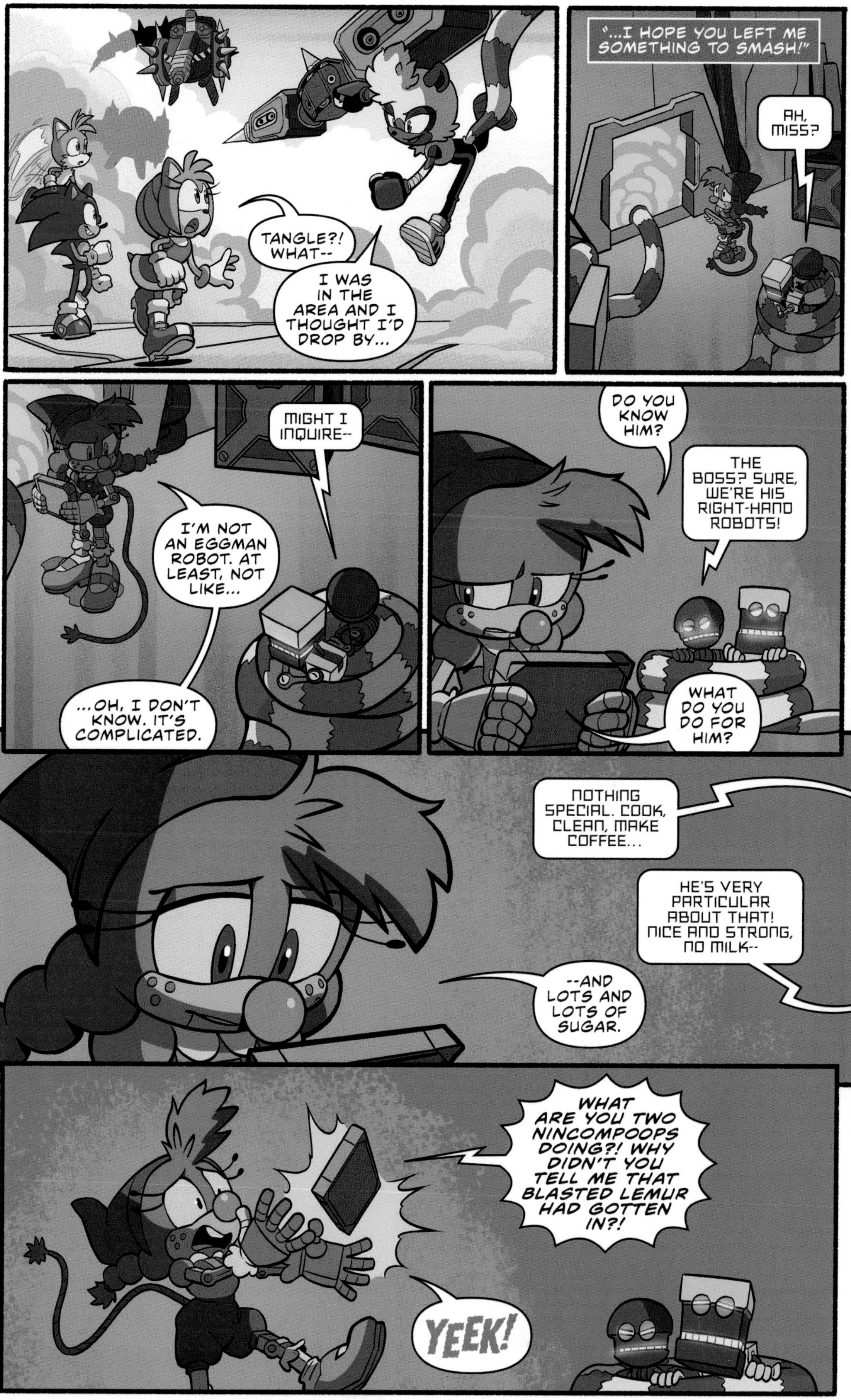

TANGLE?! WHAT--
I WAS IN THE AREA AND I THOUGHT I'D DROP BY...
"...I HOPE YOU LEFT ME SOMETHING TO SMASH!"
AH, MISS?
MIGHT I INQUIRE--
I'M NOT AN EGGMAN ROBOT. AT LEAST, NOT LIKE...
...OH, I DON'T KNOW. IT'S COMPLICATED.
DO YOU KNOW HIM?
THE BOSS? SURE, WE'RE HIS RIGHT-HAND ROBOTS!
WHAT DO YOU DO FOR HIM?
NOTHING SPECIAL. COOK, CLEAN, MAKE COFFEE...
HE'S VERY PARTICULAR ABOUT THAT! NICE AND STRONG, NO MILK--
--AND LOTS AND LOTS OF SUGAR.
WHAT ARE YOU TWO NINCOMPOOPS DOING?! WHY DIDN'T YOU TELL ME THAT BLASTED LEMUR HAD GOTTEN IN?!
YEEK!

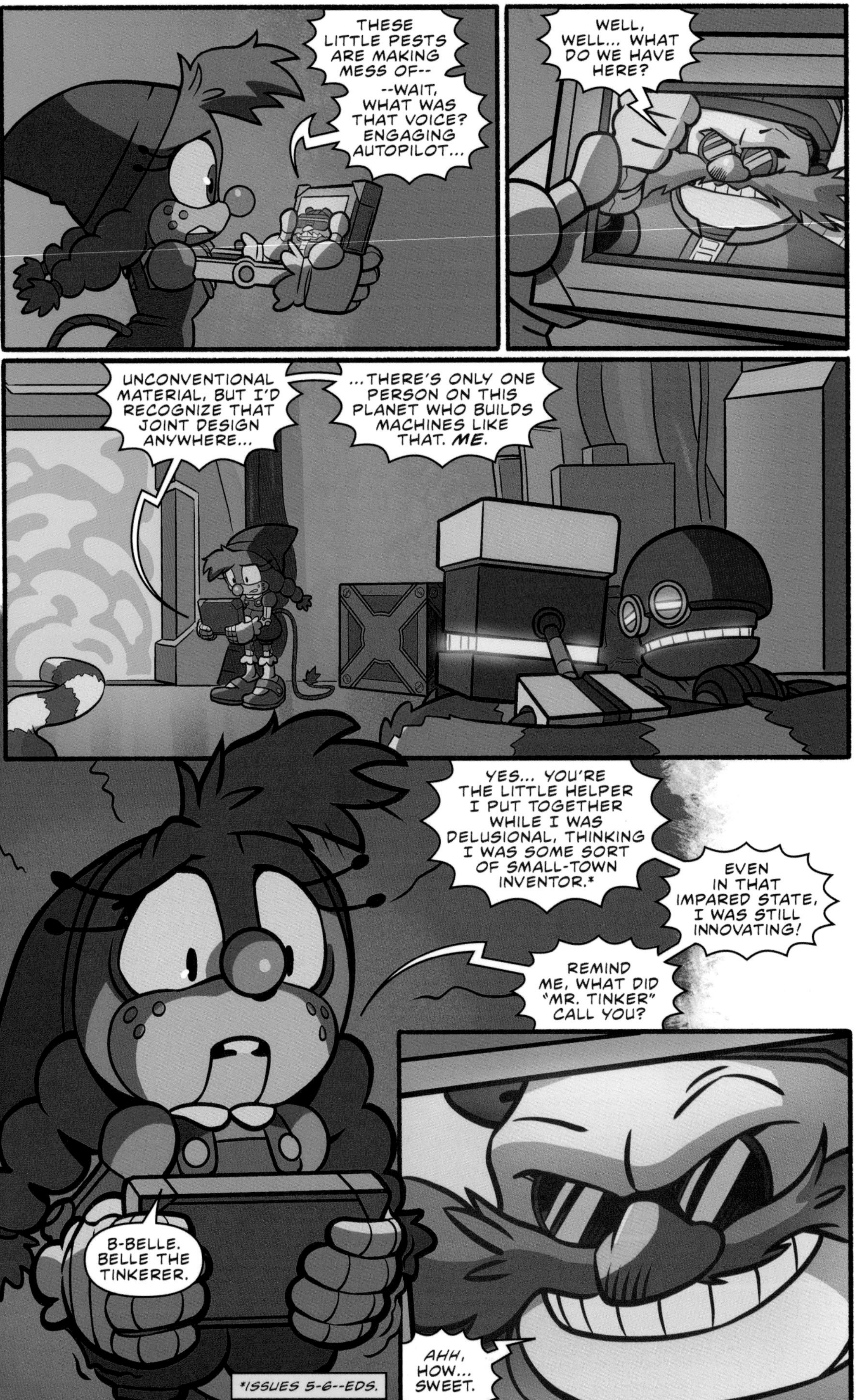
THESE LITTLE PESTS ARE MAKING MESS OF--
--WAIT, WHAT WAS THAT VOICE? ENGAGING AUTOPILOT...
WELL, WELL... WHAT DO WE HAVE HERE?
UNCONVENTIONAL MATERIAL, BUT I'D RECOGNIZE THAT JOINT DESIGN ANYWHERE...
...THERE'S ONLY ONE PERSON ON THIS PLANET WHO BUILDS MACHINES LIKE THAT. *ME*.
YES... YOU'RE THE LITTLE HELPER I PUT TOGETHER WHILE I WAS DELUSIONAL, THINKING I WAS SOME SORT OF SMALL-TOWN INVENTOR.*
EVEN IN THAT IMPARED STATE, I WAS STILL INNOVATING!
REMIND ME, WHAT DID "MR. TINKER" CALL YOU?
B-BELLE. BELLE THE TINKERER.
*ISSUES 5-6--EDS.
AHH, HOW... SWEET.

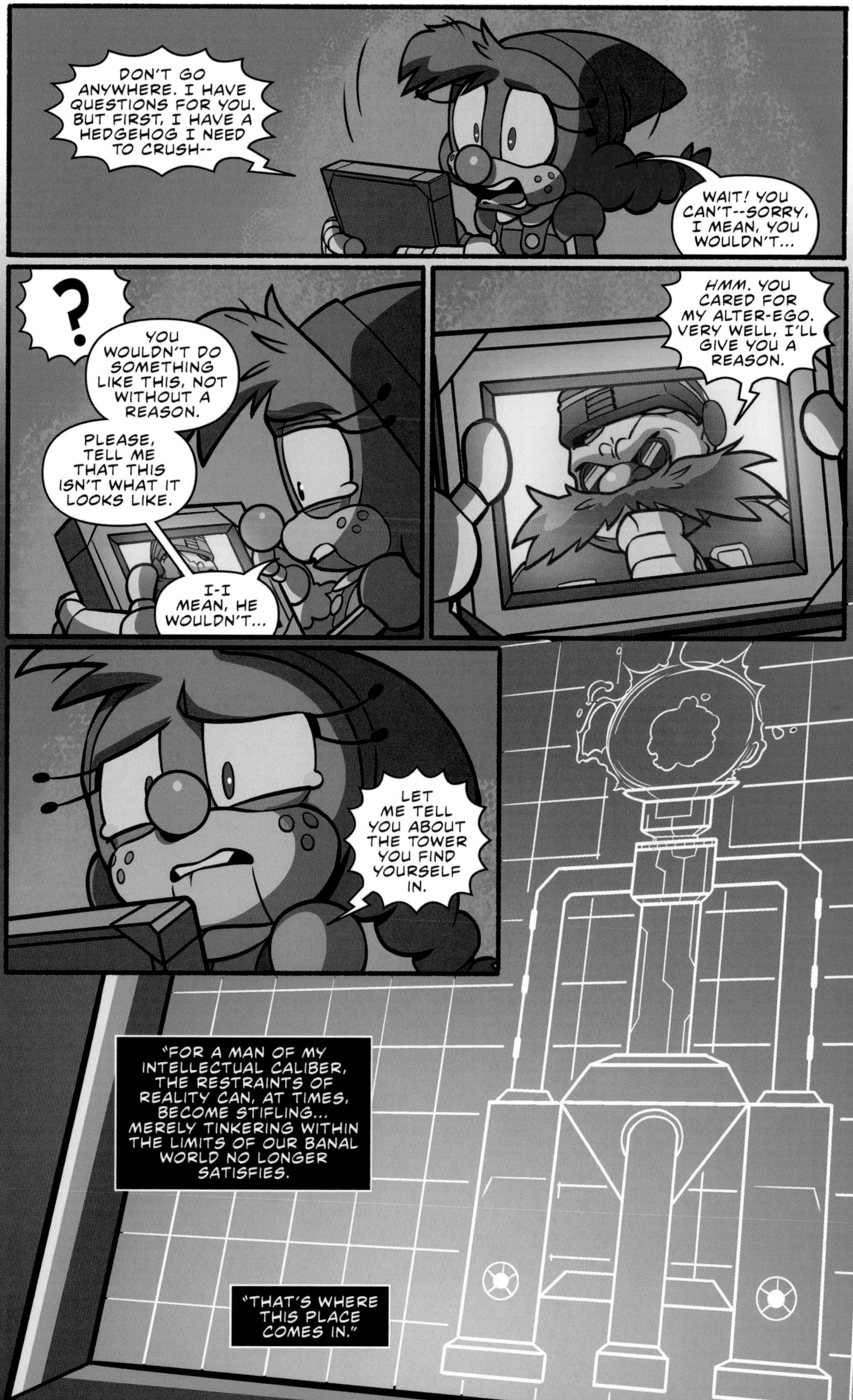
DON'T GO ANYWHERE. I HAVE QUESTIONS FOR YOU. BUT FIRST, I HAVE A HEDGEHOG I NEED TO CRUSH--
WAIT! YOU CAN'T--SORRY, I MEAN, YOU WOULDN'T...
?
YOU WOULDN'T DO SOMETHING LIKE THIS, NOT WITHOUT A REASON.
PLEASE, TELL ME THAT THIS ISN'T WHAT IT LOOKS LIKE.
I-I MEAN, HE WOULDN'T...
HMM. YOU CARED FOR MY ALTER-EGO. VERY WELL, I'LL GIVE YOU A REASON.
LET ME TELL YOU ABOUT THE TOWER YOU FIND YOURSELF IN.
"FOR A MAN OF MY INTELLECTUAL CALIBER, THE RESTRAINTS OF REALITY CAN, AT TIMES, BECOME STIFLING... MERELY TINKERING WITHIN THE LIMITS OF OUR BANAL WORLD NO LONGER SATISFIES.
"THAT'S WHERE THIS PLACE COMES IN."

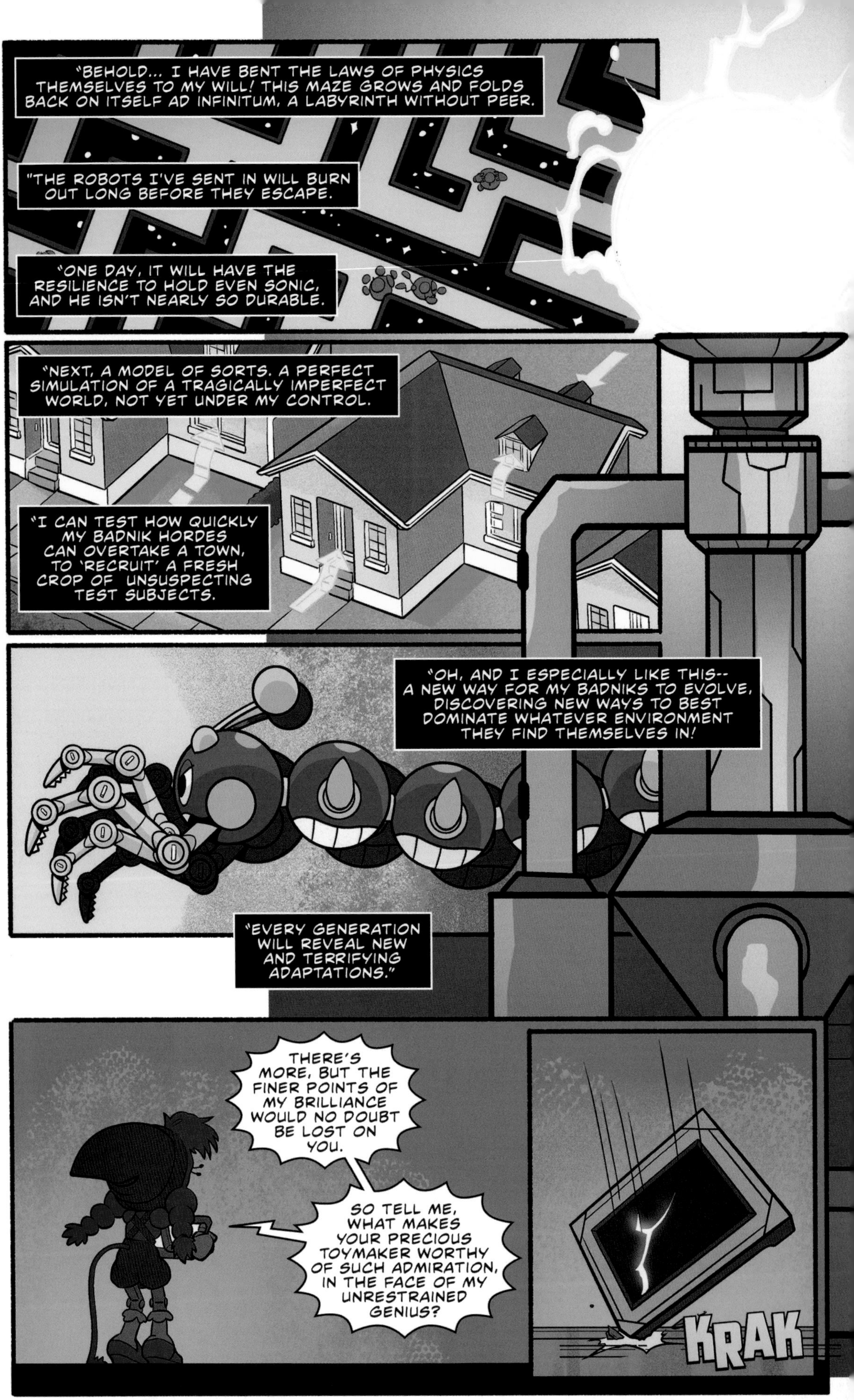
"BEHOLD... I HAVE BENT THE LAWS OF PHYSICS THEMSELVES TO MY WILL! THIS MAZE GROWS AND FOLDS BACK ON ITSELF AD INFINITUM, A LABYRINTH WITHOUT PEER.
"THE ROBOTS I'VE SENT IN WILL BURN OUT LONG BEFORE THEY ESCAPE.
"ONE DAY, IT WILL HAVE THE RESILIENCE TO HOLD EVEN SONIC, AND HE ISN'T NEARLY SO DURABLE.
"NEXT, A MODEL OF SORTS. A PERFECT SIMULATION OF A TRAGICALLY IMPERFECT WORLD, NOT YET UNDER MY CONTROL.
"I CAN TEST HOW QUICKLY MY BADNIK HORDES CAN OVERTAKE A TOWN, TO 'RECRUIT' A FRESH CROP OF UNSUSPECTING TEST SUBJECTS.
"OH, AND I ESPECIALLY LIKE THIS-- A NEW WAY FOR MY BADNIKS TO EVOLVE, DISCOVERING NEW WAYS TO BEST DOMINATE WHATEVER ENVIRONMENT THEY FIND THEMSELVES IN!
"EVERY GENERATION WILL REVEAL NEW AND TERRIFYING ADAPTATIONS."
THERE'S MORE, BUT THE FINER POINTS OF MY BRILLIANCE WOULD NO DOUBT BE LOST ON YOU.
SO TELL ME, WHAT MAKES YOUR PRECIOUS TOYMAKER WORTHY OF SUCH ADMIRATION, IN THE FACE OF MY UNRESTRAINED GENIUS?
KRAK

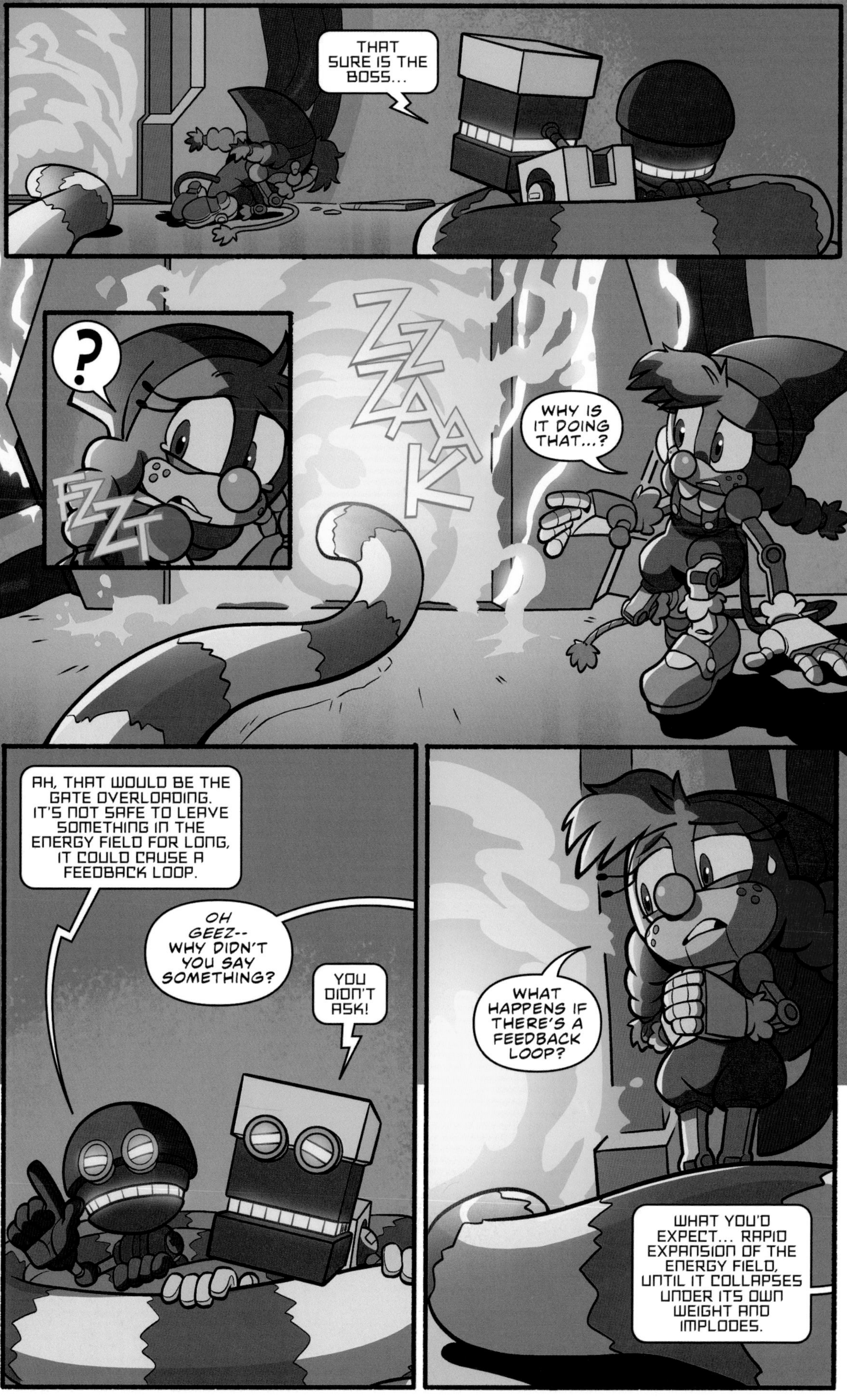
THAT SURE IS THE BOSS...
?
FZZT
ZZZAAAK
WHY IS IT DOING THAT...?
AH, THAT WOULD BE THE GATE OVERLOADING. IT'S NOT SAFE TO LEAVE SOMETHING IN THE ENERGY FIELD FOR LONG, IT COULD CAUSE A FEEDBACK LOOP.
OH GEEZ-- WHY DIDN'T YOU SAY SOMETHING?
YOU DIDN'T ASK!
WHAT HAPPENS IF THERE'S A FEEDBACK LOOP?
WHAT YOU'D EXPECT... RAPID EXPANSION OF THE ENERGY FIELD, UNTIL IT COLLAPSES UNDER ITS OWN WEIGHT AND IMPLODES.

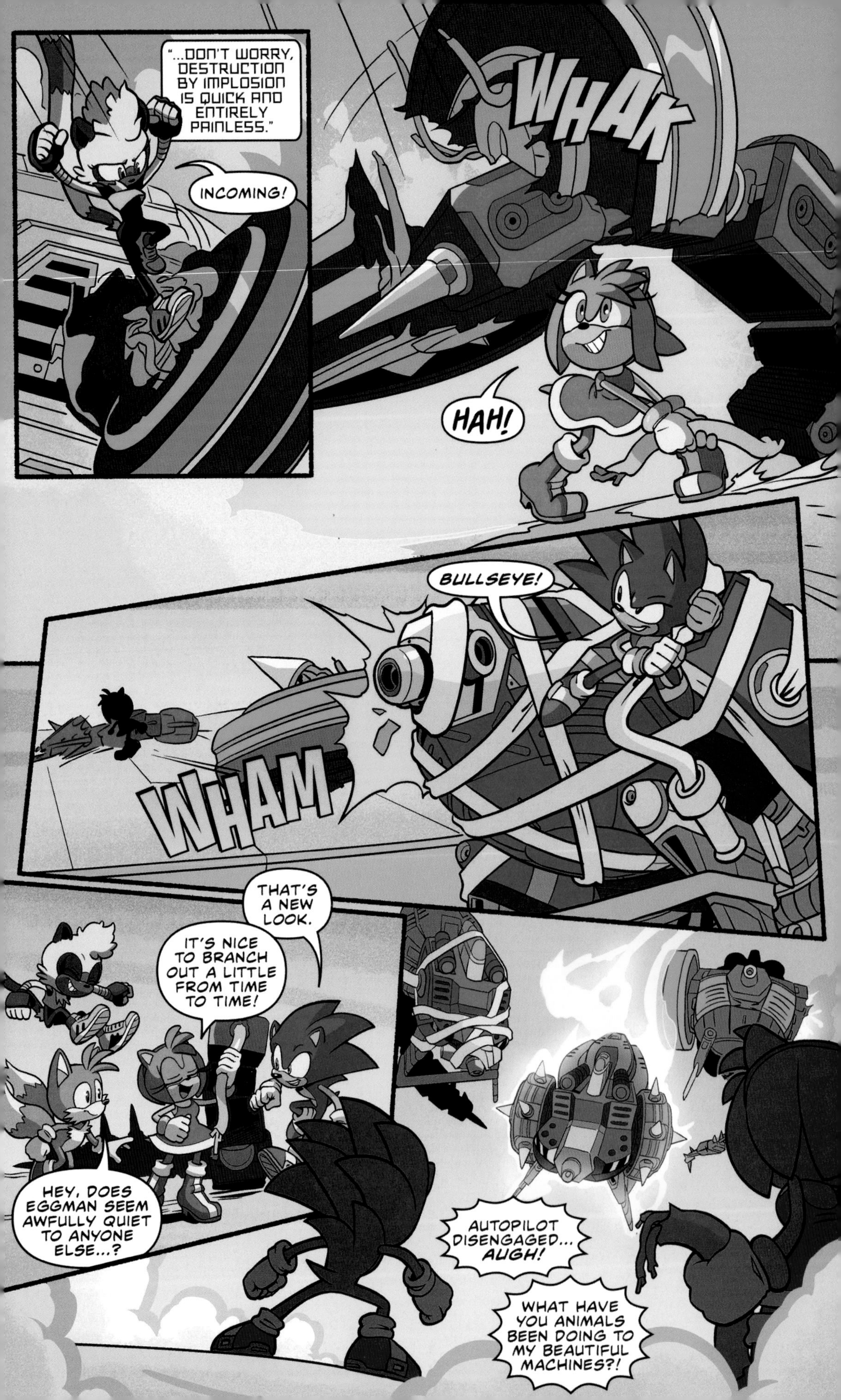

"...DON'T WORRY, DESTRUCTION BY IMPLOSION IS QUICK AND ENTIRELY PAINLESS."
INCOMING!
WHAK
HAH!
BULLSEYE!
WHAM
THAT'S A NEW LOOK.
IT'S NICE TO BRANCH OUT A LITTLE FROM TIME TO TIME!
HEY, DOES EGGMAN SEEM AWFULLY QUIET TO ANYONE ELSE...?
AUTOPILOT DISENGAGED... AUGH!
WHAT HAVE YOU ANIMALS BEEN DOING TO MY BEAUTIFUL MACHINES?!

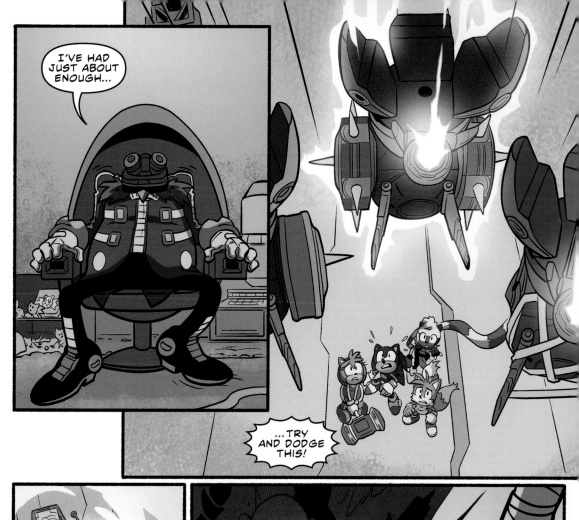

I'VE HAD JUST ABOUT ENOUGH...

...TRY AND DODGE THIS!

UP HERE!

CRASH

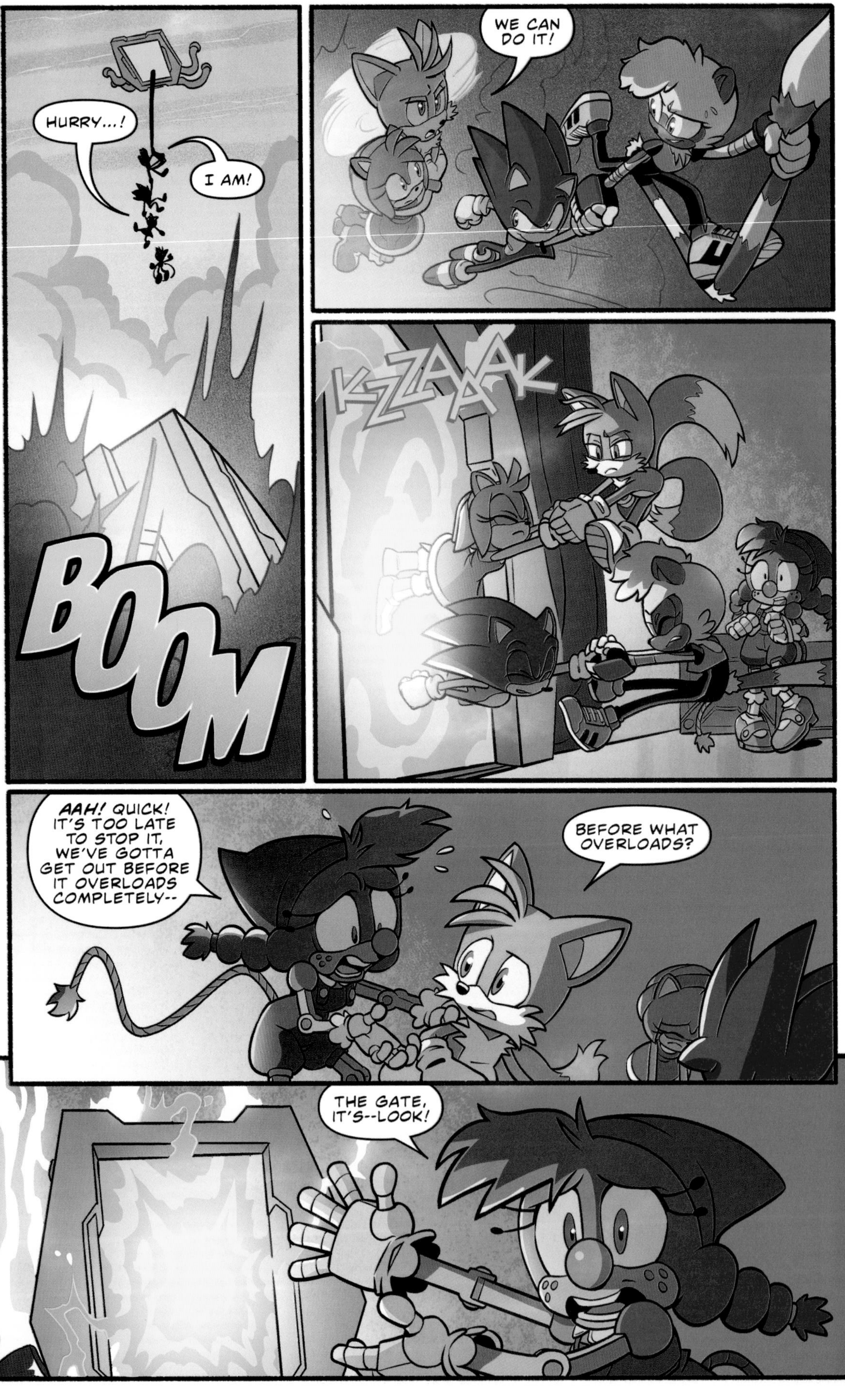
HURRY...!
I AM!
BOOM
WE CAN DO IT!
KZZAAAK
AAH! QUICK! IT'S TOO LATE TO STOP IT, WE'VE GOTTA GET OUT BEFORE IT OVERLOADS COMPLETELY--
BEFORE WHAT OVERLOADS?
THE GATE, IT'S--LOOK!

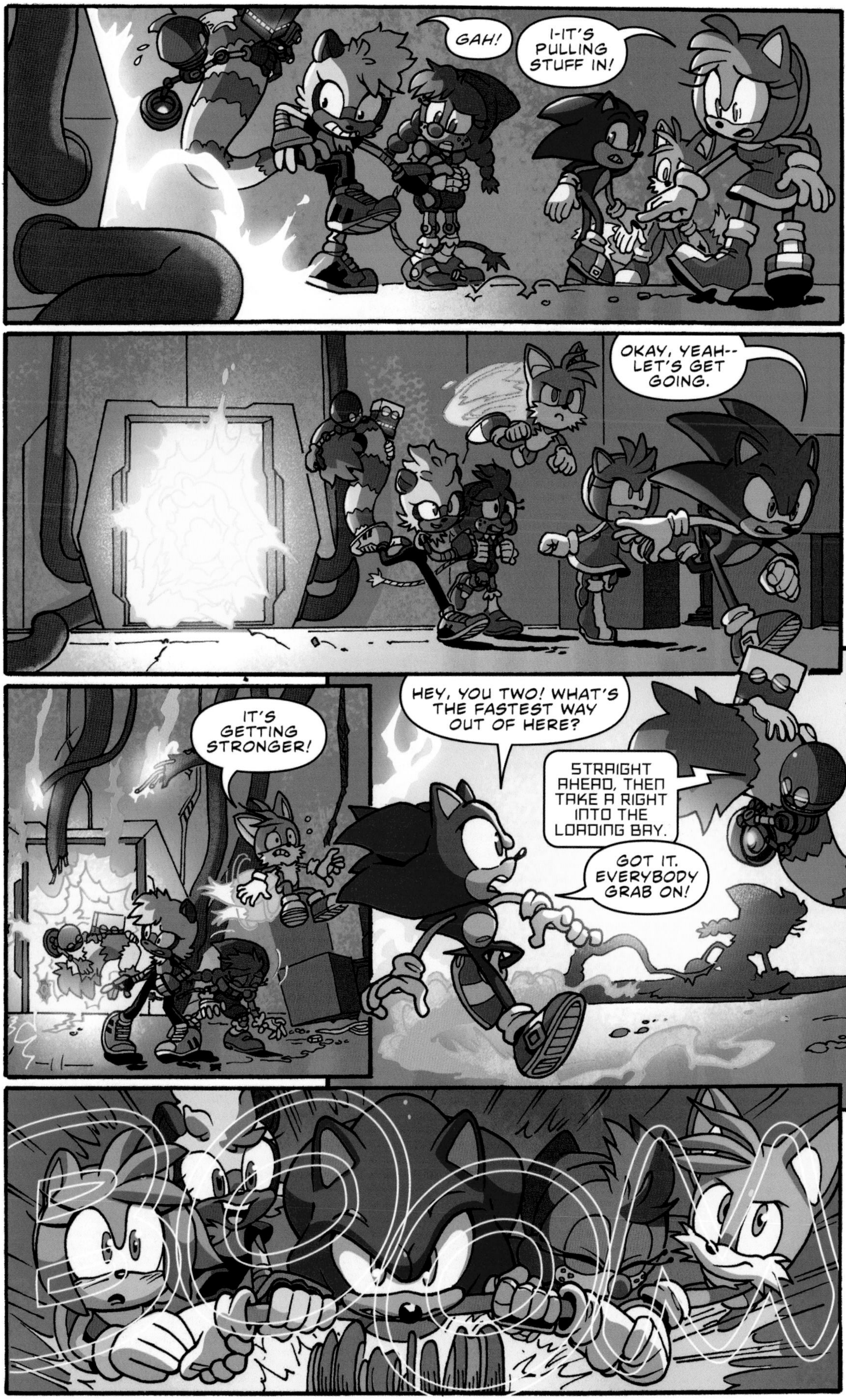
GAH!
I-IT'S PULLING STUFF IN!
OKAY, YEAH-- LET'S GET GOING.
IT'S GETTING STRONGER!
HEY, YOU TWO! WHAT'S THE FASTEST WAY OUT OF HERE?
STRAIGHT AHEAD, THEN TAKE A RIGHT INTO THE LOADING BAY.
GOT IT. EVERYBODY GRAB ON!
BOOM

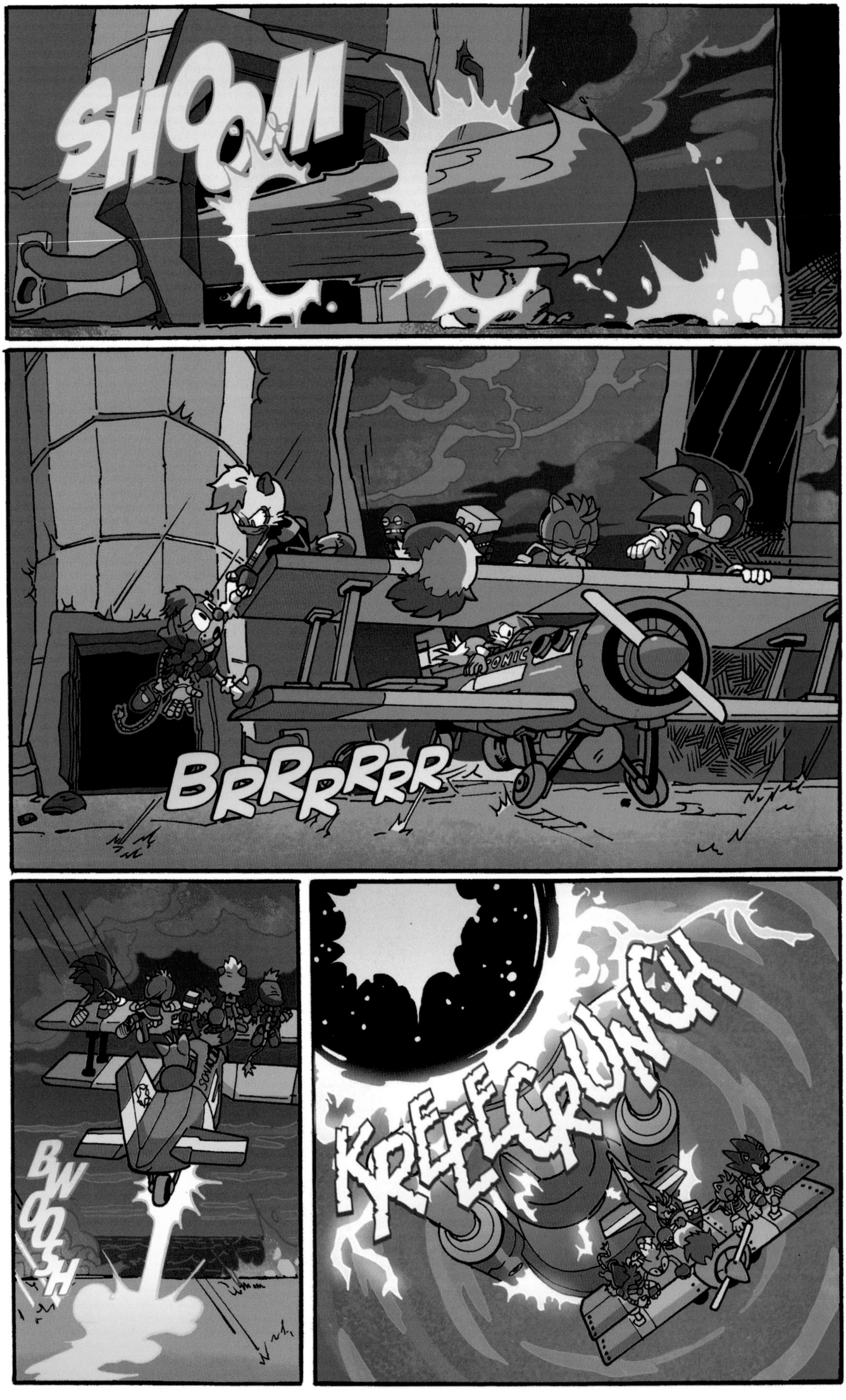
SHOOM
SONIC
BRRRRRR
SONIC
BWOOSH
KREEECRUNCH

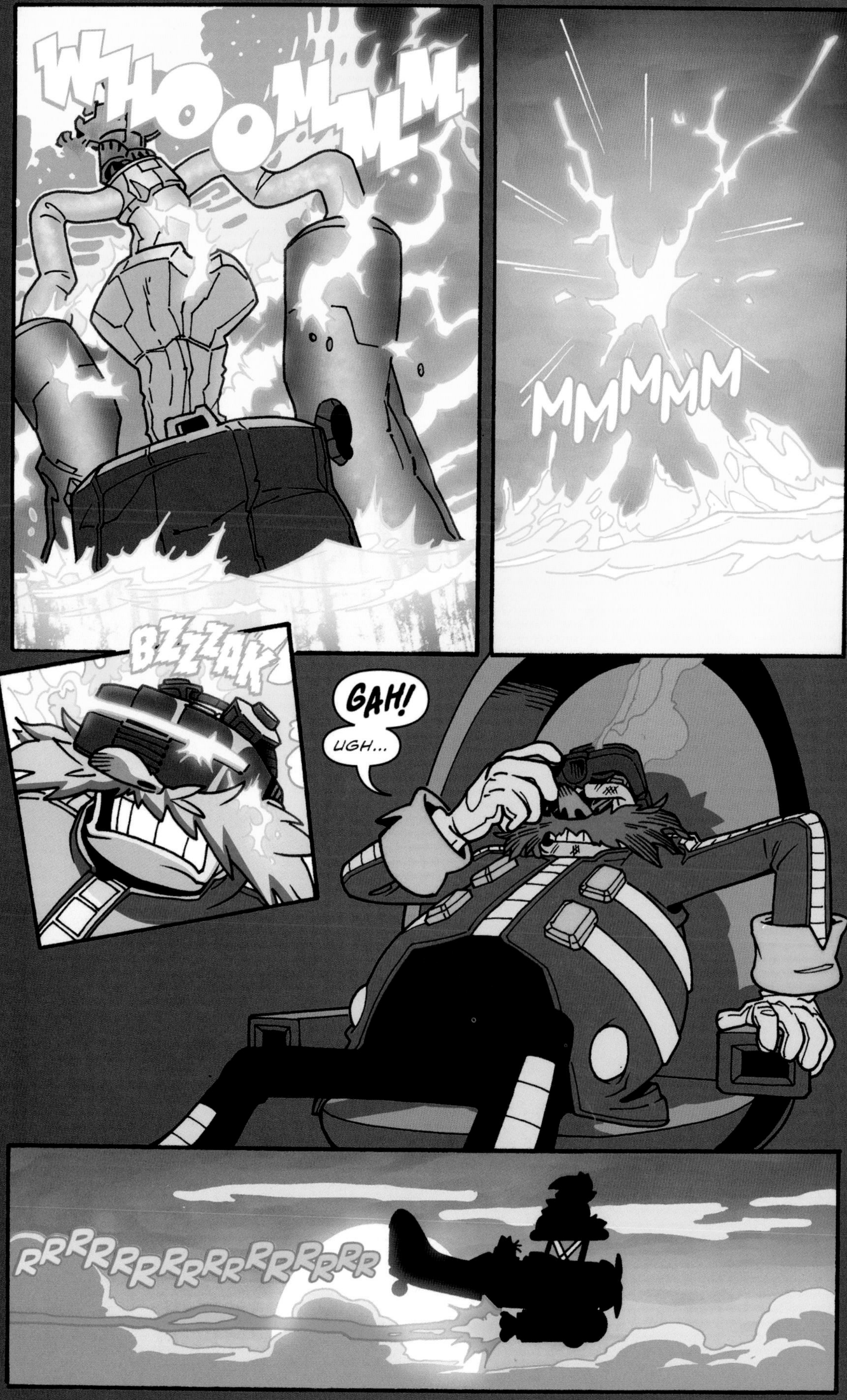
WHOOMMM
MMMMM
BZZZAK
GAH!
UGH...
RRRRRRRRRRRRRRRR

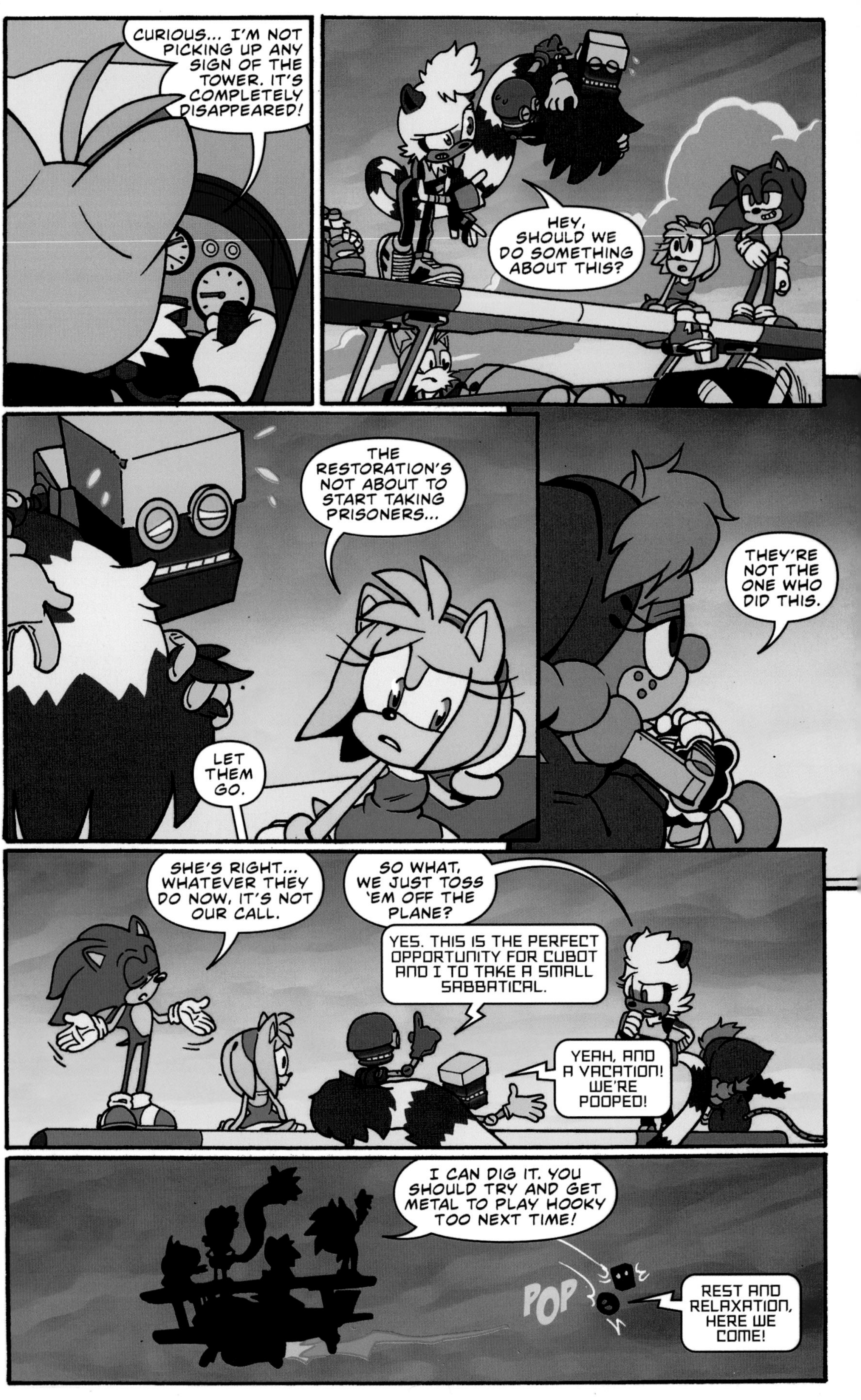
CURIOUS... I'M NOT PICKING UP ANY SIGN OF THE TOWER. IT'S COMPLETELY DISAPPEARED!
HEY, SHOULD WE DO SOMETHING ABOUT THIS?
THE RESTORATION'S NOT ABOUT TO START TAKING PRISONERS...
LET THEM GO.
THEY'RE NOT THE ONE WHO DID THIS.
SHE'S RIGHT... WHATEVER THEY DO NOW, IT'S NOT OUR CALL.
SO WHAT, WE JUST TOSS 'EM OFF THE PLANE?
YES. THIS IS THE PERFECT OPPORTUNITY FOR CUBOT AND I TO TAKE A SMALL SABBATICAL.
YEAH, AND A VACATION! WE'RE POOPED!
I CAN DIG IT. YOU SHOULD TRY AND GET METAL TO PLAY HOOKY TOO NEXT TIME!
POP
REST AND RELAXATION, HERE WE COME!

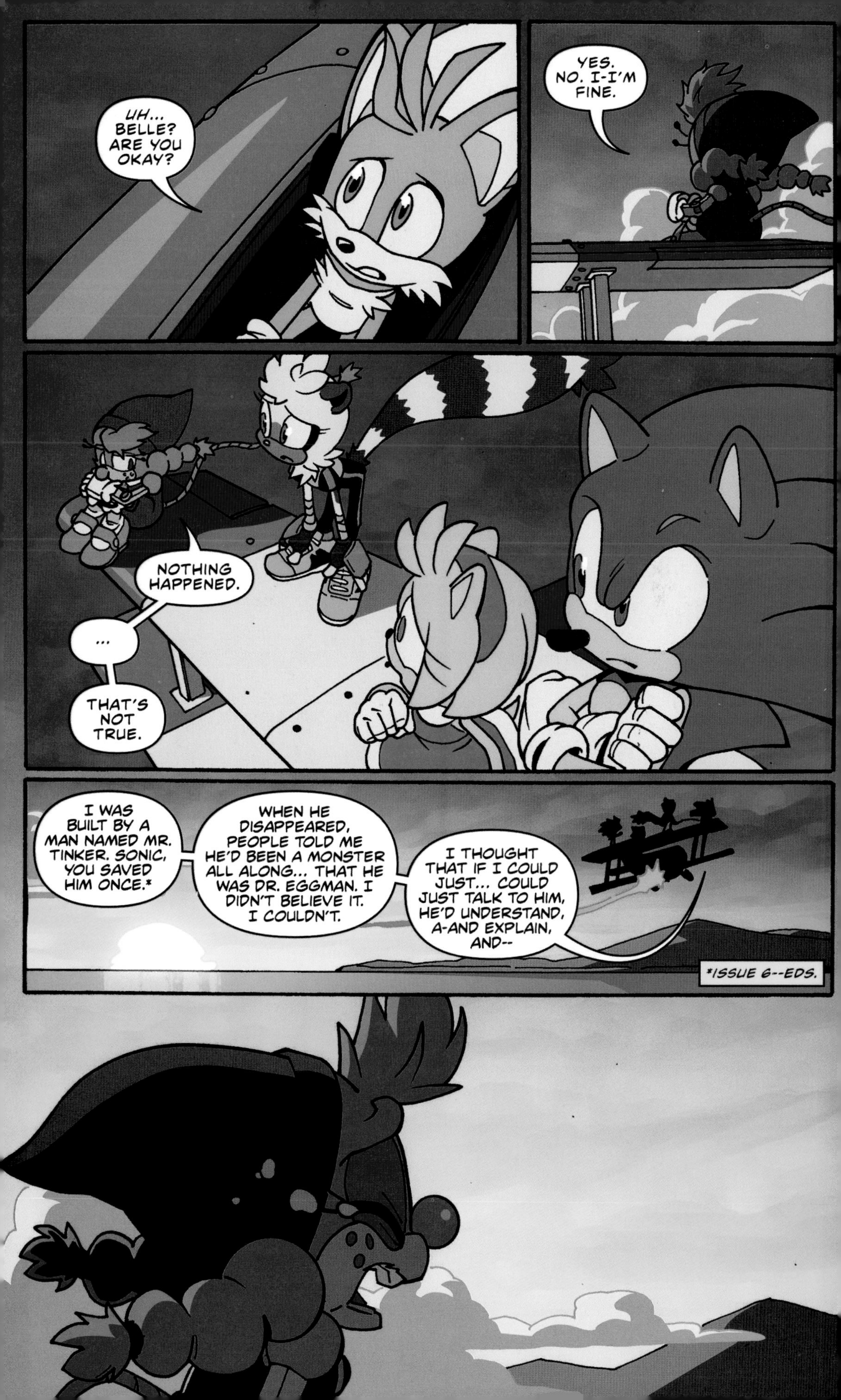
UH... BELLE? ARE YOU OKAY?
YES. NO. I-I'M FINE.
NOTHING HAPPENED.
...
THAT'S NOT TRUE.
I WAS BUILT BY A MAN NAMED MR. TINKER. SONIC, YOU SAVED HIM ONCE.*
WHEN HE DISAPPEARED, PEOPLE TOLD ME HE'D BEEN A MONSTER ALL ALONG... THAT HE WAS DR. EGGMAN. I DIDN'T BELIEVE IT. I COULDN'T.
I THOUGHT THAT IF I COULD JUST... COULD JUST TALK TO HIM, HE'D UNDERSTAND, A-AND EXPLAIN, AND--
*ISSUE 6--EDS.

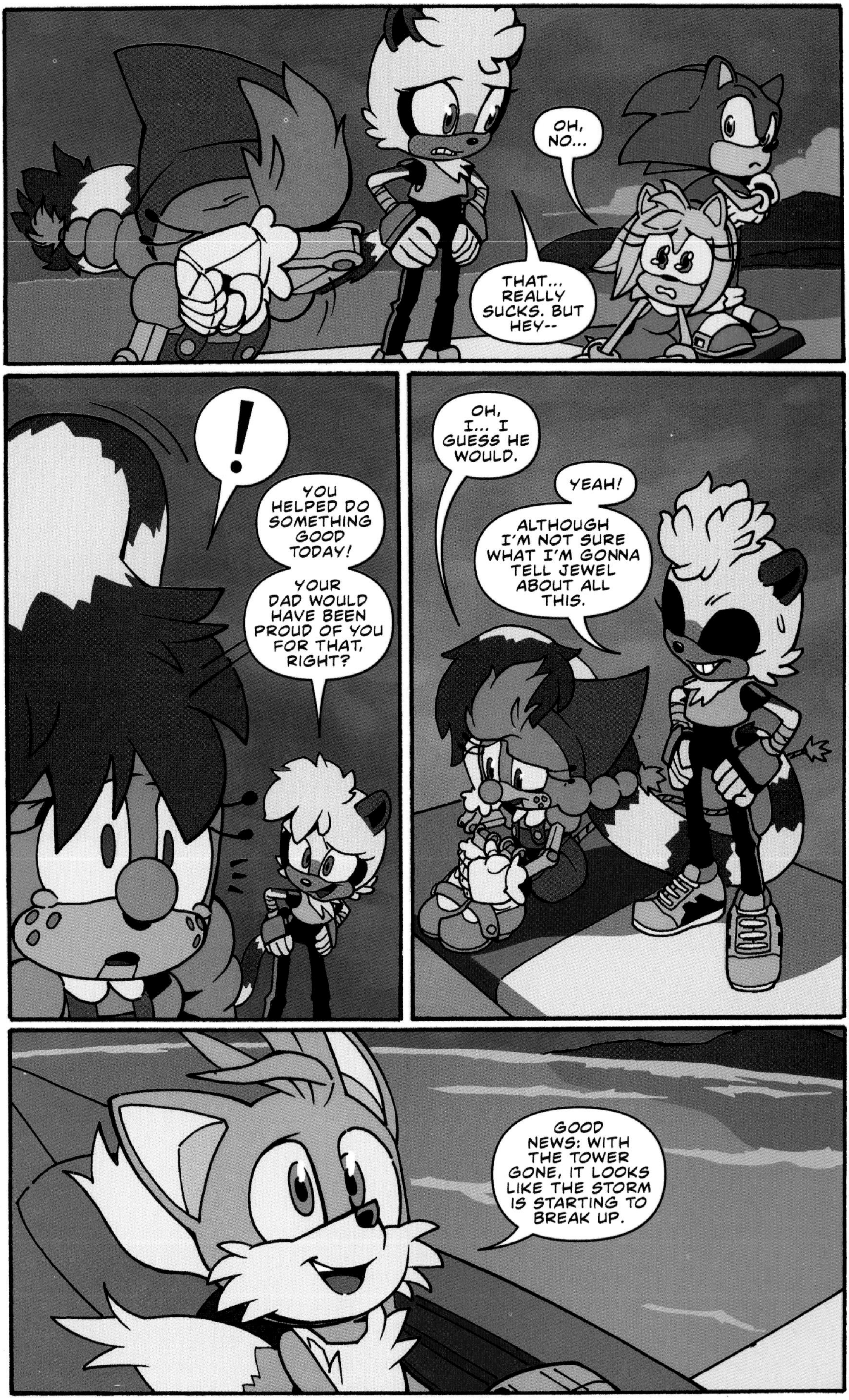
OH, NO...
THAT... REALLY SUCKS. BUT HEY--
!
YOU HELPED DO SOMETHING GOOD TODAY!
YOUR DAD WOULD HAVE BEEN PROUD OF YOU FOR THAT, RIGHT?
OH, I... I GUESS HE WOULD.
YEAH!
ALTHOUGH I'M NOT SURE WHAT I'M GONNA TELL JEWEL ABOUT ALL THIS.
GOOD NEWS: WITH THE TOWER GONE, IT LOOKS LIKE THE STORM IS STARTING TO BREAK UP.

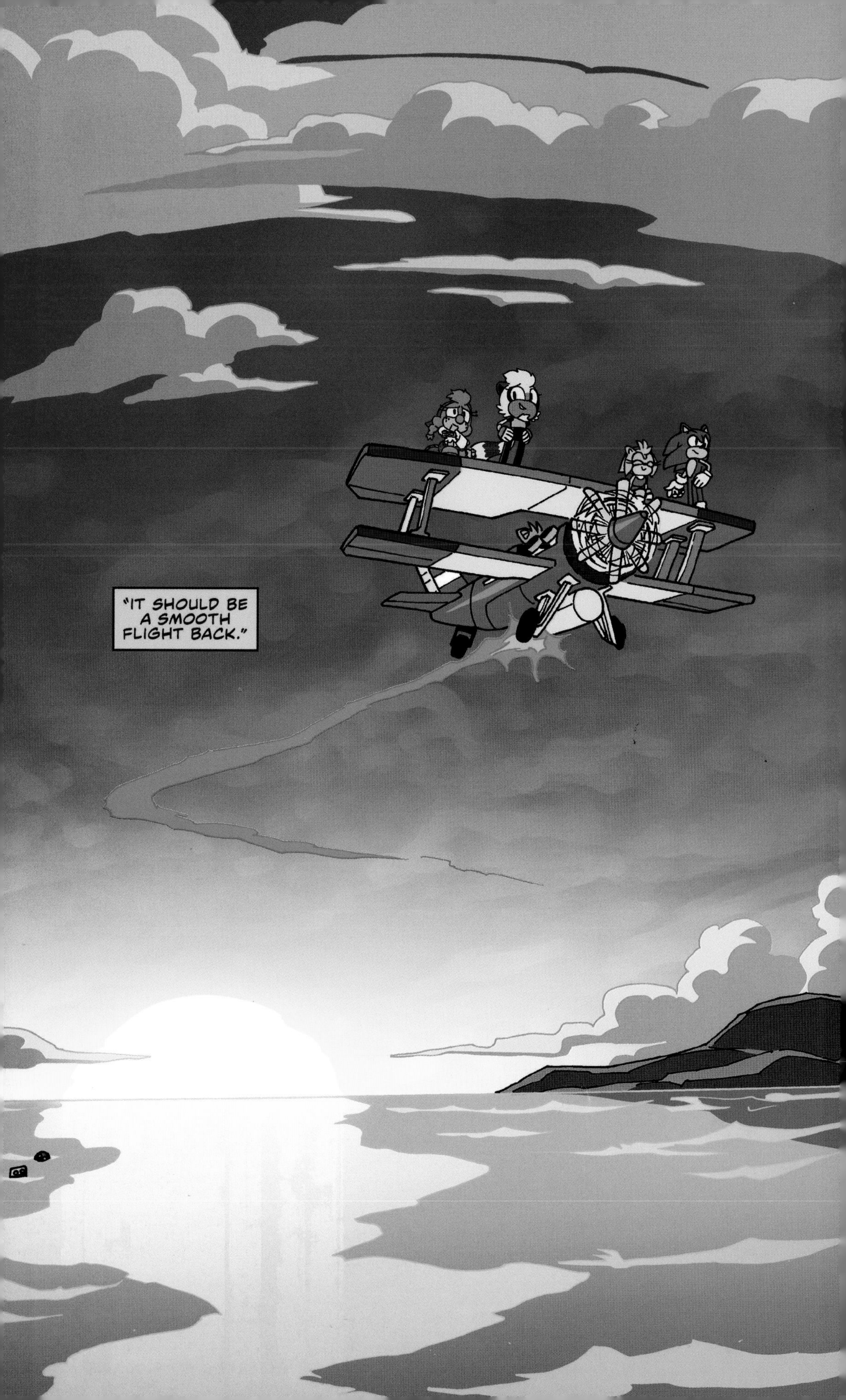
"IT SHOULD BE A SMOOTH FLIGHT BACK."

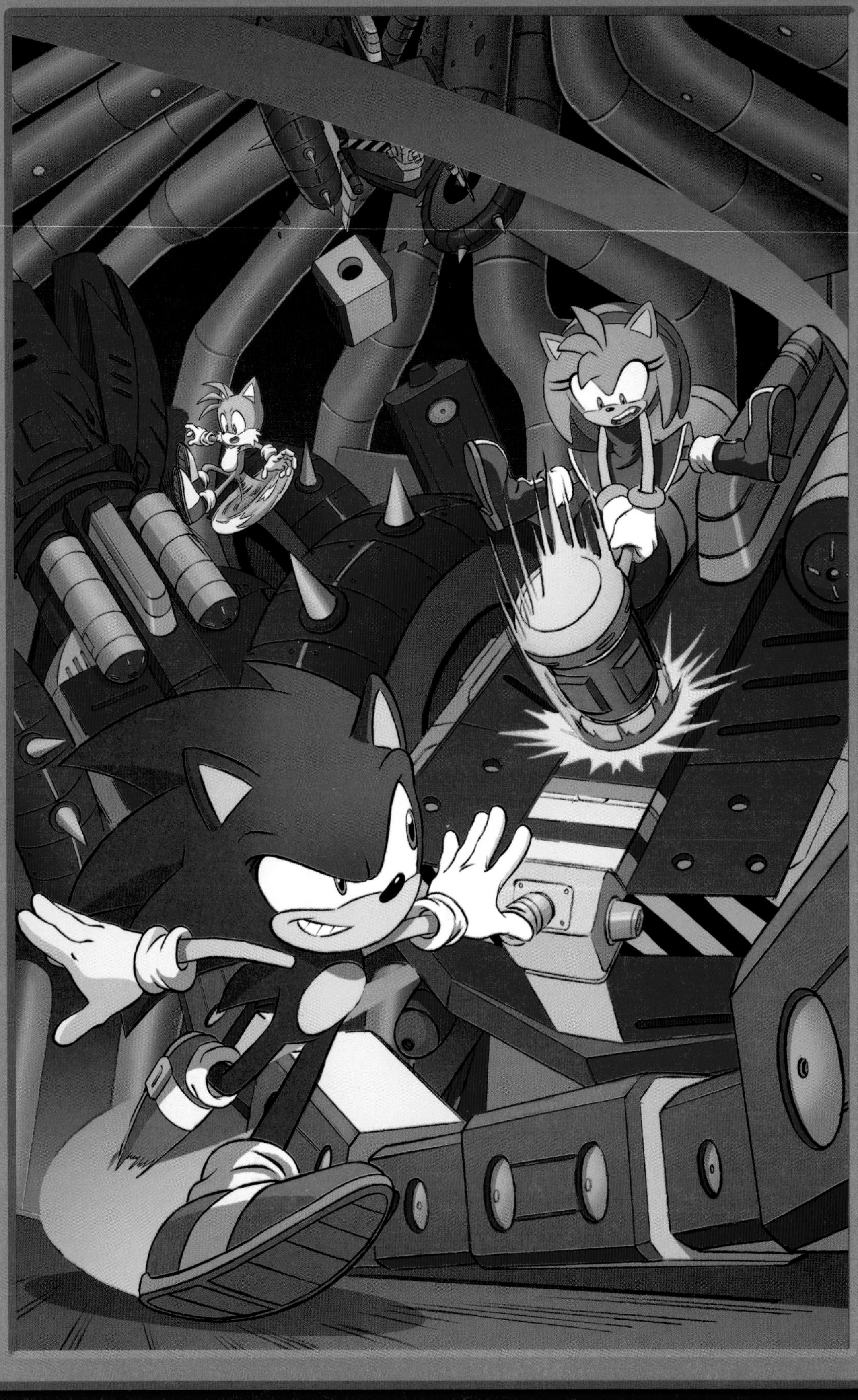

ART BY **DAN SCHOENING** COLORS BY **LUIS ANTONIO DELGADO**

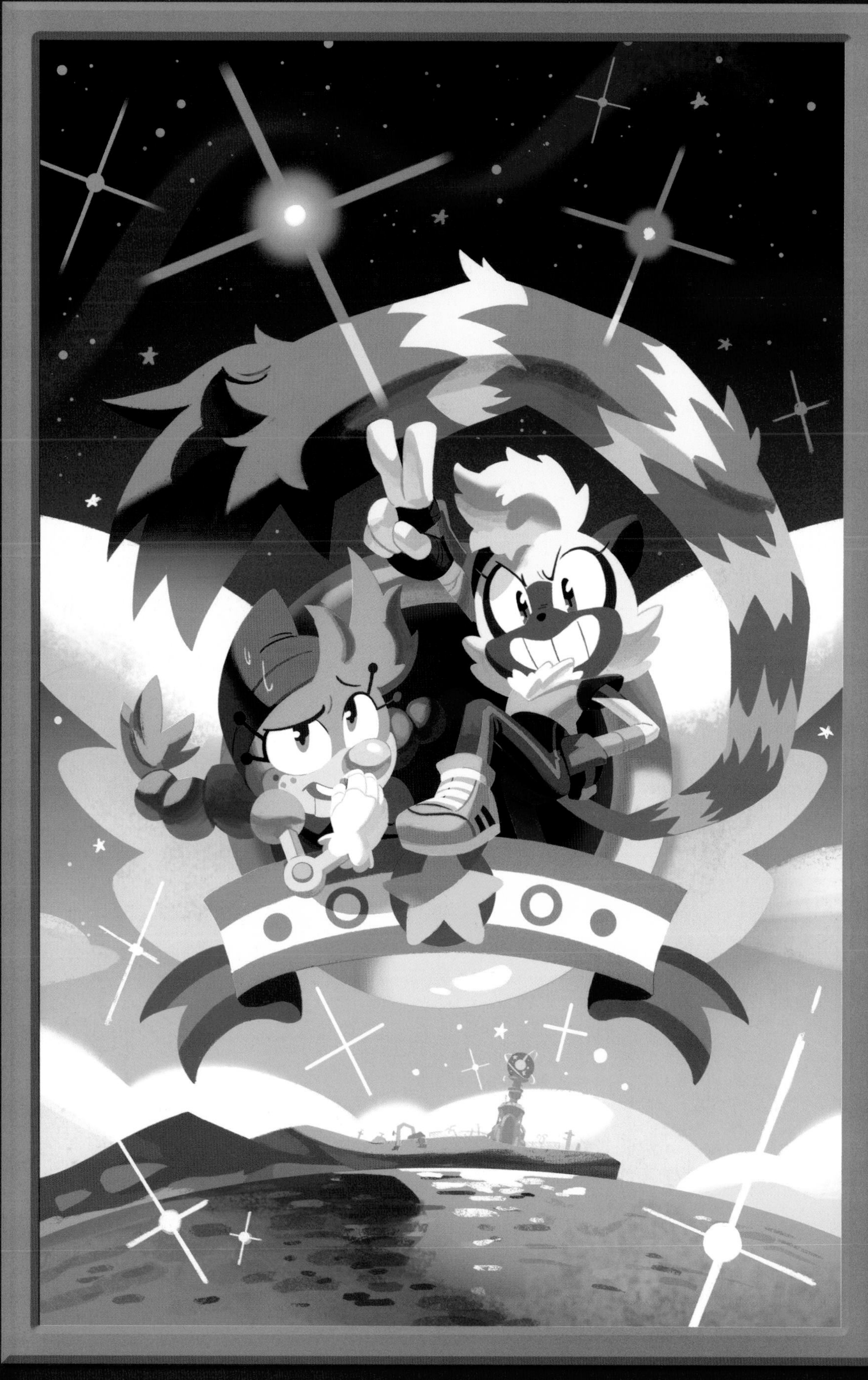

ART BY **NATHALIE FOURDRAINE**

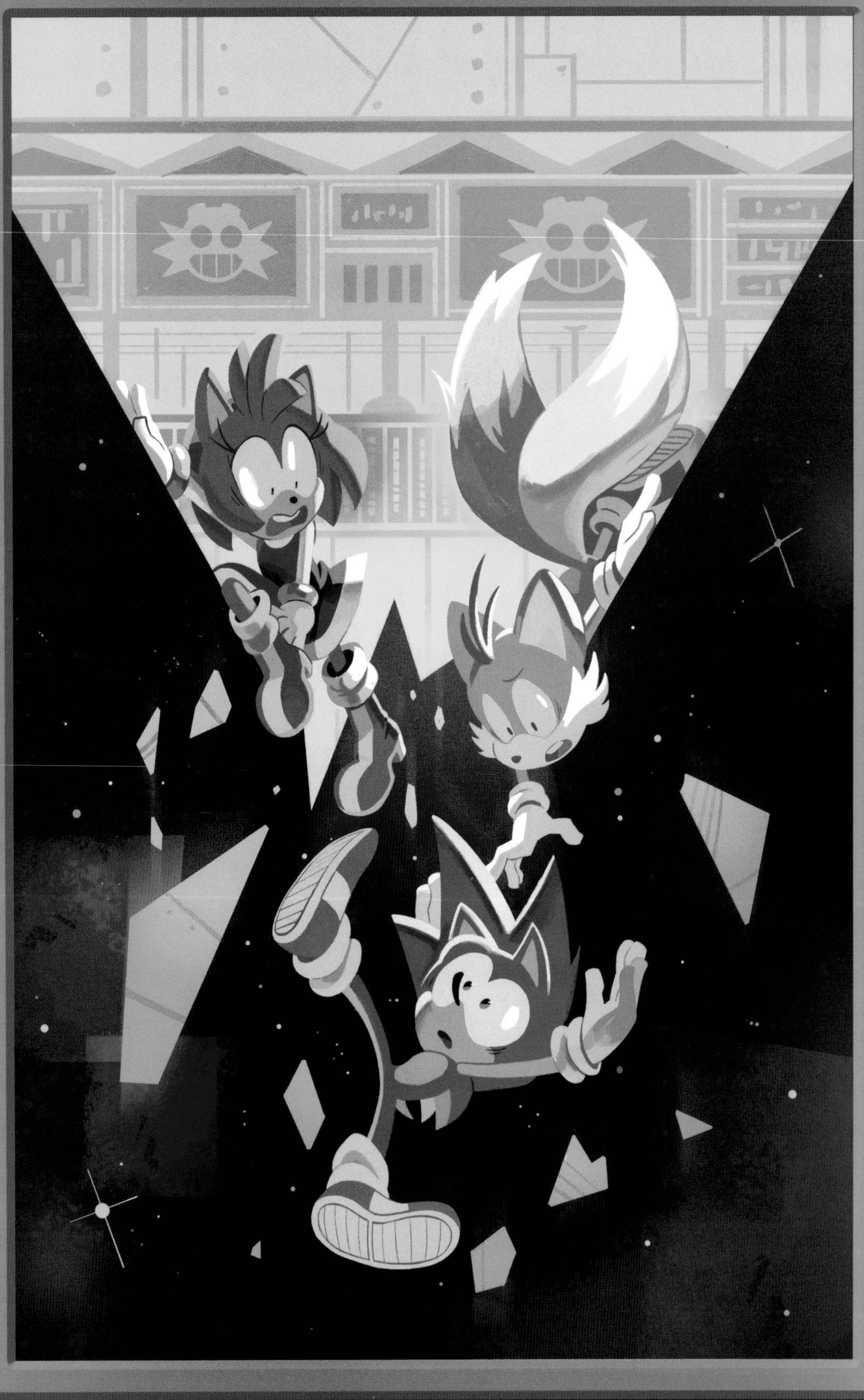

ART BY **NATHALIE FOURDRAINE**

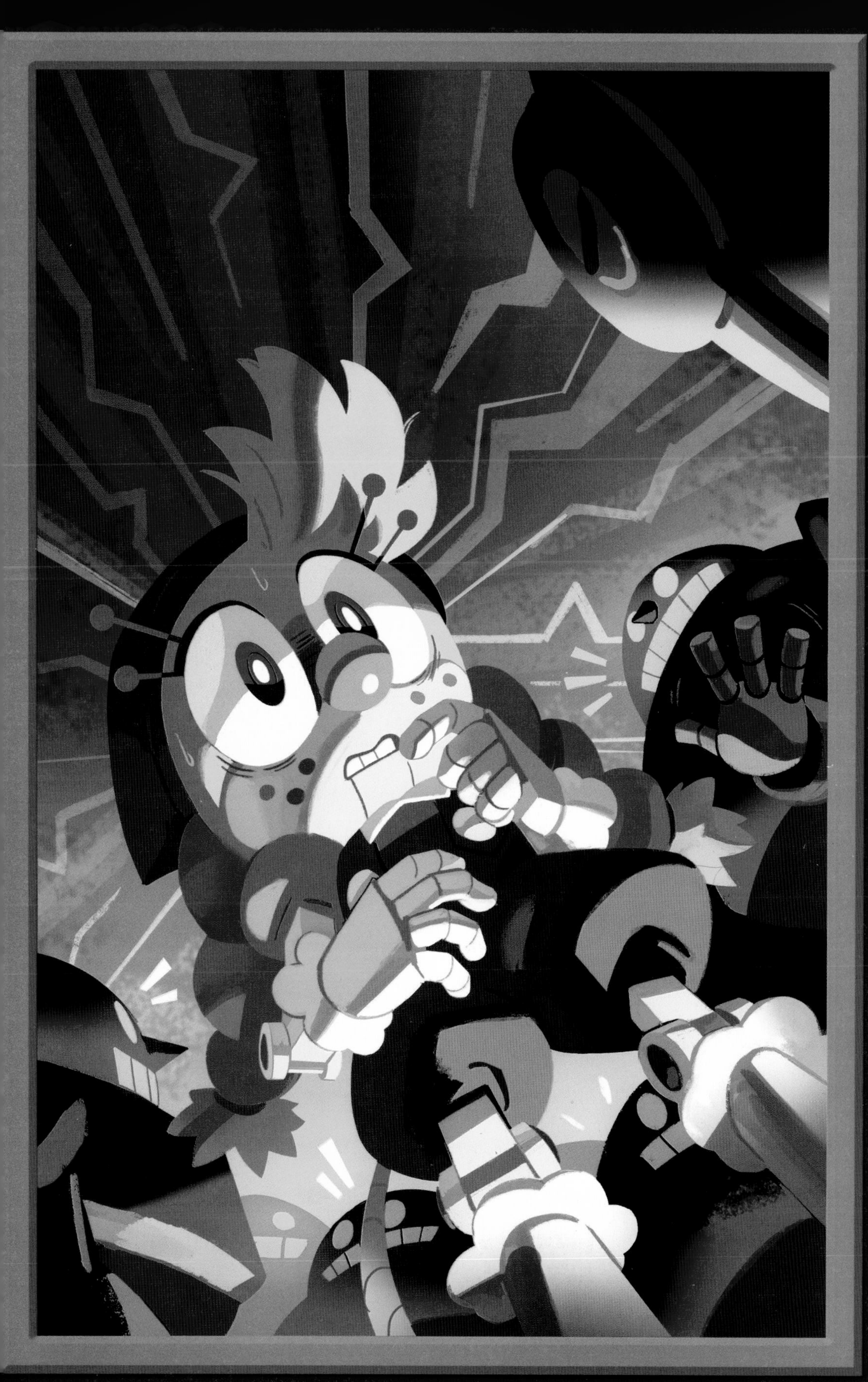

ART BY **NATHALIE FOURDRAINE**

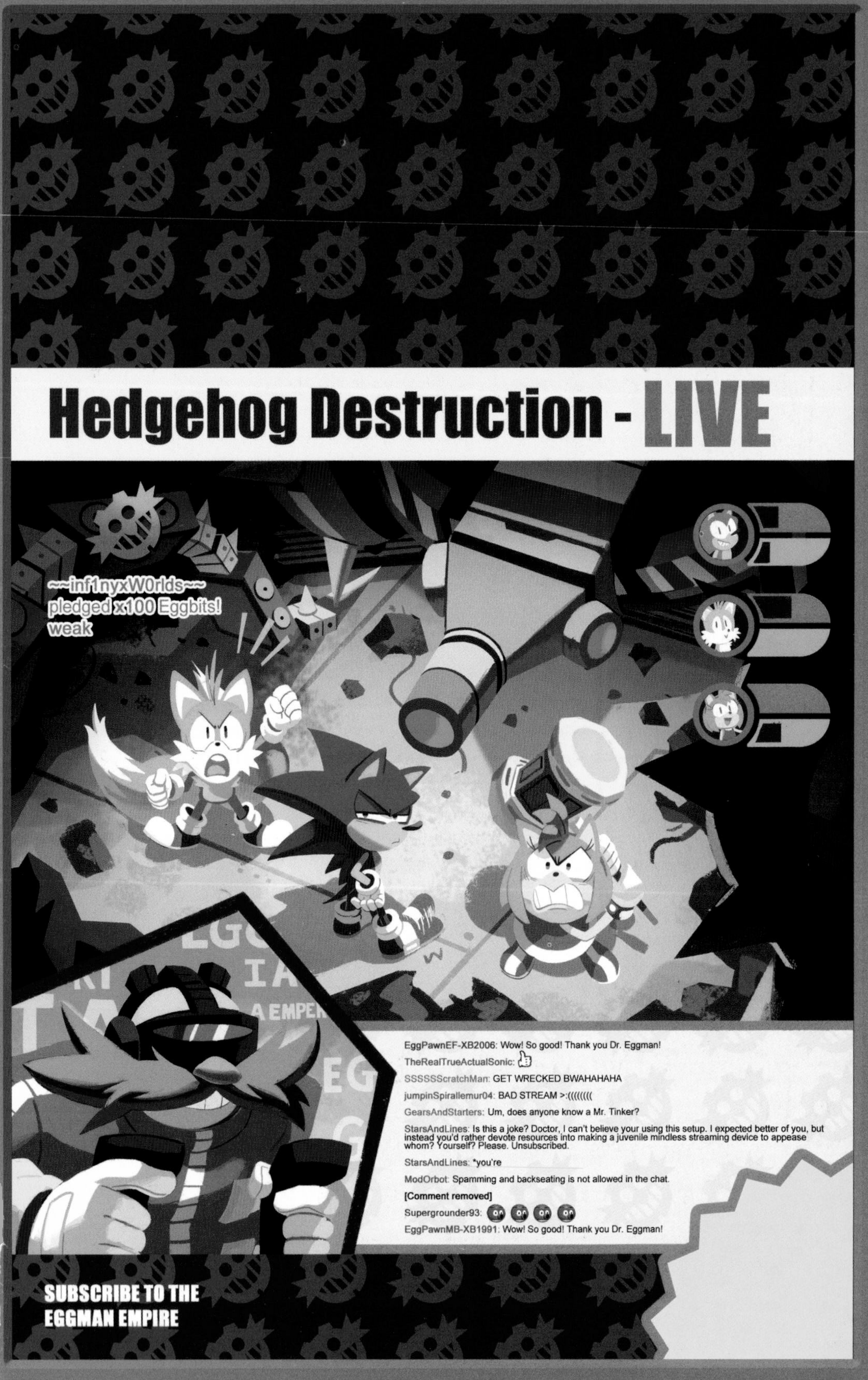
Hedgehog Destruction - LIVE
~~inf1nyxW0rlds~~
pledged x100 Eggbits!
weak
EggPawnEF-XB2006: Wow! So good! Thank you Dr. Eggman!
TheRealTrueActualSonic:
SSSSSScratchMan: GET WRECKED BWAHAHAHA
jumpinSpirallemur04: BAD STREAM >:((((((((
GearsAndStarters: Um, does anyone know a Mr. Tinker?
StarsAndLines: Is this a joke? Doctor, I can't believe your using this setup. I expected better of you, but instead you'd rather devote resources into making a juvenile mindless streaming device to appease whom? Yourself? Please. Unsubscribed.
StarsAndLines: *you're
ModOrbot: Spamming and backseating is not allowed in the chat.
[Comment removed]
Supergrounder93:
EggPawnMB-XB1991: Wow! So good! Thank you Dr. Eggman!
SUBSCRIBE TO THE
EGGMAN EMPIRE

ART BY **NATHALIE FOURDRAINE**

SONIC™
THE HEDGEHOG

TEST RUN!

Facebook: **facebook.com/idwpublishing**
Twitter: **@idwpublishing**
YouTube: **youtube.com/idwpublishing**
Instagram: **@idwpublishing**

Cover Art by
Tracy Yardley

Cover Colors by
Leonardo Ito

Series Assistant Edits by
Riley Farmer

Series Edits by
David Mariotte

Collection Edits by
Alonzo Simon
and **Zac Boone**

Collection Design by
Shawn Lee

ISBN: 978-1-68405-851-8   25 24 23 22   1 2 3 4

Originally published as SONIC THE HEDGEHOG issues #37–40.

Nachie Marsham, Publisher
Blake Kobashigawa, VP of Sales
Tara McCrillis, VP Publishing Operations
John Barber, Editor-in-Chief
Mark Doyle, Editorial Director, Originals
Erika Turner, Executive Editor
Scott Dunbier, Director, Special Projects
Lauren LaPera, Managing Editor
Joe Hughes, Director, Talent Relations
Anna Morrow, Sr. Marketing Director
Alexandra Hargett, Book & Mass Market Sales Director
Keith Davidsen, Sr. Manager, PR
Topher Alford, Sr. Digital Marketing Manager
Shauna Monteforte, Sr. Director of Manufacturing Operations
Jamie Miller, Sr. Operations Manager
Nathan Widick, Sr. Art Director, Head of Design
Neil Uyetake, Sr. Art Director Design & Production
Shawn Lee, Art Director Design & Production
Jack Rivera, Art Director, Marketing

Ted Adams and Robbie Robbins, IDW Founders

Special thanks to Mai Kiyotaki, Michael Cisneros, Sandra Jo, Sonic Team,
and everyone at Sega for their invaluable assistance.

SONIC™
THE HEDGEHOG

TEST RUN!

SEGA®